To conquer . . . or to be conquered?

Miles drew Mathilda towards the punt.

At last he would have her all to himself again, and the possibilities made his blood race. This decisive step in his scheme for Mathilda's downfall had been planned long ago, but now that the moment was upon him, Miles could think of nothing but the velvety texture of her skin, the promise of surrender in her amber eyes, the seductive invitation of her soft mouth, already parted in anticipation of the inevitable kisses they would share. This was what he had waited ten years for, he reminded himself to stem the rising euphoria of emotions. This was his moment of victory.

And then Mathilda smiled up at him, and Miles felt his bones melt and his heart take wings. A heart that had betrayed him. . . .

Broken Promises

Patricia Oliver

A SIGNET BOOK

SIGNET
Published by New American Library, a division of
Penguin Putnam Inc., 375 Hudson Street,
New York, New York 10014, U.S.A.
Penguin Books Ltd, 27 Wrights Lane,
London W8 5TZ, England
Penguin Books Australia Ltd, Ringwood,
Victoria, Australia
Penguin Books Canada Ltd, 10 Alcorn Avenue,
Toronto, Ontario, Canada M4V 3B2
Penguin Books (N.Z.) Ltd, 182–190 Wairau Road,
Auckland 10, New Zealand

Penguin Books Ltd, Registered Offices:
Harmondsworth, Middlesex, England

First published by Signet, an imprint of New American Library,
a division of Penguin Putnam Inc.

First Printing, May 2001
10 9 8 7 6 5 4 3 2 1

Copyright © Patricia Oliver, 2001

All rights reserved

 REGISTERED TRADEMARK—MARCA REGISTRADA

Printed in the United States of America

PUBLISHER'S NOTE
This is a work of fiction. Names, characters, places, and incidents either are the product
of the author's imagination or are used fictitiously, and any resemblance to actual
persons, living or dead, business establishments, events, or locales is entirely
coincidental.

Contents

The Elopement

London
June 1808

The bell towers of London chimed the hour of midnight as the light travelling chaise bowled smartly over Westminster Bridge and turned right onto the Portsmouth Road. To one of the occupants of the carriage, the sound held ominous overtones, which she found hard to ignore. In another twelve hours these same bells would be ringing out again, particularly the bells of St. George's Church in Hanover Square, to celebrate the union between Miles William Stephens, Viscount Halifax, heir to the sixth Earl of Southmoor, and Miss Mathilda Heath, both of Bath.

Except that now there would be no wedding. There would be no bride. The bells would ring for an empty church. If things went as planned, Miss Mathilda Heath would be miles away, boarding the *Peregrine* in the seaport of Portsmouth, bound for Calcutta, India.

And she would be married to another man.

The enormity of the step she was taking caused Mathilda a moment of panic. An involuntary shudder shook her, and she pulled the light rug that lay across her lap more closely about her to ward off the chill that had nothing to do with the swirls of mist that rose from the dark recesses of the river they were leaving behind.

"Having second thoughts again, my darling?"

Her companion, who had sat opposite Mathilda since handing her into the chaise in the mews behind her Aunt Agatha's house, leaned forward and gently traced the curve of her cheek with his finger. The gesture was infinitely comforting, and Mathilda felt herself relax.

"You trust me, do you not, Mathilda?"

His voice was warm and tender, and Mathilda felt her anxiety dissolve. She nodded and smiled. "Oh, yes, James, of course I do," she murmured, gazing at the dark form of the man who now held both her gloved hands in his. He bent his head to kiss her fingers, and a sliver of moonlight briefly outlined the strong line of his jaw.

"It is not as though we are running off to Gretna Green, love," he said, and Mathilda could hear the smile in his voice. "We agreed that the dash up the Great North Road was far too havey-cavey for us. I, for one, have no desire to be wedded by some castaway Scotsman over an anvil. No, love, nothing so ramshackled will do for my Mathilda." He raised her fingers to his lips again.

"But you still believe everyone will think we are on our way to Scotland?"

She caught the flash of white in the dimness when he smiled. "That is bound to be the first place old Miles will think of when he hears the news. No doubt he will set out after the coach I hired to travel north."

"Will he not be furious when he discovers the trick?" Mathilda could not believe they would get away so easily.

James laughed shortly. "I daresay he will be as sore as a bear, but by the time he discovers that the runaway lovers are two actors from Drury Lane, it will be too late, my love. We shall be aboard the *Peregrine* and on our way to Calcutta."

"And I will be your wife," Mathilda murmured shyly, her need for reassurance turning the statement into a half question.

Events had swept her into a whirlwind of intrigue ever since the moment when she had accepted that first waltz with the elegant Elizabethan courtier at the Countess of Mansfield's masquerade ball. Mathilda was dressed as an Elizabethan lady herself, so it had seemed entirely appropriate to dance with this stranger whose costume complemented her own. She had wanted to dance the waltz with the viscount, had specifically saved it for him on her dance card, but he had failed to claim it.

Typically, Viscount Halifax had not worn a costume, limiting himself—at his mother's insistence—to covering his aristocratic features with a plain black domino. Mathilda had been disappointed. She had not dared say anything to the viscount, but had suggested to his mother that his lordship would look rather dashing as a pirate with a patch over one eye. The countess had laughed at this idea, as well she might, Mathilda recalled. Her only son, insufferably stiff-necked and punctilious in all things concerning the dignity of his name, had initially refused to attend the masquerade. Only a chance remark from his mother that he was denying Mathilda the pleasure of an evening organized by one of London's premier hostesses had changed his mind.

He had looked straight at her then—a thing he rarely did—and Mathilda had quailed under the cool grey stare, sorely tempted to deny any desire to attend the Mansfield masquerade. At Lady Southmoor's prodding, she had acknowledged a curiosity to see if the much-touted Mansfield masquerade would live up to her expectations. And, much to her surprise, the viscount had relented. He would escort both ladies to the masquerade, on the condition they did not pester him to wear a costume.

Where would she be now had her betrothed denied her that pleasure, as he obviously had intended? Had he refused to escort her to the ball; had he danced that first waltz with her; had he shown himself even marginally interested in their upcoming nuptials. Had the viscount shown the least hint of romantical interest in her . . . Mathilda sighed. Had he done any of these things, she would not be here in this chaise with another man.

Mathilda smiled a little shakily at the man who held both her hands in his and gazed at her so earnestly.

"How can you doubt it, love? It is what I most desire in all the world, and in a few hours, a *very* few hours, you will be mine, Mathilda."

Mathilda sighed, and her smile brightened. Was this not exactly as she had imagined it in her dreams? A gentleman who promised to cherish her for the rest of her life? A perfectly gorgeous gentleman, whose easy smile and warm charm had unexpectedly won her heart. A thrilling, secret, illicit courtship straight out of Mrs. Radcliffe's latest novel. A veritable shower of posies and *billets doux* that kept her heart in a constant flutter. And now a romantical flight in the dead of night to a ceremony that would join her to the man of her dreams, the dashing Sir James Parmenter.

The irony of it all was that the viscount himself had brought them together. Mathilda could not believe that it was barely two months ago that she had first met the adult James at a small soirée at the Southmoor London residence. She remembered chaffing at the rigidity of social etiquette that demanded unrelieved white for young girls making their entrance into society. She found the colour insipid and longed to wear apricot silk or the pale green satin her mother had refused to purchase for her. The green in particular would have complemented her dark colouring.

But her mother had been adamant. "White is the only acceptable colour for a girl who has yet to celebrate her eighteenth birthday," Lady Heath had insisted, the slight frown on her lovely face a clear indication that it would be futile for her daughter to argue with the arbiters of fashion.

"Never fear, my dear Mathilda," her Aunt Agatha, swathed in gorgeous purple silk with a turban to match, consoled her. "When you are the Viscountess Halifax, you may wear any colour you choose. Just have a little patience, dear. June will be here before you know it, and then you will be a married lady with unlimited allowance for clothes and gewgaws. Gentlemen are all too often tiresome and overbearing, but they do have certain advantages. Especially when they are handsome, titled, and full of juice," she added with a merry wink.

"Agatha," her mother cut in plaintively, "I have begged you not to use stable language in front of Mathilda. You will put outlandish notions into the child's head."

"I am *not* a child, Mama," Mathilda had protested, although the insipid white gown with its modest décolletage belied her words. "In June I will be married, and can do as I wish." She sounded petulant even to her own ears, and was not surprised when her mother's frown deepened.

Lady Heath's fingers were busy with the clasp of the slim pearl necklet she was fastening around her daughter's throat, but her eyes met Mathilda's in the bevelled mirror. "I warn you, child, if you give Halifax a disgust of you with your whining, there will be no marriage. His lordship is not a man to tolerate your foolish starts."

"He already has a disgust of me," Mathilda mumbled, half to herself.

"Now you *are* being foolish, dear," her mother chided. "The man dotes on you. Why do you suppose he pressed your father for an early wedding date? Had your father not stood firm, you would have been a viscountess six months ago."

"I still think he does not even like me, Mama," she insisted, never having witnessed the least sign in her betrothed of the attachment claimed by Lady Heath. "He is barely civil to me, and I have yet to receive a *billet doux* from him or even a speaking glance that might reveal his feelings."

Lady Heath bristled. "And I should hope not, child. Halifax has too much respect for his consequence and for your reputation to indulge in clandestine foolishness. You should be thankful that he comports himself with such exemplary restraint. Not all gentlemen do, I might add."

Mathilda had discovered that very evening that her mother was right. Not all gentlemen were so restrained. From the moment the viscount had brought their childhood friend and neighbour to her, and Mathilda had recognised him as the mysterious Elizabethan gentleman from the masquerade ball, she sensed that Sir James Parmenter regarded her with anything but indifference. His attentions became so marked as the evening wore on that Mathilda had more than once glanced apprehensively at her betrothed. The viscount had appeared either ignorant of or indifferent to his friend's predilection for Mathilda's company.

But it was Sir James's confession that she reminded him of an angel in her white gown, and needed but a pair of wings and a halo to take him back to the happy days of their childhood that had intrigued her. At her surprised expression, he had explained a young boy's dreams of meeting a being as beautiful and pure as the angel that watched over the worshippers in the chapel at Rose Park, his family seat.

Mathilda had been enchanted at the unexpected compliment and blushed in confusion. "You are a sad tease, sir. It is unkind of you. Besides, I doubt his lordship would be amused if he heard you compare me to an angel."

Sir James had laughed that deliciously carefree laugh of his and raised her fingers to his lips in an exaggerated salute. "But he did not hear it, now did he? And I promise not to tell. If Miles were not such a dry old stick, he would have told you himself that you are indeed an angel, except that I have never seen an angel with such enchanting eyes. They have quite stolen my wits away."

Unaccustomed to these pointed blandishments, Mathilda had at first been disconcerted at the young baronet's audacity. But as the days went by and Sir James became a fixture in the Southmoors' London residence, she began to look forward to his lively presence. When the viscount had, not unexpectedly, withdrawn from a much anticipated visit to the animals in the Tower, Sir James had stepped in, undaunted by the inclusion of his friend's two young sisters in the party with their nursemaid.

Mathilda had taken this desertion as further evidence that the viscount had so little interest in her that he would allow his friend to escort his betrothed on the promised outing. Her disappointment had been acute, but the balm of Sir James's sunny disposition had soon eclipsed her annoyance at the viscount's disinterest.

As the Season progressed, the viscount had appeared more than happy to allow his good friend to assume the duty of squiring his country-bred betrothed around London. Mathilda's reticence had gradually given way to delight at being the centre of male attention she had dreamed of at her surprise betrothal to the heir to the Earl of Southmoor. Her Aunt Agatha's invitation to spend the Season with her in London to shop for her bridal clothes and acquire a little Town Bronze had capped Mathilda's happiness. Or so she had thought at the time.

If only Viscount Halifax had lived up to her expectations, Mathilda might have been the happiest bride in London. She felt a pang of regret at the thought of the gorgeous lace wedding gown delivered only last week from the atelier of Madame Dupont, the most sought-after modiste in the Metropolis. She had left it, with so many other lovely things, in the clothespress at her aunt's house on Mount Street, taking with her only what she could cram into a small valise and a bandbox.

Mathilda felt a rush of tears gathering in her throat. Why, oh why had the eligible viscount not been the man of her dreams? She might have borne the cool demeanour he affected in public. Mathilda understood the importance of family dignity; but when this coolness had carried over into their private moments, she had begun to despair of ever finding happiness in such a match.

In a way, the viscount had brought about his own fate, she had argued to herself only yesterday. Why had he offered for her if he was unwilling to escort her around Town, drive her in his fancy curricle in Hyde Park as Sir James had done, or dance more than the perfunctory cotillion with her at the many soirées they attended? Unlike Sir James, the viscount had never invited her to enjoy ices at Gunther's or taken her to a balloon ascension. Could it be that he did not wish to be seen with a raw country girl among his aristocratic friends? Had he agreed to the match only to oblige his mother, Mathilda's godmother and a bosom bow of her mother and aunt?

Or worse yet, had he realised that she was not the wife he had expected and, too much the gentleman ever to jilt her openly, counted on his deliberate aloofness to create an irreparable rift between them?

The thought chilled her. But once having reared its head, the fear of being unwanted, unworthy, unloved, tainted her happiness. Her nuptials with the viscount began to appear like a sacrifice on his part. Her romantical heart quailed at the thought of wedding a gentleman whose affections were so obviously not engaged. And from that state of mind, it was but a short step to accepting Sir James's protestations of undying love and his proposal that they elope together.

Mathilda shook off her apprehensions and smiled encouragingly at her future husband. "That is what I desire, too, James. I have no regrets. Except . . ." she added.

"Except?" he prodded.

"Except that I wish my mother could be with me. And Aunt Agatha, who has been so good to me. And, of course, the countess. I fear she will be most disappointed in me. She is devoted to her son, you know."

Sir James murmured reassuringly as he tightened his grasp on her hands, but since at that moment the chaise rattled into the churchyard at Guilford, no more was said on the matter.

The lights were on in the vicarage, and as Mathilda stepped down onto the cobbles, she saw a portly figure approaching briskly, waving his arms and calling out an exuberant welcome to Sir James.

"Uncle Ben," James exclaimed, casting his arm about the shoulders of the vicar and bestowing an affectionate hug on him. "I apologise for keeping you up so late, but our ship leaves Portsmouth on the evening tide and we could not leave Town until nearly midnight."

"Say no more, lad, say no more," the vicar interrupted,

thumping Sir James on the back with considerable gusto. "And this must be the bonny bride," he added, turning to take Mathilda's hands in his and draw her towards the lighted vicarage. "James here has been full of your praises, but I must say he has not done you justice, my dear." He laughed gleefully at his own compliment and called out to the coachman and outriders to go round to the kitchen for a bite and a mug of ale.

"I trust Aunt Peggy and the children are well," James said as they made their way up the brick path to the door. Before the vicar could reply, the door was flung open and out tumbled a smiling woman jostled by a crowd of offspring of various sizes, all talking at once.

From the moment they stepped into the warmth of the vicarage, welcomed effusively by James's Aunt Peggy, events rushed forward with frightening speed. Enveloped in the haze of motherly affection showered upon her by Mrs. Parmenter, Mathilda was whisked upstairs to refresh herself, escorted by a vociferous army of little Parmenters into the chapel next door, and united by special licence in holy wedlock with a gentleman who was not her official betrothed.

After the ceremony was over, and duly entered into the parish records, the party returned to the vicarage to settle around the family table in noisy anticipation of the hearty repast Mrs. Parmenter had prepared for the bridal couple.

"Our Church of St. Anne's may not be as fashionable as St. George's in Hanover Square," the jovial vicar remarked after everyone had been served, "and the wedding breakfast does not include lobster patties or braised pheasant, which I hear is *de rigueur* in grand houses, but this toast is as sincere as any you will hear in London." As he spoke, the vicar raised his glass and wished the happy couple much joy and fulfillment in their new life together.

Overcome with emotion, Mathilda could barely eat more than a few morsels of the feast prepared by her hostess. Not to be outdone, Mrs. Parmenter prepared a basket of choice victuals to sustain the couple on their long journey down to Portsmouth.

"I cannot thank you enough, Mrs. Parmenter," Mathilda began as the hour of their departure drew near.

"Please call me Aunt Peggy, dear. You are one of the family now." She smiled with genuine affection, and Mathilda knew her cheeks were damp as her new aunt folded her in a warm embrace. A brief pang of longing for her mother was soon replaced by the bustle of departure and last good-byes.

It was too late now for regrets, Mathilda told herself as the coach swung out of the churchyard and the coachman pointed his horses south towards the Channel. Too late to wonder if her carefully worded note to the viscount had adequately conveyed her regret that their match had been so unsuitable, and that she had failed to please him.

Resolutely putting the viscount and what might have been behind her, Mathilda snuggled into the warmth of her new husband's embrace and began to dream of their future together in India.

ONE

The Homecoming

Hoarse shouts and the clatter of feet on deck jerked her wide awake in the predawn light. Momentarily disoriented, Mathilda sat up and gazed around the Spartan room, which her brain, fuzzy with sleep, gradually recognised as the cabin she had occupied for more weeks than she cared to remember. Could it be that the *Peregrine* had actually reached its destination as Captain Jack Mansford had promised only last night at the dinner table?

With a thrill of anticipation, Mathilda glanced around the cabin. The cot, wedged between the bottom of her own narrow bed and the old-fashioned chest of drawers, was empty and neatly made, a sure sign that Nurse Grey had risen betimes to oversee the boys' breakfast. Mathilda sighed, drew back the covers, and slid out of bed.

Mrs. Hettie Grey had been a godsend when Christopher was born the year following the Parmenters' arrival in Calcutta. Not having brought any servants with her on that hurried departure from London, Mathilda was relieved when Mrs. Grey had preferred to stay in India to care for a new baby rather than return to England with her three previous charges, the care of whom she shared with a tutor.

The arrangement had been perfect, and Nurse Grey had been there to take charge of Brian the moment he was born, and she seemed to be genuinely fond of both boys. So much so that she had allowed herself to be persuaded to accompany Lady Parmenter back to England after Sir James's death.

As Mathilda sat pondering what to wear for her first appearance on English soil in ten years, Nurse Grey burst into the cabin, carrying a tray with a steaming cup of hot chocolate and a plate of toast.

"G'morning, milady," she said cheerfully, setting the tray down on the dresser and handing Mathilda the chocolate. "'Tis true what Captain Jack told us last night. We are entering the harbour as I speak, and should be tied up all right and tight within the hour, the captain says. You had best let me help you into this gown," she added, abruptly changing the subject, "or we shall have you walking down the gangway in your shift."

Mathilda smiled indulgently at this forthright speech, and gave herself up to the nurse's ministrations. One of the first items on a long list of things she had to attend to upon reaching London was the hiring of a lady's maid. Mrs. Grey had offered to take on those additional duties during the voyage home, but once on shore, the boys would demand her full attention. Mathilda was counting on Aunt Agatha to recommend a trustworthy abigail who would not mind removing to Bath.

The thought of Aunt Agatha reminded Mathilda that she would soon be back in the bosom of her family. What was left of it. Her father had died the year following her clandestine marriage to Sir James, heartbroken—or so her mother claimed—over his daughter's shameful behaviour and misalliance. Her brother Reginald—or Sir Reginald as he was now—had openly disowned her and forbade her to set foot on the family estate near Bath. Only her Aunt Agatha had stood her friend, cheerfully opening her London residence to her disgraced niece. And of course her mother.

When the time came to disembark, the boys refused to be parted from their Captain Jack without extracting his solemn promise to visit them in Bath on his next voyage to England.

"I trust you are not put out by this imposition, my lady," he murmured a little later, handing her into the hired chaise that would take the Parmenters to London. "I have truly become attached to the lads, and value their affection," he added, raising Mathilda's gloved hand to his lips with a roguish grin.

Before Mathilda could guess his intent, the captain leaned forward and kissed her on the cheek. "Godspeed, lass. Take good care of yourself."

And then he stepped back, that crooked grin back on his handsome face, and the chaise jerked forward, leaving the inn yard and all reminders of her previous life behind her.

Their arrival in London was everything Mathilda could have wished for. As their chaise drew up before her aunt's residence at No. 5 Mount Street, it was obvious that they were expected. The carved oaken door was thrown wide, and an army of footmen trooped out, led by Lady Agatha in a startling afternoon gown in cerise satin, trimmed with bunches of cherries around the hem and a profusion of cherry-coloured French-knots on the low-cut bodice.

Mathilda blinked. It was obvious that her aunt, never a conservative dresser, had blossomed over the years into a flamboyant showcase for London's more adventuresome modistes. Even the boys remained unnaturally quiet as this red whirlwind descended upon them and enveloped them in a series of hugs accompanied by a steady flow of chatter and squeals of delight. Mathilda returned her aunt's exuberant reception with a tremulous smile, her eyes blurring with unshed tears.

"Oh, Aunt, how good it feels to be back," she managed to say when Lady Agatha paused a moment to catch her breath. "I missed you so much." She nestled in her aunt's comforting arms, stifling a sob while scanning the steps expectantly for the first sight of her mother.

"Where is Mama?"

"Angela will be down directly, dear. She developed a megrim after tea this afternoon and went up to rest. Lady Bristol—you remember what a gossip that woman is—had been sitting with us for over an hour, teasing poor Angela for news of your return to England. I despaired of her ever leaving. And you know how much your mother dislikes that old Tabby."

Mathilda drew back in surprise, a flash of annoyance marring her joy. "Is the news of my return common knowledge, then? I had hoped to get back to Bath without any fanfare."

"Oh, no, dear—not that I am aware of. Lady Bristol was no doubt fishing for any information she could get. She is distantly related to the Earl of Southmoor on her mother's side of the family, remember, so is naturally interested in any crumbs of news related to the old scandal."

This information disturbed Mathilda more than she cared to admit. "But that was ten years ago, Aunt," she protested, as her aunt drew her up the steps and into the hall. "Have there been no new scandals since then to give the busybodies fresh fodder for their everlasting tattling?"

"You may count upon it, my dear girl, but it so happens that you have returned at a rather awkward time. Everyone expected the earl to come up to scratch this Season and finally make an offer for the Pritchard chit. It was the talk of the Town. Her mother, that obnoxious Lady Pritchard, has been preening and posing for months now in anticipation of what she called the 'grand event.' Smirking on the other side of her face now, she is, the old harridan."

Mathilda stared at her aunt in dismay. "Are you saying that he is still—that he never married?"

"If you mean Southmoor, that is exactly what I am saying, love. Sore as a bear with the earache, he was, when you ran off with Parmenter. Raged around Town like a Bedlamite. I never would have given him credit for so much passion. In fact, I wrote him off as a sanguine, care-for-nobody myself, but I was wrong. You would not believe the dust he kicked up. Of course, it was no small thing for the heir to an earl to be jilted the day before his wedding." She paused and patted Mathilda's shoulder reassuringly, all the while directing the removal of her niece's luggage upstairs. "Luckily it turned out to be a nine-day-wonder, and by the end of June it was all over."

"I am glad to hear he recovered so quickly," Mathilda murmured, not quite sure that this was entirely true. "Brian, do not touch that, dear," she interjected, momentarily distracted by the interest her youngest was showing in a Chinese vase perched on a narrow rosewood table against the wall.

"Oh, no!" her aunt exclaimed with a trill of laughter, apparently impervious to the danger stalking the vase. "No such thing, dear. One day we heard he had left London and retired to Southmoor Grange. As far as I know, the poor boy never set foot in Town until three years ago, when he suddenly started squiring his mother to all the *ton* parties. Rumour had it that Lady Southmoor had prevailed upon him to marry and produce an heir. He had recently come into the title, of course, and that may have brought him out of hiding."

"Hiding? Surely you exaggerate, Aunt?"

Lady Agatha threw an enigmatic glance at her niece, who carefully fixed her attention on Brian, who was now rummaging through a bulging carpet-bag and holding up the procession of servants on the marble staircase. "I do not mean to tease you about it at this late date, my dear," her aunt added, "but you could scarcely have chosen a more public forum for casting the poor man aside. It was pure coincidence that Southmoor was not standing at the altar when he received the news. Given his strict sense of propriety, he must have suffered a severe blow."

Wishing she had not broached the subject of her aborted betrothal to Miles Stephens, Mathilda was grateful when she spied Lady Heath coming down the staircase in a cloud of sprigged lilac muslin. Angelic was a word often used to describe the ethereal Lady Heath, and Mathilda's first impression of her mother confirmed that the years had not weakened that lady's conviction that she was indeed closely related to those divine beings. "How else was she to account for her name?" was one of her favourite expressions. Angela. There was no room for coincidence in the choice of name. Her parents must have had a sudden flash of insight the moment she was born—

without a single ugly wrinkle and with a full head of pale curls—as she was happy to inform all skeptics.

"Mama!" Mathilda exclaimed with genuine affection. "Come, boys, it is time you made the acquaintance of your grandmother." Catching each son by one hand, Mathilda pulled them towards the stairs, where they were instantly enveloped in Lady Heath's perfumed embrace.

"Heavens, Agatha," she chided her sister gently. "Why must we stand about in the hall when we have a perfectly good drawing room where we might all be comfortable? Come along, boys," she added, "You must be hungry after that long drive up from Portsmouth. You shall have some of Cook's famous pastries to last you until dinnertime."

Mathilda watched her mother slowly ascend the stairs, a chattering grandson on either side. She smiled at the sight of her family reunited after so long. They made a pretty though deceptively domestic picture, and Mathilda sighed, wondering how long it would be before Brian got himself into the briars. He was not a naughty lad, merely high-spirited and full of curiosity. While Christopher was often content to sit reading a book, Brian's idea of a quiet afternoon was dismantling a clock to discover how it worked.

Her smile faded at the memory of the father who was no longer there to guide her sons. There was always Nurse Grey, and Mathilda knew she would immediately hire a tutor, of course, but there was no substitute for the firm hand of a father to keep two unruly boys in line. Now that James was gone, Mathilda wished she were on better terms with her only brother, but Reginald was, if anything, more stiff-rumped than Miles had been.

On impulse, she turned to her hostess. "How is Reginald, Aunt? Has he softened at all towards me?"

Lady Agatha's eyebrows rose expressively, and she shrugged one elegant shoulder. "What can I say, dear? You know what a nodcock your brother always was—still is for that matter. Once an idea gets lodged in his mind, there is no

moving him. Frankly, I was not surprised when Reginald publicly sided with Southmoor after the scandal broke. Blood is
not always thicker than water, dear, and your brother set such
store by his connexion with the Southmoors. He vaunted his
friendship with Miles at every opportunity, and suffered ago-
nies when the earl appeared to prefer Sir James's company. Of
course, when James fell from grace . . ." Lady Agatha let the
rest of the sentence hang in the air, but her rueful smile told
Mathilda the painful story.

"He gloated, no doubt," she commented bitterly.

Lady Agatha's laugh was not a pretty sound. "If only that
were the whole of it, dear. But the foolish man had to make a
complete cake of himself by riding hell-for-leather up the
North Road after Miles in pursuit of you and James. Naturally,
by the time Miles discovered he had been led on a wild-goose
chase, you were on the high seas and beyond his reach."

"And what did Reginald do?"

"He swore he would tear you limb from limb, but since that
was impossible, he settled for banishing you from Heath
House forever. Rather excessive, I always thought, but that is
Reginald for you."

Mathilda sighed audibly. "I gather he is still set against
me?"

Her aunt's face took on a roguish expression. "The only
way your pompous brother would even consider taking you
back into the fold would be if Miles were to take an interest in
you again, dear. And I gather that is not likely to happen if you
bury yourself in Bath."

Mathilda paused to gape at her aunt. "That is a *ridiculous*
notion, Aunt," she managed to say after a moment. "And I beg
you will not put such an outlandish idea into Mama's head. I
tremble to think what a muddle she might make of it."

Her aunt's casual remark had shaken her up considerably.
Not only was the possibility of a reconciliation with Miles utterly impossible—not for one moment had it entered her

mind—but he must despise her for jilting him, and Mathilda could not blame him.

No, the notion was indeed ridiculous, she told herself for the tenth time that evening as she climbed into her comfortable tester bed. It would be laughable if it were not so awful.

Bath would be her salvation. And Mathilda vowed to make all possible speed to Rose Park, where she was sure neither the Earl of Southmoor nor her estranged brother would dare to disturb her.

TWO

The Encounter

Miles Stephens, former Viscount Halifax, now the Earl of Southmoor, liked to take an early breakfast.

In this peculiarity he differed from the vast majority of the *haut monde,* and certainly from the rest of his own household, which suited him very well. He enjoyed the relative peace and quiet that reigned in the elegant mansion his grandfather, the fifth earl, had built at No. 17 Belgrave Square over fifty years before.

Therefore, when the door of the breakfast room opened while Harris was serving the earl his usual second helping of ham, kippers, and coddled eggs, Miles did not take his eyes from the butler hovering over the chafing dishes on the sideboard. Thinking it was one of the footmen with fresh toast, he was considerably startled to hear the melodious voice of his mother wishing him a good morning.

"Mother!" he exclaimed, lurching to his feet and dropping his serviette to the floor. "You are down early this morning," he said, automatically stating the obvious. "Is there something amiss?" He could imagine no other reason for his mother's leaving her rooms before noon. "One of the girls?"

The countess smiled enigmatically and sat down gracefully in the chair he held for her. She had chosen to sit beside him, instead of in her usual place at the end of the table. This appeared to Miles as a bad omen, and he braced himself for disaster.

"No, dear," the countess replied airily, waving away Harris's offer of a serving of ham. "Your sisters are still fast asleep after our excursion to the opera last night. I must say, it was good of you to accompany us, Miles. It made all the difference to them to have you in attendance at their first appearance at the opera. They are getting to that age when such things acquire an enormous importance to young girls. Which reminds me, we must start thinking of their come-out next Season. I do believe we may bring them out together, do you not agree, Miles?"

Miles regarded his mother with a hint of frustration. "So you left your bed betimes this morning to discuss my sisters' presentation to the *haut monde,* which is still a year in the future, if I understand you correctly, Mother? I would hesitate to call that unnecessarily precipitous, but the thought does cross my mind that there is no particular urgency for this discussion." He raised an eyebrow enquiringly.

Lady Southmoor took a sip of the tea Harris had set before her. "No, of course not, you tiresome boy. That was not it at all. I merely wished to mention it while I have your full attention, Miles."

The earl held his peace, limiting himself to a slight smile. "Well, yes. And now that you have mentioned it, Mother, and I can guarantee you have my full attention, perhaps you will tell me what other piece of news could not wait until a more civilised hour?"

"You are obnoxious this morning, Miles," his mother retorted. "I have a good mind to return to my bed and leave you in abysmal ignorance of what the *ton* is saying about you."

Miles felt the smile slip from his face. "I have no burning desire to be *au courant* with the latest tattle going the rounds, Mother. Perhaps you would be better advised to go upstairs to continue your rest."

"Oh, no, you will not fob me off so easily, dear. There are two rumours that concern you—well, strictly speaking one is not a rumour at all—and which I think might interest you."

"I take that to mean that the rumours interest *you,* Mother," the earl drawled, lifting a substantial piece of ham to his mouth and chewing it methodically.

"Naturally, whatever concerns any of my children interests me, Miles. That hardly needs mentioning. But when I hear a downright falsehood circulating among my friends, my first instinct is to deny it, which of course I did. Later, I began to wonder if perhaps you did not—inadvertently, of course—do something to cause this quite dreadful gossip."

"I can think of nothing the tattle-mongers might say that would interest me in the slightest, Mother, so you might save your breath for more constructive things. This ham is excellent, by the way, quite the best I have tasted recently."

By this time, the earl's curiosity had been mildly piqued by the news his mother had risen so early to share with him. He knew better than to admit it, however. Lady Southmoor's conversations were notoriously convoluted at the best of times, but when there was a specific point to be made, the countess delighted in holding her audience spellbound until the last possible moment. Not infrequently, the telling became so involved that the point was entirely lost. Miles had learned long ago that pretended indifference was the best defence against his mother's verbosity. If she thought his attention flagging, she often got to the point.

In this instance, the kernel of the countess's news came so quickly, the earl nearly choked on his toast.

"Bother the ham!" Lady Southmoor exclaimed crossly. "How can you sit there eating when rumour has it that you do not intend to offer for the Pritchard chit?"

Under cover of his cough, Miles chastised himself for not warning his mother not to plan for a summer wedding at Southmoor Grange. At the very least he would have been spared this unsettling interruption in his morning routine.

"Well?" the countess insisted when he made no immediate response. "Do you wish to break your mother's heart? Again? Tell me it is not true that you failed to present yourself at Lord Pritchard's house-party last weekend?"

"That is true enough, Mother," Miles murmured with no hint of remorse.

"But *why,* Miles? Why?" the countess wailed. "I thought we had agreed that the Pritchard girl would do very nicely. I was afraid something like this would happen. I had a premonition about it, if you must know. How I wish I had gone with you, dear. Everything would have been settled by now. But no, you must dash your mother's hopes for the third time in as many years."

She sounded truly forlorn, but Miles knew his mother's show of grief was calculated to make him feel as guilty as possible.

He grinned irreverently. "Then why did you not accept Lady Pritchard's invitation, Mother? I might well be a doomed man by now had you been there to keep me on course."

The countess gave an inelegant snort of disgust. "You know I cannot abide that woman, Miles. A veritable harridan. Of course, Pritchard married beneath him, which should be a lesson to every gentleman not to get carried away by a pretty face. And Lucy Pritchard had a pretty face, I will give her that. But her mother was a mushroom of the worst ilk. But that happens in the best of families—"

"Not in ours, Mother," Miles cut in sharply. "And I refuse to be the one to introduce tainted blood into our line. I simply came to the conclusion that I had no wish to be saddled with that harridan—as you call her—for the rest of my life."

It would be quite bad enough that the dowager countess would certainly wish to continue residing at Southmoor Grange, but the thought of having Lady Pritchard continually underfoot as well had convinced Miles that he was not yet ready for that kind of torturous existence.

He heard his mother sigh and knew the argument was over. "That little Celia Pritchard would have made a docile and obedient wife, dear," she murmured without conviction. "That in itself is an asset today, when young girls' heads seem to be filled with romantic nonsense unheard of in my day."

"Yes, obedience is always to be desired in a female," the earl agreed, nodding to Harris to refill his cup. "But a modicum of intelligence is also pleasant if one is to spend any time at all with one's wife."

His mother waved this facetious remark away impatiently. "Where did you go then, Miles, if you were not at Pritchard Place?"

"I went down to the Grange. It is so pleasant in Somerset in the spring. Sometimes I marvel that we are wasting time in Town when we could be at home enjoying the bounty of nature. The roses have outdone themselves this year, Mother, and Carter tells me we can expect a bumper crop of fruit." He paused before expressing the thought that had been on his mind for the past sennight. "Would you object to leaving Town next week instead of waiting another month? It is not as though you will miss anything of any importance."

This heresy was met by a series of wails and protestations, as he knew it would be. Halfway through a litany of all the soirées, musicales, garden parties, al fresco breakfasts, and other delights she would miss if her unfeeling son insisted upon uprooting her before the end of the Season, Lady Southmoor made one of her dramatic pauses.

"Besides," she continued in a noticeably different tone of voice as soon as his attention was caught, "there is an excellent reason for you to remain in London, Miles. One I am sure that you will not bear to miss when you hear it."

Her voice quivered with excitement, but the earl gave no sign of interest in this announcement. He finished up the last of his kippers, refused another helping of ham from Harris, and drained his cup of coffee. Then he looked pointedly at the mantel clock.

"I fear I must leave you, Mother. I am engaged to meet Willy Hampton and Mansfield at Tattersall's shortly. There is a prime colt from the Lonsdale stables I have asked Hampton to evaluate for me." This was not strictly true. His appointment with his friends was not until the afternoon, but Miles was anxious to quit the house before his mother engaged him in another lengthy argument.

He stood up and brushed an imaginary crumb from his dark blue coat. "Now, if you will excuse me, Mother, perhaps we can continue this conversation over tea this afternoon."

"Brace yourself, Miles." Something in his mother's tone stopped the earl in his tracks. "I think you will want to know that Mathilda is back in London."

The earl felt his heart race uncomfortably. "Mathilda?" he echoed, although he knew instantly which Mathilda his mother meant.

"Yes, Mathilda," Lady Southmoor repeated. "Mathilda Heath. Or perhaps I should call her Lady Parmenter now. She arrived yesterday, and I hear she is quite, quite beautiful."

In spite of a Herculean effort, the earl felt his face stiffen into a rigid mask. He stared down at his mother, noting the satisfied smile on her face. Let her gloat, he thought coldly. Let them all gloat, as no doubt the *ton* was already doing at this very moment. The news had broken through the shell of reserve he had cultivated for so long and touched off the rage that had festered in his heart for ten long years. Ever since the day *she* had jilted him, practically at the altar, and run off with his false friend, James Parmenter.

The earl bowed stiffly and, without a word, strode out of the room.

The Park was almost deserted at the unfashionable hour of seven that morning as Lady Parmenter walked briskly beside the Serpentine. Ahead of her, Christopher and Brian raced along the footpath, stopping every so often to pick up some treasure, which they ran back to exhibit with boyish pride. Mathilda had already been required to examine and give her approval to several odd-shaped stones, a pale blue eggshell from which the occupant had long since hatched and flown away, a number of bedraggled feathers from the waterfowl that inhabited the lake, and a grubby mitten with a gaping hole, in a particularly ugly shade of green.

"Put that dirty thing down immediately," she commanded when Brian presented this pathetic object for her inspection. "We cannot know who wore it last or whether he had some dreadful disease that you would not wish to catch, dear."

"I told him not to pick it up, Mama," Christopher remarked in that superior tone he used when his brother ignored his advice. "It would serve you right if you caught chicken pox and came out in horrid red spots all over," he added, addressing Brian.

His brother was undismayed. "If I catch it, so will you. Is that not so, Mama? And then you will have spots, too, and have to stay in bed and go without pudding for a week. So there."

"I daresay neither of you will catch anything if you throw it away this instant, Brian."

Her youngest promptly ran to the edge of the lake and tossed the mitten into the water. Instantly, a fat duck seized it—no doubt thinking it edible—and swam off with a trail of noisy competitors in its wake.

"Oh, look, Mama," Christopher cried suddenly, pointing towards Rotton Row. Mathilda turned and her heart caught in her throat. A fashionable racing curricle, drawn by four high-stepping blooded horses, came dashing past, its yellow wheels a blur of speed. Mathilda followed it with her eyes, memories of her last sojourn in London rushing back to tease her.

Miles Stephens had owned just such a sporting vehicle, although he had never invited her to ride out with him in it. Too dangerous for a lady, he had responded when she had dared to admire the racy-looking curricle with its four matched greys. She had longed to sit close beside him on the blue leather seat and enjoy the thrill of driving in Hyde Park at the fashionable hour, nodding regally to her acquaintances, who would all be agog at seeing little Miss Mathilda Heath so elevated in the world.

Mathilda sighed at the memory. That had never happened, of course—like so many of her romantical fantasies about her former betrothed. When he had condescended to take her driving at all, it was in the Southmoor landau, a staid, cumbersome vehicle—at least in the eyes of a young girl—drawn by two chestnuts that seemed to have exhausted all their fire. Nor were they ever alone, as Mathilda had so often wished they might be. His mother and two young sisters invariably made up the party, and occasionally Aunt Agatha. Sir James would often ride beside the carriage and his steady flow of merry conversation kept Mathilda from being bored to tears.

How she missed James. She stood for a moment looking out over the placid waters of the Serpentine, remembering the many afternoons they had walked there together, with the casual supervision of her aunt or one of the maids. Her betrothed had never seemed to care what she did.

A warning shout from one of the boys brought her attention back to the present. Christopher and Brian had reached a small wooden dock beside the lake, evidently used for boarding the brightly painted rowboats moored there. Her youngest and most adventurous son was in the process of stepping into a garish red boat that rocked alarmingly, while Christopher, always the cautious one, watched in obvious alarm.

"Brian!" Mathilda shouted. "Get out of that boat this instant." When her son paid no noticeable attention to this command, she picked up her skirts and hurried along the path, hoping she would not have to jump into the water to save him from drowning. "Christopher," she fussed, "how could you let your brother get into that boat? You know he cannot swim."

Mathilda stood as close as she dared to the edge of the dock and extended her hand to her son. "Take my hand, you naughty boy. How dare you get into a boat without permission?"

"I w-wanted to see how it f-felt," Brian responded bravely enough, although Mathilda could see his face was pale.

"I shall show you how it feels to be tanned on the seat of

your pants when we get home, young man," Mathilda scolded. "Now, take my hand."

Crouched down, holding the sides of the boat with his hands, Brian tried to stand, but the movement caused the boat to rock alarmingly.

"I cannot, Mama. The boat will tip over if I stand up." A note of panic was creeping into his voice.

"Of course, you can. Give me your hand, and I will help to keep the boat steady."

Brian stood up again, but the boat wobbled so violently that Mathilda thought she had lost him. "Oh, Mama," he wailed, now thoroughly frightened. "I cannot do it." He crouched down again abruptly.

"Yes, you can," she said bracingly, "unless you wish to spend the night down there with the ducks." This attempt at humour did not have the desired effect, and Brian showed every sign of imminent tears.

"Hold on there, lad, I doubt it will come to that," an amused masculine voice remarked from so close behind Mathilda that she jumped. "Here lad," the gentleman said in a voice that emanated a calm confidence, "stand up quickly and take both my hands as you do so. We shall have you out of there in a jiffy. Are you ready, lad? On the count of three, then."

Before Mathilda could collect her wits, the jolly stranger had grasped Brian's hands in his and heaved him up onto the dock in one swift movement. The rescue was so quick and effortless that it was all over before Mathilda could say Jack Robinson.

Her immediate reaction was to hug her son tightly against her, ignoring his embarrassed protests at this maternal demonstration. "You are a very naughty boy," she scolded, running her fingers over him as if to assure herself that her son had suffered no harm. "I swear you have aged me by ten years at the very least. No pudding for you today, my lad, and you may be thankful it is nothing worse."

"Now there is an exaggeration if ever I heard one," Brian's saviour remarked with a chuckle.

"Exaggeration?" Mathilda looked up quickly and found herself gazing into twinkling brown eyes. "I think going without pudding is a small price to pay for this new mischief my son has discovered, sir."

"Oh, I was not referring to the pudding, ma'am, although that does sound a little severe to me. I have always been partial to sweets myself, as you can see." He gestured at his ample figure, that Mathilda would have to agree certainly bordered on the corpulent, as if to prove his point. "I meant the whisker about you aging ten years. That cannot possibly be true, unless you became the mother of these two charming lads when you were in the schoolroom yourself."

Mathilda stared at him, silently digesting this rather impudent remark. She should not be standing about in the deserted Park, talking to a stranger, but for some odd reason, she felt as though she had known this short, rather plump gentleman with the merry face forever.

"Now who is exaggerating, Mr. . . . ?"

He reacted instantly, with a deprecating grin. "I do most sincerely ask your pardon, ma'am. I fear my manners have gone begging. Willoughby Hampton at your service." In spite of his ample girth, Mr. Hampton executed an excessively elegant bow, his graceful movement calling Mathilda's attention to his superbly cut dove-coloured unmentionables and spotless white-topped boots sporting the silver tassels affected by the Corinthian set.

Mathilda could not resist smiling. "We are glad to meet you, sir. I am Lady Parmenter, and these are my sons, Christopher and Brian. We are infinitely obliged to you, Mr. Hampton, and I am sure Brian has something he wishes to say to you." She nudged her youngest pointedly.

Brian stepped forward, a lopsided grin on his face. "Thank you, sir, for getting me out of that nasty fix. I cannot swim, you see, and I would have been duck food had you not come along when you did."

"Nothing to it, lad," Mr. Hampton said, shaking the boy's hand vigorously. "Besides, I could hardly stand around and watch those dastardly ducks nibble you down to the bone, now could I?"

Brian giggled. "You do not like ducks, sir?"

"Only on my dinner table, lad. There I like them very well." He laughed at his own witticism, and Mathilda smiled.

"I say, sir, is he yours?"

They all turned to find Christopher gaping in admiration at a tall grey horse, whose lines shouted thoroughbred, fidgeting under the watchful eyes of a groom on a bay cob. As if sensing that he was the centre of attention, the grey pricked his ears and swung round to observe them, pawing the turf impatiently.

"Yes. Ain't he a beauty?" Mr. Hampton replied with obvious relish. "Only had him for a couple of months, but I plan to hunt with him come November up in Melton Mowbray."

"Oh, Mama, when can we get the horses you promised us?" Christopher demanded excitedly. "I want to learn to hunt."

"I believe I said ponies, dear," Mathilda replied quietly.

"Nobody joins the hunt on a pony," her eldest protested disgustedly. "I shall be laughed off the field."

"Hold your horses, lad," Mr. Hampton exclaimed with a laugh. "You must learn to jump before you can hunt, and a pony is a good place to start. I learned everything I know from my first pony, Puck."

"I want a horse like yours, sir," Christopher insisted.

"What do you call him?" Brian wanted to know.

"Horatio."

"The man who kept the bridge over the Tiber?" Christopher enquired smugly, never missing an opportunity to display his learning.

"The very same, lad, although I doubt any Roman horse could match him."

"He looks like a prime goer, sir." Christopher's voice was so full of awe that Mathilda's heart contracted.

"Do you race him, sir?" Brian asked, moving closer to the magnificent animal. "He looks as though he could beat anything on four legs."

"Oh, he is fast enough, to be sure, lad. But hunting is my true passion."

"How old is he, sir?" Christopher extended a cautious hand to stroke the sleek grey neck.

"Boys, that is quite enough," Mathilda broke into her sons' eager voices. "You must not pester Mr. Hampton with any more questions. It is time we went home, dears. You will not wish to be late for breakfast."

"That would be a major disaster in my book," chortled the genial Mr. Hampton. "A pleasure to have met you, Lady Parmenter." He made another courtly obeisance, shook hands with both boys, and mounted his horse.

"Do you ride every morning, sir?" Brian called as Hampton turned to ride away.

"Even if it rains, lad," came the laughing response, before the impatient grey carried Mr. Hampton away at a canter along the path.

"What a nice man," Brian declared, putting his seal of approval on the generous stranger as they turned homewards.

"Gentleman, you oaf," his brother corrected him. "Is that not so, Mama?"

"Mr. Hampton is most definitely a gentleman of the first stare, dear," she agreed.

The name *Hampton* sounded familiar, but Mathilda could not recall ever meeting anyone by that name. It did occur to her that he might well know the Earl of Southmoor, since most gentlemen of the *haut monde* frequented the same clubs. And if so, it was inevitable that Mr. Hampton would, sooner or later, identify her as the female who had jilted his friend ten years before.

How long would it be before Miles himself heard of her presence in London? And what, if anything, would he do?

Mathilda glanced around her anxiously as though expecting the earl to pounce on her from behind one of the spreading oaks along the banks.

Finally, she confronted the question that had plagued her since her return, and which she had studiously avoided. What would she do if she came face-to-face with her former betrothed again? If she could believe her aunt, sadly prone to exaggeration, Miles had not taken her desertion calmly. But ten years was a long time to harbour a grudge, and Mathilda had expected to find him married with a nursery full of little ones upon her return. Apparently, this had not happened. She wondered briefly if she had misjudged Miles's feeling for her, but brushed the notion aside as absurd.

It did not bear thinking of, but the sooner she left London for the safety of Bath the better.

With one last glance over her shoulder, Mathilda called to the boys, then hurried out of the Park and mounted the steps of her aunt's house with a sense of relief.

THREE

Enter the Countess

"Why would I need another evening gown, Aunt, much less a fancy ball gown? I do not expect to go to many grand balls in Bath, if any. The town cannot have changed that much in ten years. Besides, I am still in half-mourning."

Lady Denton ignored her niece's protest and instructed the modiste to show them the latest bolts of silks and satins received from the Orient. "It is high time you put off those pallid lilacs and greys, dear. High time. I think that green silk will do wonders for you," she added, reminding Mathilda vividly of the time when she had yearned to wear such a colour instead of the insipid white her mother had insisted upon. Perhaps if she had worn green silk, with a more revealing décolletage, Miles might have paid her more attention and . . . But it was senseless to waste time on what might have been. She had made her choice and had two beautiful boys to show for it. And all those wonderful years with James.

"It might surprise you to know that Bath has much to offer nowadays, dear," her aunt said as she rummaged through a selection of gloves and laces laid out on the counter. "We have a regular theatre season now, with visiting troupes from London and Edinburgh. There is a new Assembly Hall, several new tea shops, and the circulating library has grown to double the size. The summer months are filled with dinners and garden parties at the big houses in the neighbourhood. And of course, the Countess of Southmoor still holds her annual Bazaar in July. I can assure you there will be no shortage of invitations the moment everyone learns you are back, dear."

Mathilda cringed at the mention of the countess. Miles's mother, a childhood bosom-bow of both the Heath ladies, had been so very kind to Mathilda, almost like another aunt. Besides being her godmother. How she could ever face her again, Mathilda could not imagine. If anything, it would be worse than seeing Miles.

Perhaps coming back to Bath had not been such a good idea after all.

"It behooves you to look your best," her aunt continued. "Unless of course you intend to remain single for the rest of your days."

As soon as they were ensconced in the Denton carriage on their way home to Mount Street, her aunt took up the subject again.

"I meant what I said just now about turning yourself into an old matron before your time, dear. Poor James has been gone almost a year now, if my memory serves me. And here you are, an utterly stunning young widow, with a very comfortable fortune, a house in the country, and two perfect little boys. What a shame to waste it all sitting around Rose Park growing old gracefully. I will not hear of it, so say no more."

"But I do not *need* to marry again," Mathilda protested.

Her aunt gave one of her exasperated snorts. "You have lost the wits you were born with, girl, if you believe those boys will not need a man about the house to teach them how to go on in life. This is a man's world, you know, and it will do the lads no good to bring them up with a feminine attitude towards it."

"I had counted on Reginald to mentor them in those things—"

"Bosh!" her aunt exclaimed crossly. "Not only is that sapskull dead set against receiving you at Heath Hall, but I would not wish any son of mine to ape that stiff-rumped, odious coxcomb for all the tea in China. He is quite insufferable."

"Well, it is too early to start teaching them to be men, Aunt. They are still my babies."

"Balderdash, girl. They already need a man's guidance. Especially that scamp Brian. Why do you think they can talk of nothing but that Hampton fellow you met in the Park two days ago? By the way, in case you have not guessed it, your admirer is no ordinary gentleman. The Honourable Willoughby Hampton, of the Devonshire Hamptons, is the nephew and heir to Baron Hampton, one of the plumpest men in the south of England, and I am not speaking of his physical aspects, although all the Hamptons run to portliness. He is prime husband material, although wily as a fox, they say."

"Well, I am not interested in Mr. Hampton or any other gentleman."

Disregarding her niece's attempt to close the subject, Lady Denton continued enthusiastically. "Hampton is one of the original Seven Corinthians, the wealthiest and most elusive rakes in London at one time. Most of them have fallen to parson's mousetrap of course, which is just as it should be. There is something immoral about letting all those fortunes and titles go to waste in senseless philandering. I believe Hampton is one of the last holdouts now that the infamous Marquess of Monroyal was safely hogtied last year to the Hancock chit."

Mathilda descended from the carriage in Mount Street and turned to assist her aunt. "And just what is your point in reciting all this history, Aunt?"

"It has just occurred to me that Willy Hampton might be ripe for plucking, dear. And what a magnificent catch he would be," she added with a sigh. "Rich as Croesus and a thoroughly charming gentleman to boot. A noted connoisseur of horseflesh, is Willy Hampton. He would be delighted to guide you in choosing ponies for the boys, I am sure."

"Once he discovers who I am, his interest will disappear, so do not get your hopes up too much."

"Oh, I am sure he already knows who you are, dear. He is bound to know Southmoor. They all go to the same clubs, these bachelors. And you may also be sure that Miles knows you are back in London."

Mathilda directed the footman to gather their parcels from the carriage before accompanying her aunt up the shallow steps. "And what possible significance might that have? It is hardly likely that he cares where I am."

Lady Denton grinned wickedly. "We shall see, dearest. We shall soon see about that. Gentlemen are such odd creatures."

"You will never guess whom I met in the Park this morning, Miles," Willy Hampton said conversationally as the friends strolled up the steps of White's to keep their engagement to spend a quiet evening at the card tables.

The Earl of Southmoor was not in a conversational mood, and merely grunted. He was still smarting from his mother's recent announcement that his former betrothed, Mathilda Heath, was back in London. Having expected the news for years now, he had even looked forward to it with a perverted kind of pleasure. Visualising all the indignities and savouring the humiliations he would heap upon her head had kept him in a white heat for several months following her unexpected defection. But when the scandal subsided and he retired to his family estate near Bath to nurse his hurt, that first incandescent flash of fury that had driven him rampaging up the North Road, hands itching to encircle that white throat and choke the deceitful breath out of it, had melted to a hard core in his chest that flared up sporadically at any mention of the traitorous hussy.

And now she was back in London.

Within his grasp again.

His fingers closed convulsively around the ivory head of the malacca cane he affected. He had waited so long . . .

"Well?" he said, pulling himself back from the past as they chose a table in a cosy nook of the room and ordered claret from the steward. "Am I supposed to guess who this new conquest of yours is, old man?" Actually, Miles had no interest in his friend's amorous dalliances, just as long as they did not lead Hampton down the treacherous path of matrimony.

His friend laughed, but his eyes were fixed speculatively on the earl's face. "No conquest this one, Miles, my lad. Rather frosty to tell the truth, but a real Beauty. Not your usual pale simpering miss with incessantly fluttering eyelashes and lisping inconsequentials, but a true thoroughbred."

"A thoroughbred, eh? In that case I shall take your word for it. She must have been dazzling indeed to remind you of a horse, Willy."

Willy laughed again, evidently enjoying a private joke. "The lady thawed noticeably when I saved one of her boys from falling into the lake. Very attached to her boys, she is; a fine strapping pair of lads."

Miles took a sip from his glass and regarded Hampton over the rim. A sudden sense of uneasiness stole over him.

"And the name of this paragon of motherly virtue?" he enquired, a cynical twist on his lips.

"Lady Parmenter."

Miles felt his insides clench and his jaw harden.

Was that a hint of derision he detected in Hampton's voice? Of pity? Or was it his own mind playing tricks on him? Miles could not be sure, so he took another sip of claret to steady his nerves.

"I gather you knew she was back in London?"

"Yes," Miles growled, surprised that he could talk at all. "My mother is a friend of Lady Denton."

Hampton's sunny expression disappeared. "You are not contemplating anything foolish, are you, Miles?"

The earl's black eyebrows lifted contemptuously, and he felt his lips stretch into a thin line bordering on a sneer. "And what foolishness would that be, Hampton?" His voice was dangerously quiet.

His friend backed off. "None at all, I am sure, old man. After all, we are dealing with water under the bridge, are we not?"

Ignoring the question, Miles picked up a pack of cards and shuffled. His mind was not on his game, however, and within two hours he had lost over two thousand pounds and drank more claret than was his wont.

On impulse, he invited Hampton to join him at Southmoor Court for dinner, but as the two friends strolled along the darkened streets together, his thoughts returned to the subject that had eaten away at him for ten years.

"What about those boys?" he asked abruptly, hating himself for this show of interest. "Do they favour their mother?"

"Oh, no, old man," Hampton responded, evidently in no need of further clarification. "Spitting image of Parmenter; the eldest has his father's fair hair and blue eyes. The youngest, Brian, is fixing to be a rare handful. Reminds me of my nephews. A daredevil if ever I saw one. Was planning to invite them to the balloon ascension next week." He paused, glancing briefly at his companion. "That is if you ain't got any objection, old man."

Miles did not respond. He had ceased to listen to his friend's litany of praise for the two young Parmenters. He found nothing to interest him in two boys who should have been his. An unexpected rush of jealousy jolted the core of hatred in his heart, and he cursed silently as they mounted the steps at No. 17 Belgrave Square.

For some odd reason, he thought of the Pritchard chit, whom he had fully intended to offer for last week. At the last moment, his courage had faltered, and he had been unable to bring himself up to scratch. She had been so frighteningly young and innocent. She and the one before her—whose name he had already forgotten. Both girls of excellent families, quiet and respectful and obedient; both unexceptional candidates for the wife of an earl. Just as Mathilda Heath had been ten years ago—all accomplished and biddable, eager to please him, or to grasp the position of rank and fortune he could offer them.

No, he reminded himself. Mathilda had not been interested

in rank or fortune. She had run off with a baronet with half the earl's income. She had chosen a mere baronet over him.

The earl had waited years for this moment, and he intended to savour it fully. Sweet little Mathilda had humiliated him before the entire world; mocked him, tossed him aside for a man he had always held his friend. How wrong he had been, he thought grimly, grinding his teeth in suppressed rage. How they must have laughed as they sailed away and left him to bear his shame alone.

Well, the day of reckoning was upon her. The treacherous jade would pay the price, and Miles Stephens was looking forward to extracting it in full measure.

The spring skies had clouded over during the afternoon, and as the Denton carriage stopped before the front door on Mount Street, several footmen hurried down the steps with umbrellas to ward off the first fat drops of rain that were beginning to fall.

"You have quite worn me out with all this shopping, Aunt," Mathilda murmured as they entered the hall, where Benson waited to relieve them of their smaller parcels. "Where do you get the energy? I declare I have never seen such fascinating places as those furniture warehouses. I could spend a week in that George Walters Import Emporium without exhausting my curiosity."

"Walters is the premier source in London for all imported goods, dear. I confess I spend too much of my own money there. George Walters is one of the richest men in Town, by the way. A Cit, of course, but exquisitely charming. His daughter— Angela I believe her name is, just like your mother—recently wed Harry Davenport, the Earl of Castleton. Her mother was the daughter of an earl, so the match was not quite the mésalliance it appears."

Mathilda stared at her aunt in consternation. "Is there anything you do not know about *anyone* in Town, Aunt?" she demanded, pulling off her pale yellow gloves and handing her reticule to Benson. "I find that quite disconcerting if you must know."

Lady Denton laughed gaily, the ruffled trim on her striped turquoise walking gown quivering in rhythm with her merriment. "I know everyone of any importance in Town, dear, and many who are of no importance whatsoever. I cannot hold a candle to old Lady Stevens down in Brighton, of course. Lady Emmaline, who is Willy Hampton's aunt, by the way, and a fearsome harridan by all accounts, is quite the hub of all news worthy of the name in the country. My dear George did not move in the Regent's intimate circles, but he knew all those who did, and rumours have a way of filtering down to me sooner or later. For example, did you know that the Duchess of Glouschester's last son is thought to be—"

"Aunt, please," Mathilda exclaimed quickly, conscious of the servants all around them. "I am anxious for my tea. Is my mother already in the drawing room, Benson?" she continued, addressing the butler.

"Yes, milady, indeed she is. Cook has just sent up the tea-tray." He paused for an instant before adding, "The Countess of Southmoor is sitting with her ladyship."

Mathilda froze and glanced at her aunt, who appeared unconcerned by this disturbing news. "I believe I shall take my tea in my sitting room," she murmured as they trod up the stairs together.

"Nonsense, dear. I am delighted that dear Claire has decided to acknowledge you. Before you know it, you will be invited everywhere."

"I hope not, Aunt," Mathilda exclaimed, dismayed at the thought, "for I shall certainly not accept. I have no wish to be gawked at and scrutinised by all the Tabbies in Town."

No amount of remonstrating from her aunt could change Mathilda's mind, but she had barely had time to take off her bonnet and tame a wayward curl or two before there was a discreet knock on her door. She was not surprised when a footman delivered a summons from Lady Heath to join the ladies downstairs.

Since she could think of no reasonable excuse for not doing so, Mathilda glanced at herself in the bevelled mirror, pinched some colour into her pale cheeks, and entered the drawing room a few minutes later, her heart in her throat.

She soon discovered that her fears were misplaced, for the countess rose at once and embraced her with so much affection that Mathilda was soon drawn into talking about her Indian experience as though it were the most normal thing in the world. Tactfully, she did not mention James, but the countess displayed such interest in the boys that they were called down from the schoolroom for her inspection.

"I understand you have made quite an impression on a good friend of mine, Mr. Willy Hampton," the countess remarked to Brian when the lively conversation permitted.

"Oh, yes, my lady," Brian responded without hesitation, not being shy with strangers. "He is quite top-of-the-trees with us and a real hand with horses. Did you know that he let me ride his grey Horatio, a bang-up piece of blood and bones if ever there was one?" He grinned with pleasure. "And I did not fall off, either," he added with a smug glance at his brother, who had, it turned out, not been so lucky.

The tea hour passed very pleasantly indeed, and when the countess rose to take her leave, she pressed Mathilda to accompany the elder ladies to a small musicale she was holding at Southmoor Court in two days' time.

"A very small affair, I can assure you. Only my particular friends and a few musicians I like to sponsor. I know you have a sweet singing voice, Mathilda, and I shall look forward to hearing you again."

Mathilda could not find the courage to refuse this generous invitation directly to her ladyship, but she resolved not to set foot in Miles's house under any circumstances.

How could she? Mathilda asked herself as she lay awake that night long after the clock in the hall had struck midnight.

The earl would surely give her the most crushing set-down imaginable. She was not yet ready to face the man she had so mistreated on the eve of her eighteenth birthday. It had been a coward's way out to entrust the news of her change of heart to a few cold lines on a damp note delivered by a servant. At the time, she had been relieved to escape Miles's inevitable wrath, but when it was too late to change those heartless words, Mathilda had come to realise that, however little he had appeared to care for her, her former betrothed had received very shabby treatment indeed.

Perhaps one day she would have the opportunity to beg his forgiveness, she told herself, turning over again in a vain attempt to sleep. He would never grant it, of course, but she owed it to herself, and certainly to Miles Stephens, Earl of Southmoor, to make the attempt.

But not yet.

FOUR

Cat and Mouse

"Top of the morning to you, Miles." This cheerful greeting heralded the appearance of the Hon. Willoughby Hampton, better known to his intimates as *Sweet Willy,* at the library door. He paused on the threshold, raised a jewelled quizzing-glass to his right eye, and surveyed the room lazily. "Harris said I would find you here."

Miles glanced first at the clock on the mantel, then at his friend and forced a smile. "What brings you out of bed at this early hour, Willy? You did not leave the Jameson ball last night until nearly dawn."

"Gad!" Hampton exclaimed, strolling across to a deep leather armchair and sinking into it with a contented sigh. "Runs in the blood, old man. The Hamptons are farmers, always have been. Up at cock-crow and all that."

"And you came here to impress me, I suppose?"

As an early riser himself, the Earl of Southmoor was usually to be found comfortably ensconced in his library every morning after breakfast, reading the *Gazette.* That sunny morning in mid June was no exception. The state of the paper, spread around him on the floor and furniture in its customary disarray, suggested that his attention had been directed not so keenly on foreign affairs, the controversial bill recently presented to Parliament, the racing prospects in Newmarket, or the latest news from the former colonies, but on the large section of print consecrated to the social gatherings and gossip of the *ton.*

He had been perusing a list of guests at three of the main social affairs held the previous week, and the fact was not lost on his visitor. Hampton peered at the page through his glass and his ruddy face took on an amused expression.

"I see," he remarked, nodding his head owlishly at the column. "Checking out the latest toilettes sported by this year's crop of marriageable chits, are you? I noticed an alarming preponderance of pink at Jameson's affair last night. Not my favourite colour, I regret to say. Now, I could not but admire the temerity of Lady Jarvis in her tangerine ensemble with the little green beads on that enormous ruff around the hem. And Mrs. Cartwright quite outdid herself with those monstrous yellow ostrich feathers in her purple turban. Pity she is so tubby, for on another that ball gown in ruffled puce satin might possibly have shown to more advantage."

Miles looked up from his perusal, a reluctant smile dispelling his gloom. "Whatever are you blathering on about, Willy?" He paused to watch his friend savour the fresh cup of coffee Harris had set beside him. "Do you realise, old man, that if ever you fell on hard times and those prize sheep of yours in Devon succumbed to murrain and perished *en mass*, you might easily earn your keep as a gossip columnist for the daily rags. Imagine how much the general tone of the population would be elevated by your descriptions of Lady Jarvis swathed in tangerine satin."

Hampton gazed reproachfully over the rim of his cup. "You choose to mock my artistic talents, Miles, but do not think such radical ideas have never crossed my mind. I daresay if I set my mind to it, I would be lionized or crucified quite as immoderately as this half-Scots fellow has been. All on account of some limp, jangling *ottava rima* ramblings immortalizing— if I may quote the press—the licentious, irrelevant escapades of a misguided Prometheus."

Miles laughed shortly. "I gather you do not like Byron."

"Quite the contrary, I find him vastly amusing. His satirical voice is one of the best, but all too often he sacrifices the deli-

cacies of style for revolutionary bombast. Let us hope he im-
proves with time."

"You amaze me, Willy. Not only are you an arbiter of feminine fashion in London saloons, but a literary wit and critic in
the bargain."

The earl leaned back in his chair and crossed his long legs.
"Now that we have all the preliminaries out of the way, my
friend, perhaps you will tell me the real reason for this enjoy-
able call of yours."

Hampton grinned broadly and helped himself to one of the
warm scones the earl's butler had thoughtfully provided.

"The truth of the matter is that I have just come from a delightful lake-side encounter with Lady Parmenter in the Park."

Although Miles had begun to suspect as much, this bald announcement turned his stomach into a hard knot. It was all he
could do not to toss his cooling coffee into his friend's smiling
face. The depth of his fury alarmed him. He bit his tongue and
said nothing.

"I thought you would like to know that she grows more delightful with every encounter. One would never guess her age
to be—what is it?—six-and-twenty."

"Eight-and-twenty," Miles cut in without thinking, then
cursed himself for betraying his interest.

"Whatever you say, old man," Hampton concurred. "Much
to my regret, I did not know the lady when she and you . . .
that is to say, during the year of your betrothal. I do recall that
you were pretty cagey about the whole affair. Kept her to
yourself, so to speak—for which I cannot blame you. Of
course," he continued delicately, "there is always the proverbial fly in the ointment, as my Aunt Stevens would say."

"I suggest we leave all talk of flies out of it, Hampton,"
Miles snapped brusquely. "I do not wish to discuss it."

"Of course," his friend hastened to say. "Could not agree
more, old boy. Pesky things that they are. I only mention it
because—"

"What is your drift?" the earl enquired in a deceptively soft voice. "Are you telling me that you have developed a *tendre* for the lady?"

Miles could hear the challenge implicit in his question, and regretted his inability to dismiss the subject as inconsequential.

Hampton grinned sheepishly. "I confess the idea did occur to me. But I want to be sure that you will not be bent out of shape if I trespass on that ground, Miles. No sense in jeopardizing a perfectly sound friendship, if you know what I mean?"

Miles knew all too well what his friend was saying. Unfortunately he could not forget—or forgive—that other friend from long ago who had not been so scrupulous.

He shrugged. "Appreciate your candour, Hampton, but that is all water under the bridge," he responded with calculated indifference. "I wish you well." He did no such thing, of course, but how could he admit the unthinkable, even to one of his closest friends? How could he say that the notion of Mathilda—*his* Mathilda—finding solace with yet another gentleman turned his soul to ashes?

"What do you say we drop in at White's for a little sustenance and perhaps a game of whist?" he heard himself say, although he had no appetite at all, and cared little if he never saw another pack of cards in his life.

"Splendid idea, Miles." Hampton helped himself to another scone. "Let me just polish off these delicious morsels. Would not want your excellent Cook to think I disparage her offerings."

Moments later they collected their hats and gloves and sauntered out into the sunshine of Belgrave Square. The earl twirled his malacca cane with a nonchalance he was far from feeling.

"So, Miles," his friend exclaimed as their path took them towards the club, "am I to understand you have not yet seen the lovely Mathilda?"

The sound of his former betrothed's name on another man's lips offended him, but Miles controlled his rush of anger.

"No, but I expect to do so tonight at my mother's musicale."

"If you care to take a turn in my new curricle this afternoon, I think I can guarantee you shall set eyes on the Beauty sooner than that."

Miles was suddenly not so sure that he wished to take this decisive step in bridging the distance of years that stretched between the Mathilda he had once known and the female who had reentered his life as Lady Parmenter, a widow with two children. A radiantly lovely widow, if Hampton's account could be trusted.

Before he could decipher this odd reluctance to reacquaint himself with the female who had so disastrously changed his life, Miles succumbed to the long buried urge to hunt down the source of his humiliation and destroy her. The sooner that hunt began, the predator in him urged, the sooner Miles Stephens would enjoy retribution.

"Sounds like an excellent idea, old man," he drawled, a slow smile of anticipation curling his lips.

"I swear you shall not escape so easily from accompanying us, dear," Lady Denton protested loudly when Mathilda complained of a racking megrim after tea on the day of the countess's musicale. "I shall instruct Cook to prepare a draught of her Scottish potion for such ailments. It does taste a little like . . ." She paused in mid-sentence. "Perhaps I should not tell you what it tastes like, dear, or you will not want to drink it. But it is wonderful stuff and works like a charm. Ask your mother."

Mathilda glanced at Lady Heath, who was busy cutting up a slice of seed cake into bite-sized pieces. Her mother looked particularly fetching in a fluttery pale primrose gown of the finest muslin, picked out with deeper yellow rose-buds on the brief bodice that revealed a perfect expanse of white throat and bosom enviable in a female half her age. It was no surprise to Mathilda that her father had been utterly besotted by this wispy creature whose pale curls were as untouched by grey as they had been ten years ago.

Had she been born with the fragile beauty of her mother, Mathilda had often asked herself, would Miles have been more attentive? Would he have looked at her more often, smiled at her with secret admiration, touched her with those strong, slender fingers of his that she had—in a flutter of romantical yearning—longed to feel against her cheek?

At one time—in her extreme youth—Mathilda had bitterly resented her mother's perfect looks. She had been rather gawky as a girl, a phase she could not imagine her mother ever experienced. As she grew older, Mathilda realised that she would never enjoy her mother's beauty. She was a Heath like her father and Aunt Agatha, like her brother Reginald, whose hair had been the identical shade of dark auburn when they were children. The resemblance was so startling that Lady Denton had often been taken for her mother, a state of affairs that Mathilda had resented, until James had told her that he had first been seduced by her dark tresses and darker eyes. No pale blond Beauty could hold a candle to his Mathilda, he had always said.

"Is this true, Mama?" she enquired. "I hate potions of any kind, but if you swear by it . . ." Mathilda let the words hang there, hoping her mother would not remember that her only daughter had rarely been afflicted by megrims in the past. She was quite determined not to attend the musical evening even if she was obliged to drink some disgusting draught or other concocted by her aunt's Scottish cook.

Lady Heath popped a small piece of cake delicately into her mouth and nodded. "Your aunt is correct, dear. A small dose of Cook's magic potion and an hour or two's rest will work wonders."

"Magic?"

Her aunt laughed. "You must know how these Scots are, dear. They still honour the old Celtic ways and believe in all sorts of spells and witchcraft that it is best not to examine too closely."

"Witchcraft?" Mathilda echoed with growing astonishment. "You are beginning to sound like those old Indian holy men one encounters in Calcutta who have herbs and charms and amulets for every conceivable ill that might befall mankind. Christopher is the one who could tell you what to take for an earache or loss of hair. He picked up an incredible amount of the lore from our old gardener in Calcutta, who was a practicing healer."

The older ladies looked dubious. "I think we had better stick with Cook's potion, dear," her aunt insisted. "You will be as right as rain in a trice. I shall send down to her immediately." After relaying her order to the butler, she turned to her sister-in-law, and Mathilda saw a twinkle of amusement in her aunt's dark eyes.

"May we expect to encounter Lord Snowburn tonight, Angela? I hear he is excessively fond of music."

To Mathilda's astonishment, her mother blushed a rosy pink that gave her the appearance of a young girl. "I believe his lordship has expressed a notion to attend the musicale," she murmured, her attention fixed on the tiny morsels of seed cake she had aligned on her plate.

"Lord Snowburn?" She glanced enquiringly at her aunt.

"Yes, Aloysius Augustus Snowburn," Lady Denton said with relish. "A charming gentleman of the old school, and an excellent fourth at whist. A tidy fortune in the Funds, I hear, and a prosperous estate up in Lancaster. His nephew is the Marquess of Gresham, old Wexley's heir. Good connexions on his mother's side, too."

"And this paragon likes music, I gather?" Mathilda prodded when her aunt paused to replenish her tea-cup.

Lady Denton laughed, her throaty voice conveying all sorts of salacious nuances. "That is what he would have you believe, dear. Personally"—her voice lowered conspiratorially—

"I think your mother is the attraction, because he is forever underfoot wherever we go."

"Your aunt exaggerates as usual," Lady Heath put in quickly, the glow lingering on her cheeks. "It so happens that Aloysius was a suitor of mine before I met your father, dear. He is Reginald's godfather and has always stood my friend. When he heard I was coming to London to meet you, he offered to escort us about Town." She glanced defiantly at her hostess. "And even your aunt must admit that it is convenient to have a gentleman at our disposal for social occasions."

Reminded that she had pleaded a megrim, Mathilda refrained from pursuing this startling new insight into Lady Heath's gentlemen admirers, excused herself, and retired to her room to await Cook's magic potion. She slept the rest of the afternoon away, awakening only when Lady Denton slipped into her room before dinner. Her aunt showed such concern that Mathilda felt guilty for her subterfuge, and as a result allowed herself to be bullied into drinking a bowl of chicken broth, which she loathed. If this was the price she must pay to avoid an encounter with the earl, Mathilda was happy enough to pay it.

At breakfast the following morning, Lady Denton reported that not only did Mr. Hampton appear utterly downcast at Mathilda's indisposition, but that the earl himself had taken particular note of her niece's absence.

"Most condescending of him, to be sure," she said with sly pleasure. "You could have knocked me over with a feather when he addressed me, dear. He is usually so starched up that I never know what to say to him."

The notion of her loquacious aunt bereft of speech was so unusual, Mathilda had to smile. "Was Lord Snowburn present?" she asked, more to divert the topic to safer ground than out of any real interest in her mother's ancient beau.

"Indeed he was," Lady Denton responded promptly. "And I have invited him to take tea with us this afternoon. He is most desirous of renewing his acquaintance with you, Mathilda. I was tempted to include Willoughby Hampton in the invitation. The poor boy stood there looking so cast down at your absence that my heart was touched. It appears you have made a conquest there, dear, and who am I to stand in the way of true love?"

"You are being quite absurd, Aunt," Mathilda responded quickly, before she saw the tell-tale glint of amusement in Lady Denton's eyes. "Or a sad tease, I know not which. But in any case, I have no particular interest in Mr. Hampton, although the boys dote on his every word."

"I would have invited him for my own pleasure, dear, for Hampton is quite charming; but Southmoor chose that moment to approach me, and I could not extend an invitation to one and not the other."

"Thank you for that small kindness, Aunt," Mathilda said tersely. "I am glad to know you have some consideration for my feelings."

Lady Denton laughed. "I was sorely tempted to find out if Southmoor would actually accept my invitation," she confessed. "I would be willing to wager a pony that he would," she added gaily, accepting a plate of eggs and bacon from Benson, hovering beside her chair. "I felt it in the air, and my instincts are rarely wrong."

"They are wrong in this case, Aunt, so perhaps it is as well you did not make that foolish wager. You would have lost your twenty-five pounds."

Dismissing what she considered her aunt's purely imaginary claim of any interest on the earl's part, Mathilda put her former betrothed out of her mind and gave herself up to the pleasures of a day spent with her boys.

FIVE

Encounter at Hatchard's

Willy Hampton had been true to his word. After less than an hour tooling around London in his friend's new curricle and four, causing not a few heads to turn among the shoppers along Piccadilly, Miles was favoured with a glimpse of the female he was determined to destroy.

He had noticed the two young boys first. Their fair colouring had reminded him instantly of James Parmenter, and brought back memories of happy summers at Southmoor Grange. James had been his closest neighbour and friend in those days, and had shared his every secret. How often had they conspired together to elude Reggie Heath, whose family estate lay to the north of Southmoor Grange. A lad their own age, Reggie had been too timorous for their youthful bravado, invariably finding fault with every piece of fun they dreamed up. He had ratted on them, too, an unforgivable sin.

Reggie had held the trump card in the end, of course—his only sister, Mathilda.

Miles remembered all too well that summer little Mathilda Heath had emerged from the schoolroom transformed from the painfully shy blue-stocking into the dark-eyed slip of a girl who had turned his head and stolen his heart with the first flutter of her incredibly long lashes. At four-and-twenty, Miles had considered himself a man of the world, and had fancied himself infatuated with other females before.

But Mathilda was different. She left him tongue-tied. How he wished that James had not been called away to Scotland that summer to visit his ailing grandfather. James had the gift of the gab and would have known what to say to a young lady of refined sensibilities. James could recite poetry, quote witticisms, and provoke laughter at whim. Miles had needed his friend with him that summer, but had somehow muddled through alone.

When his mother had proposed a match between the families, Miles had been simultaneously astounded at his good luck and petrified with fear that Mathilda would refuse him. His mother had called him a nodkin even to imagine such a nonsensical thing.

"You are Southmoor's heir, dear," she had said confidently, as though that fact alone could overcome all obstacles. "And Mathilda is a girl of sense. She will see the advantages and do as her father bids her."

His mother had been right, of course. When he had presented himself at Heath Hall to make his offer, his success had been a foregone conclusion. That officious Reggie had told him so, meeting him in the hall and throwing an arm across his shoulders in an offensively familiar way. Sir John Heath had been equally unambiguous. His jovial welcome had confirmed Miles's fear that Mathilda had been primed to accept him, no matter how he phrased his offer.

The inevitability of the affair had depressed him. When Sir John had sent for his daughter and left them alone, with what could only be termed a fond smirk on his face, Miles's mind went blank. Later, he had no recollection of what he had actually said to Mathilda, although it must have been what she expected, for no sooner was it said than she summoned her father, who congratulated him enthusiastically and called in the rest of the family to celebrate the event.

He had not even sealed their agreement with a kiss.

Come to think of it, he had never kissed his affianced bride. It was one of the things Miles had looked forward to after the wedding.

A wedding that, thanks to his good friend James, had never

taken place. James had kissed the bride instead. For his Mathilda had become James's bride, and Miles had never forgiven him. Never forgiven her.

Miles ground his teeth as his gaze moved from the two handsome boys to the woman with them. She was as radiant as Hampton had promised. He was momentarily struck dumb, as he had been so long ago, at the first glimpse of her perfect profile. She wore a fashionable bonnet of deep lavender, festooned with pink roses, that shaded her face, but he saw her laugh at a comment from the younger boy, and his stomach clenched. A happy picture indeed, he thought, bitterness rising in him in a nauseated wave, a picture that should have included him.

A sharp jab in the ribs from his companion brought Miles out of his daze.

"Well?" Hampton demanded, his attention on a bright red gig blocking the road ahead. The two young dandies in the gig took one look at the driver of the spanking team of bays and fell over each other trying to coax their wall-eyed chestnut aside. They only succeeded in spooking the animal into rearing up and backing the gig into a heavy dray-horse hitched to a wagon unloading barrels of goods to a grocer's establishment. The dray-man did not take kindly to this cow-handed behaviour of his betters and made no bones about telling them so at the top of his voice.

In the ensuing commotion, Miles lost sight of the Parmenters, but that first glimpse of Mathilda burned into his brain like a fever. He noticed with dismay that his hands were trembling, and he clenched his fists instinctively.

"Well?" his companion insisted. "Was I not correct in my assessment of the lady's charms? What a lovely sight for a poor old bachelor's eyes. Makes me wonder why I never surrendered long ago to the lures of parson's mousetrap."

Coming from Willy Hampton, who had outsmarted the most tenacious mamas on the Marriage Mart since the day he came down from Oxford as one of the prime catches of the Season, this pronouncement sounded ludicrous. Miles wondered how much truth there was in his friend's casual remark. He hoped that Hampton was merely jesting. If his friend developed a *tendre* for Mathilda, it might complicate Miles's plans, but not deter him from the vindication he had come to believe was his due.

"You cannot be serious, old chap," he said bracingly. "Only think what would happen to the reputation of the infamous Corinthians if you succumb to the yoke of matrimony."

Hampton's face took on a glum expression. "The Corinthians are a lost cause, my dear fellow. Every last one of them felled by Cupid's arrow. And with the demise of old Monroyal last summer—"

"Robert Stilton is dead?"

"Aye, indeed," Hampton said mournfully. "*Slain by a fair sweet maid,*" he recited melodramatically.

"I heard that he was caught with the wrong *maid* under compromising circumstances," Miles said bluntly.

"Poor Robert's hand was forced, that is true enough. He took on one wager too many. And now that Robert has fallen, I am the only one left unshackled. What is a man to do?"

He sounded so woebegone that Miles had to laugh. "No sense in attending a wake until a man has been decently laid out, old boy."

Although they did catch several glimpses of Lady Parmenter and her aunt tooling about town, it was not until the next evening at the opening of the Italian opera with Nina Caravaggio at the Opera House that Miles was permitted his first prolonged inspection of his former betrothed.

Accompanied by old Lord Snowburn, the three Heath ladies slipped into their box moments before the lights dimmed for the first act. During the intermission, Hampton paid his respects, but Miles was unable to escape the tiresome chatter of two young friends of his mother's who vied for his attention.

As a result he felt frustrated at not being able to approach Mathilda, and disgusted with himself at his sudden desire to do so.

*   *   *

Accompanied by Lord Snowburn, the Heath ladies arrived at his lordship's box as the lights dimmed on the first act. Lady Denton whispered that Hampton and Southmoor were both present in the latter's box, accompanied by the countess, his mother. The presence of two younger ladies, whom her aunt pronounced as of little consequence, made Mathilda feel easier at first. But during the interval she could not help noticing— since the Southmoor box was directly across from their own— that both ladies were vying for the earl's attention in a manner she considered immodest to say the least.

Mathilda told herself she should be grateful to the ladies who kept the earl fixed to his seat. Mr. Hampton was the only one from the Southmoor party who came to pay his respects to the Heath ladies. He was so very charming that Mathilda was beguiled into granting him permission to bring one of his ponies to the Park the following morning.

"It occurred to me that the boys would enjoy a canter on an animal more suitable than my Horatio," Hampton murmured as he made the request. "Only say the word, my lady, and I shall bring a mount for you as well. There is nothing like a canter in the early morning to get the blood flowing."

While refusing this kind offer, Mathilda found herself admitting that she would be glad of some guidance in choosing ponies for her sons when they repaired to Bath.

"I know there are no horses in the stables at Rose Park at present, except the work horses and the agent's cob. I suppose I could instruct Barnes to procure mounts for us, but—"

"My dear lady," Hampton interrupted with a smile, "one cannot always depend on an agent to find a good horse in the country. Nothing would give me greater pleasure than to scout out a safe lady's mount for you and reliable ponies for the boys. It would be my delight, I assure you, and even if I do say so myself, I am accounted a rare hand at horse trading."

So it was that Mathilda found herself consulting with Mr. Hampton about all details regarding the purchase of horses and a light travelling chaise to take them to Bath. That led to

Mr. Hampton's offering his escort into Somerset, which Lady Denton accepted with alacrity, despite Mathilda's protestation.

"I wonder a gentleman of his many pursuits would find time to waste on three widowed ladies and two small boys on such a tedious journey," Mathilda remarked waspishly when the gentleman had taken his leave.

Lady Denton smiled. "I daresay he has his reasons, my dear Mathilda," she replied mildly.

"Then I trust he will not bring all his rakish friends with him," was all Mathilda could find to say.

Her aunt's delighted laughter caused Lord Snowburn and Lady Heath to glance over with interest.

"My dear girl," Lady Denton spoke as soon as she had recovered her composure. "Never in my life did I think to hear poor Southmoor referred to as a rake. If indeed that is who you mean. And as for Hampton himself, I daresay he may have his rakish side—he used to run with gazetted rogues like Gresham, Wolverton, Monroyal, and Mansfield, you know—but a more mild-mannered gentleman it would be hard to find in a month of Sundays."

Conscious of the others in the box, Mathilda kept her thoughts on the matter to herself.

Two afternoons later, as the friends made their now habitual parade down Piccadilly, Hampton impulsively turned off on St. James's with the intention of stopping at their club for nuncheon. Out of the corner of his eye, Miles caught the flutter of green as a lady descended from her coach and entered Hatchard's Bookshop. The two boys with her were unmistakable, and before Miles quite knew what he was about, he had jumped from the moving curricle.

"Hatchard's," he called over his shoulder. "Meet you at White's later," he added and strode away. The scent of his prey heady in the air, even as his rage surged anew at the sight of the lady in green.

The sudden hush that greeted him as he stepped into the

sanctum of London's most popular bookshop made him pause. Several elderly gentlemen sat in the reading nook, perusing the daily papers, while two matrons examined the latest arrivals at a small table near the door.

Mathilda was nowhere in sight.

The murmur of a boy's voice alerted him, and he moved along the rows of bookcases, glancing down each aisle until he found her. She was standing near the end of the aisle, gazing up at the highest shelf. The two boys milled about, evidently seeking a specific title.

The earl strode quietly down the adjoining aisle, his nerves prickling with anticipation. At the end of the row, he turned into the next aisle, knowing she would be almost within the grasp of his hand. He came to an abrupt halt, his breath caught in his throat.

She had not heard his approach, and as he stood watching, so close he could detect the faint lavender perfume she wore, she reached up for a book on the top shelf. Conscious of every detail of the scene, passing in slow motion before his eyes, Miles saw her gloved fingers fumble with the volume. She stood on tiptoe, but the book stubbornly refused to be jostled away from its companions.

"Allow me." Before he realised what he was doing, Miles stepped forward, bridging the gap between them, and slid the recalcitrant volume from its slot, holding it in his hand.

Lady Parmenter flinched visibly and turned a startled gaze towards him. After the briefest hesitation, she recognised him, and Miles distinctly heard her gasp. Lips parted, eyes wide, she gazed up at him, and Miles felt as though he had been dealt a particularly punishing blow to the solar plexus. With a great effort, he pulled himself out of his paralysis and forced his lips to move.

"Welcome back to England, Mathilda."

She made no reply, staring at him with an expression he could not read in the dimness of the aisle. Her eyes were luminous, filled with emotions that flitted through their amber depths in bewildering succession.

Miles was momentarily captivated by their intensity, before he remembered why he was there.

"I trust I may still call you Mathilda?" His voice was low, cajoling, and slightly hoarse. She never took her eyes from his, returning his gaze steadily, without any hint of the painful shyness he remembered in the girl he had once known. He saw her lips part, and a sudden desire to claim that kiss that had been denied him long ago overtook him. The urge was so strong, Miles had to exert his will to recall his anger.

Her lips moved, but her first words were not those he had expected.

"Still?" she echoed with a hint of puzzlement. "Never once did you call me Mathilda, my lord. It is one of the things I particularly remember about you."

She did not drop her eyes, as he was accustomed to females doing in his presence. The notion that she had remembered him, thought of him at all, thrilled him until it struck him that her words were almost an accusation. How dare she accuse *him* of the very crime she herself had committed? With an effort he repressed an angry retort.

Had he truly never called his betrothed by her given name? He could well believe it. It sounded like the kind of thing he would do. Although now that she had mentioned it, Miles recalled that his friend—he cringed to use that term for his betrayer—had been free enough with her name. Too free, of course, but he had not thought anything of it. Until it was too late.

"Remiss of me." He could think of nothing else to say.

"Yes, my lord." Her voice was cool, and her cheeks had regained their colour. She held out her hand. "Thank you for getting the book down. These shelves are not as convenient as they appear."

He placed the book in her hand, noting that she made sure their fingers did not touch. "My mother tells me you will soon remove to Bath. Have you set a date yet?"

She clutched the book, her eyes suddenly evasive. "Our travel plans are not settled. My aunt is reluctant to leave London."

Miles did not believe this for a moment. Her reticence amused him. It was imperative that he know where his quarry was hiding, but he could find out easily enough from Hampton.

"You are looking well." He could still think of nothing meaningful to say. "India must have agreed with you."

Only after this platitude was out did Miles realise that it might be understood as an indirect reference to her marriage. And the last thing he wanted to admit was that marriage to James had made her happy. He cursed his lack of address. After all these years he still could not talk comfortably with the female who had mattered so much to him. He knew he should say something about her bereavement, but he could not bring himself to mention James's name. The sting of betrayal was still too sharp.

"Yes, Calcutta suited us very well." She was gazing up at him again, her amber eyes more beautiful than he remembered, her lashes as long and luxuriant, but far more bewitching if that were possible. He felt a tightness in his chest and searched vainly for something intelligent to say.

"Shall I see you at the Kendrick's ball tomorrow night?" Even to his ears, his voice sounded stiff.

She smiled briefly. "No, but my aunt will be there, I am sure."

He opened his mouth to respond, then shut it abruptly. How could he say that he had no interest in Lady Denton without implying that it was Mathilda he wanted to see again?

Miles was at a loss for words again. He was saved from dredging up more inanities by one of the boys, who suddenly appeared at her side.

"Mama, may we please take this one? I did not—Oh, excuse me, sir," the lad added with an embarrassed grin and ducked away.

The interruption broke the spell that seemed to hold them together. Miles felt her relief as a palpable thing spring up between them as she stepped back, murmured her thanks again, and turned to follow her son down the aisle. Where would this end? he wondered, not quite as sure of the outcome as he had been just this morning.

He watched her go with mixed emotions.

Mathilda had no clear recollection of the drive back to Mount Street. The sudden, disturbing encounter with the Earl of Southmoor in the narrow aisle at Hatchard's had rattled her nerves and given rise to all sorts of wild fantasies that assailed her no sooner had she laid her head on the pillow that night. She closed her eyes, but her mind would not stop spinning. She kept seeing his dark eyes gazing into hers as she had once dreamed they would. His gaze was every bit as mesmerizing as she had imagined it. Mathilda had been unable to look away.

He had materialized beside her—far too close for comfort— so suddenly, so unexpectedly that he had unnerved her. She had felt rooted to the floor, unable to move a muscle. The faint scent of his Holland water, assailing her as he reached up to bring down the copy of Scott's latest novel, had rendered her helpless, quite unable to turn and follow her first instinctive urge to flee. She had stood there, breathing in the well-remembered warmth of his presence, basking in it. Against all reason, she chided herself, looking back on her missish reaction to a gentleman who should, by rights, have had no effect on her whatsoever.

Evidently she had been mistaken on that account. His voice alone had shaken her so deeply she had been unable to respond to his welcome. Standing there like some gauche schoolroom chit, she had simply gazed at him, making no effort to stem the wild flood of memories that rose up to envelop her.

The spell of his presence had been rudely broken by his

next words, which brought back to her, more vividly than she had thought possible, the depth of the chasm that had separated her from this man. *I trust I may still call you Mathilda?* He had spoken without the slightest recollection of the truth. The sound of her name had never passed his lips before. How could she forget that? She had ever been a dry *Miss Heath* to him. How could *he* not remember how formal and cold their relationship had been?

She had been shocked into reminding him that his memory was faulty; there had been no such intimacy between them. Much as she had wished for it at the time, he had never so much as touched the tips of her fingers unless he could not, in all civility, avoid it. The pain of his rejection still rankled, but all he could say was some platitude about being remiss.

Remiss indeed! Her ire flared again at the irony of it. How could he be so cavalier about something that had mattered so intensely to her? He had not cared what she thought; that had become obvious as the Season progressed. What Mathilda wished had never mattered to anyone, she realised with sudden clarity. Her parents had welcomed the match; her father had even instructed her exactly what she should respond to the viscount when he made his offer; her brother had warned her not to expect romantical nonsense from a man of Southmoor's rank. They had all been in alt at the advantageous connexion, dazzled by the title and fortune the match would bring.

Mathilda had been dazzled by the man.

At seventeen, she had imagined herself in love. In spite of Reginald's warning, she had told herself that Miles's reserve would eventually give way, and he would reveal through furtive touch, or secret glance, or whispered words, that his heart was hers. None of this had happened, and in the end, Mathilda had despaired of discovering the love she yearned for under the seeming indifference of her betrothed.

No wonder she had felt such a surge of relief when James had smiled at her with admiration in his eyes.

"Who was that gentleman, Mama?"

Pulling herself from fruitless ruminations on the past, Mathilda glanced at her eldest son. Christopher often displayed an intelligence beyond his years, and since his father's death had taken it upon himself to help her keep an eye on his younger brother.

"That was the Earl of Southmoor," she replied simply. "He knew your father long ago, and has an estate to the south of Rose Park."

"He is a neighbour, then?"

"Yes, dear. He lives at Southmoor Grange, the largest estate in the area. His mother is the countess you met at tea the other afternoon."

"I like her," Christopher announced with the directness of children, and it was not lost on his mother that her son omitted any reference to the earl. "I like Mr. Hampton, too. He promised to teach me to hunt as soon as I outgrow my pony. Does he live near Rose Park?"

"The Hamptons are from Devonshire, but I believe Mr. Hampton has an aunt in Bath. And he has kindly offered to escort us there when we leave London."

"Let us leave tomorrow, Mama," Brian chipped in, his voice eager. "Mr. Hampton said I have good hands and an excellent seat. He has promised to find me a pony when we go home. Can we, Mama? Go tomorrow I mean? I want to learn to ride."

Mathilda had not considered cutting short her London stay, but Brian's enthusiasm was infectious, and she was suddenly anxious to take possession of the home she had thought to share with James. The Parmenter solicitor in the City, Mr. Hamilton, had called upon her during the first week of her return and informed her that the house could use some refurbishing.

"Of course, the good news, my lady, is that Sir James provided very handsomely for the upkeep of the estate, which has prospered under the present manager. Sir James settled a very generous portion on you, besides making you co-trustee of the heir. You will be able to live at Rose Park without sparing the expense."

Mathilda had known that James had prospered in India, but it was not until Mr. Hamilton showed her the settlements that she realised she was a wealthy woman.

"Yes, Mama," Christopher added his plea to his brother's. "Let us go home. I would like to see the place where Papa was born."

Nothing would suit her better, Mathilda thought, as the carriage drew up before her aunt's house. She had taken no pleasure in the few social gatherings she had attended with her mother and Lady Denton. Society still remembered the ancient scandal, and Mathilda fancied she saw speculation and censure in the eyes of the *ton*. Returning home, she would leave London gossip and impertinent curiosity behind her.

And she would also escape further confrontations with the earl.

Looking back on their brief encounter, Mathilda recalled the interest Miles had shown in seeing her again. Had he not enquired if she would attend the Kendrick's ball? He had sounded as though he *wished* to see her again. But surely that was impossible. Why would he wish to have anything to do with a female who had jilted him? Perhaps he had asked so that he might avoid the ball if she were there?

Perhaps he was merely being civil? That must be the explanation. He was ever oppressively polite. Besides, what possible interest could the Earl of Southmoor have in the widowed Lady Parmenter and her two boys?

Satisfied that she had nothing to fear in that direction, Mathilda mounted the steps, smiling at the excited chatter of her sons.

SIX

Rose Park

"There is no reason on this earth why you must rush off in such a bang, dear," Lady Heath remarked for the fourth time at breakfast that morning. "Do reconsider, Mathilda. I particularly wished to take you to Almack's tomorrow evening. Sally Jersey made a point of enquiring about you at the Kendrick's ball last night. She is most anxious to hear about one of her godsons who took up a post in Calcutta two years ago and has not been heard of since."

Mathilda sipped her tea and smiled affectionately at her mother. "If Lady Jersey is concerned about that rattle Mr. Farthingworth, she has every reason to be anxious, Mama. He is forever in low company and spends his time drinking and gambling instead of fostering his career. I do not envy his family, for he is bound to come to a bad end one of these days."

"Then you will stay a few days longer? I know Sally would want to hear this information from your lips."

"No, Mama," Mathilda said, quietly but firmly. "I have already made up my mind, and the boys are restless here. It is high time they returned to their father's house and learned to live like normal English boys."

"Mr. Hampton will be disappointed, dear," Aunt Agatha put in with a coy smile. "I swear the dear man was quite looking forward to playing the gallant when he offered to escort us back to Bath. If you are not with the party, he will be sadly deflated, I can assure you, for what gentleman would wish to escort two elderly ladies when he might have enjoyed your company."

"Your aunt is right, Mathilda. You are being very tiresome, and Mr. Hampton is not a gentleman to be treated lightly. You must think of the future, dear, and I can think of no one I would rather have as a son-in-law than our charming Mr. Hampton."

"You are building castles in the sky, Mama," Mathilda replied with a laugh. "I am barely acquainted with your Mr. Hampton, and from what I have heard, he is most adroit at evading matrimonial entanglements. It is a peculiarity I particularly admire in him," she added perversely.

"Fiddle!" Lady Denton exclaimed sharply. "I will not believe I have such a mutton-head in the family. Even if Hampton is merely being civil—which I take leave to doubt—his company cannot but lend consequence to us all and bring you to the notice of other eligible gentlemen who are not so skittish about getting caught in parson's mousetrap."

Mathilda shook her head in exasperation. "My dear Aunt, I have been back in London less than a month, and you would already have me on the hunt for a second husband. Believe me, I have many things to do at Rose Park, and looking for a husband is not among them. Perhaps in a few years, when the boys are older—"

"And you are also older, dear," her mother interrupted gently. "But meeting Lady Jersey is not the only reason I wished you to accompany us to Almack's tomorrow. Lady Southmoor has promised to be there, and you will never guess who is to escort her?"

From her mother's conspiratorial expression, Mathilda guessed immediately who would be the countess's escort, but she chose to feign ignorance. "Are you suggesting that her ladyship has a cicisbeo? How very pleased I am to hear it. Who is the lucky gentleman?"

Lady Denton gave an unladylike snort. "Do not be deliberately obtuse, girl. Your mother is referring to Miles Stephens, Lady Southmoor's son. Remember Miles," her aunt continued with some asperity, "the gentleman you left at the altar all those years ago?"

Mathilda raised a delicate eyebrow in mock surprise at this tactless remark. "Oh, yes. Naturally, I remember Miles, but I cannot say I am anxious to see him again. What could we possibly have to say to each other?"

Lifting her cup, Mathilda took a sip of tea and regarded the reaction of the two elder ladies to this provocative remark. She had not mentioned a word about the encounter with the earl at Hatchard's yesterday. To do so would have been to invite a flurry of questions she had no wish to answer. She had put Miles out of her life ten years before and was determined that he should stay out. That he had encroached upon her thoughts and invaded her dreams ever since she had glimpsed his tall figure at the opera was a contretemps she would have to learn to live with.

Both ladies stared at her as though she had uttered an obscenity. "The countess appears to believe her son is anxious to see you, Mathilda," her mother said carefully. "I confess I am intrigued, and if you would but accompany us to Almack's tomorrow and meet the man, the mystery might be solved."

"Then you will have to ask the countess, Mama, for I will not be there. By that time on Wednesday I expect to be at Rose Park. And now, if you will excuse me," she added, getting to her feet, "I must supervise the packing."

Conscious of the cloud of disapproval that hung over the breakfast table, Mathilda was glad to escape upstairs. Halfway through the morning, however, while she was helping Mrs. Grey fill the extra trunks with the boys' new clothes, Mathilda was surprised to see Lady Denton burst in, her face wreathed in smiles.

"Your mother and I have decided to return to Bath with you, dear," her aunt announced with evident satisfaction. "There is little to keep us in London so late in the Season if you and the boys are not here."

"Do you suppose you will be ready in time, Aunt?" Mathilda

suspected this was some trick to get her to stay a few extra days, and she was not mistaken.

"Oh, yes, dear," Lady Denton replied blithely. "Unless of course you would consider delaying your departure for a day or two to allow us to pack everything."

"The boys and I will leave tomorrow as planned," Mathilda replied firmly. "There is no need for you and Mama to accompany us. I am sure we shall manage perfectly well without your Mr. Hampton's escort."

"Nonsense!" Lady Denton countered, and Mathilda remembered belatedly that her aunt had a way of getting what she wanted, one way or another. "We shall pack only the essentials, and the housekeeper can send the rest on to Bath next week. Besides," she added with a smug smile, "I have already sent round to inform Mr. Hampton that our plans have changed."

"And he has cried off, I presume?"

"Nothing of the sort, dear. Hampton confirmed that he is entirely at our service tomorrow."

There was no more to be said, and Mathilda bowed to the inevitable.

Hampton's note, obviously scribbled in haste, was delivered to the earl at his breakfast table. Since he was alone, Miles opened it and spread it out beside his plate. As he read his friend's slanted script, a frown gathered on his brow. So the quarry was about to bolt, was she? Willy reported that Lady Parmenter had made arrangements to leave the Metropolis at dawn on Wednesday.

The news was not unexpected. Miles felt a stirring of excitement. The hunt was on in earnest now. He passed his plate to Harris, who proceeded to cut thick slices from the large York ham on the sideboard and transfer them to the earl's plate, adding a generous helping of potato omelet garnished with fresh parsley.

As he ate, the earl ran over his list of engagements, discarding all that might be cancelled without a second thought. These included the lackluster ball at the Kendrick's that evening and two morning calls he had agreed to attend with his mother. The theatre engagement he had with a party of friends next week could also be dispensed with. He was engaged to play cards with friends at the Countess of Mansfield's card-party on Thursday, but he could bow out gracefully and send Cassandra a large bouquet of the yellow roses she loved.

His mother was counting on him to escort her to the usual Wednesday ball at Almack's and this appeared to be the only engagement the earl felt obliged to keep; he was reluctant to disappoint the countess.

"Harris," he commanded between mouthfuls of the succulent ham, "I shall be leaving for the Grange on Thursday. I shall drive myself in the curricle and leave the chaise for her ladyship, who will not wish to leave Town quite so early in the Season, I imagine. Take care of things for me, will you, Harris?"

"Certainly, my lord," the old butler murmured, taking the tea-pot from a footman and pouring his master a fresh cup. "Will you require my services at the Grange, my lord?"

"No. Jackson will do nicely," he replied, referring to the under-butler. "I want you to stay here to take care of her ladyship and oversee her removal to the Grange when the time comes. I will take Kelly and my groom. No doubt Mrs. Tuttle will have everything in hand if you send to advise her of my coming."

Having thus taken care of the arrangements to his entire satisfaction, Miles removed to the library to read the *Gazette*. He paused in the act of raising his coffee-cup to his lips when his eye caught a small entry near the bottom of the social gossip page. *A fashionable single gentleman from Devon,* the officious writer gleefully informed his readers, *appears to be smitten by a lovely widow recently returned from India. The pair have been discovered in romantic rendezvous beside the Serpentine.*

Miles put his cup down with a clatter, spilling some of the fragrant liquid on the rosewood table at his elbow. "The devil fly away with Hampton," he muttered under his breath. He glowered towards the door, half expecting his friend to saunter in as was his wont. When Hampton did not appear, Miles cast the paper aside and stood up. He had a mind to call for his horse and take a turn in the Park himself. Perhaps he would catch a glimpse of this *lovely widow.* He might even surprise his friend in her company, although what he would do if that happened, he could not begin to imagine.

A glance at the bronze clock on the mantel told him it was well past ten, too late to catch early morning strollers in the Park. Miles stood a moment, indecisive. Then with another muttered oath he flung out of the room and ordered his horse. Attributing his restlessness to lack of exercise, the earl spent a full hour cantering along secluded bridle-paths, his mind full of the vindication he was about to extract from a certain lovely widow.

After an excellent nuncheon at Boodles with Willy Hampton, who confirmed that he was indeed engaged to escort Lady Parmenter and the children to Bath on the morrow, Miles returned home earlier than usual, already chaffing at the self-imposed delay in leaving London. He was sorely tempted to accept his friend's invitation to join the party on its journey into Somerset, but settled on joining Hampton at the Grange a day later.

"I trust you can stay for a month or two to keep me company," he remarked to Willy as they strolled back to Belgrave Square. "Mother will be most put out if you are in Bath and do not visit. Besides," he added carelessly, "she will be counting on you to help her entice Mathilda back to the Grange."

Hampton looked surprised. "The countess is desirous of renewing that connexion?"

"No doubt about it. Mother is Mathilda's godmother, you know. Always had a soft spot for the girl."

"Even after . . . ?" Hampton's question faded into an awkward silence.

"After the brazen little hussy left her only son at the altar?" Miles remarked sarcastically before he could stop himself.

Hampton glanced at him curiously. "I had no idea you still felt so strongly about it, old man. Are you sure you would not rather come on down to Devon with me for the summer? I can guarantee some excellent pigeon shooting, and I have some promising yearlings to show you."

Miles forced himself to smile. "Thanks, but no. It appears that the entire sorry affair was my fault. If you listen to my mother tell the story, of course. She has badgered me into promising to help bridge the awkwardness between the two families. Always was thick as thieves with the Heaths, you know. Went to Miss Mayberry's Bath Seminary together, the same one Sarah and Rose attended."

"And how are those two lovely sisters of yours, Miles? Before you know it, they will be ready to make their bow to the *ton*."

"The twins are in fine fettle," the earl replied, glad to change the subject. "Mother has decreed they will be ready to make their come-out next Season."

"So soon?" Hampton sounded slightly shocked. "It seems only yesterday they were in the schoolroom."

Miles laughed. "None of us is getting any younger, old man. Perhaps the time is come to reconsider your vow to eschew marriage, Willy," he remarked jokingly. His friend's tenacity in clinging to his single state was well known, and Miles doubted that an eight-and-twenty-year-old widow with two children would change that.

When Hampton did not respond, the earl glanced at him sharply. His friend's cherubic countenance was unnaturally pensive.

"To be quite honest with you, Miles, I have reconsidered it

more than once in the past year. The leg-shackled state becomes every day less daunting to an old bachelor like me." His face cleared and he chuckled. "It might take very little to push me over the edge, let me tell you, old friend."

This unexpected confession sat heavily on the earl's mind long after Hampton had left him. Was it possible that Mathilda Parmenter had anything to do with his friend's drastic softening towards matrimony? He had pondered the same question before, but today, for the first time since Miles had known him, Willy Hampton had sounded curiously nostalgic.

A female would be a complete fool to reject a suitor as eligible as Willoughby Hampton, he told himself morosely. And Mathilda was no fool.

The possibility of a match between his best friend and the woman he meant to destroy made Miles distinctly uneasy. He knew he must get down to the Grange and put his plan into motion before any real damage was done to Willy's heart.

As far as Mathilda's heart was concerned, Miles hoped that it would soon be damaged beyond repair.

As his own had been ten years before.

When the cavalcade set forth from Mount Street on Wednesday morning—rather later than Mathilda had planned—the cheerful demeanour of Mr. Hampton went a long way towards reconciling her to his presence. As it turned out, Hampton appeared to have considerable experience in controlling the high spirits of small boys and organizing the disposal of the two coaches hired to carry the vast quantity of baggage that had accumulated in the front hall.

Mathilda soon discovered that Mr. Hampton was endowed with an extraordinary degree of patience. Once they had left the bustle of London behind, he was easily cajoled into taking first one, then the other of the boys up before him on his fancy grey gelding, and indulging them with endless tales of his youthful exploits at his family estate in Devon.

The journey passed pleasantly and quickly, in spite of the

stops Hampton insisted on making to tempt the ladies with a succulent roast duckling served at the King's Arms along the Bath Road, and the justly famous damson and gooseberry pies offered by the innkeeper's wife at the Three Swans. He appeared to be well known at every posting inn along the Road and commanded the best service every time they changed horses.

"I have travelled this Road innumerable times since I was a boy," he explained as the party sat around a table in a private parlour at the Three Swans. "I keep horses at several of the posting houses as did my father before me. 'Tis little wonder the people hereabouts know me."

Privately, Mathilda believed that Hampton was so well liked in the area because he was considerate and generous with everyone he met. If only his good friend the Earl of Southmoor had been half as pleasant, Mathilda mused as their coach rattled past the imposing stone gatehouse guarding the entrance to Southmoor Grange, her life might have been very different.

But Miles had not been anywhere near as pleasant as his friend, and Mathilda's life was what it was, and she could not bring herself to regret a single moment of it.

Since Mathilda was not welcome at Heath Hall, and had not dared presume that Rose Park was in any condition to accommodate visitors, she had accepted her aunt's invitation to stay with her in Bath. Her days were to be spent entirely at her husband's estate, however, and at her initial visit, she was relieved to find the old manor house less dilapidated than she had feared. The original family housekeeper, Mrs. Walker, had taken pride in maintaining the house in readiness for the master's return, and although most of the rooms were still under holland covers, the master suite was aired and ready for Mathilda when she arrived.

"It is right glad we are to have you back, milady," the old retainer assured Mathilda as they climbed the curving oak stair together. "Mr. Walker and I have done our best to keep things up, but after we lost Sir George and his lady in that dreadful accident five years ago, the London solicitor closed the house and let all the servants go. Except for me and Mr. Walker in the house, of course. And a girl who comes in twice a week to help me with the heavy work. The outside staff is pretty much intact except for the grooms. Those lads were let go when the horses were sold off."

"We shall have a full staff again as soon as you and Walker can find replacements," Mathilda assured the housekeeper. "And the sooner the better. I am particularly interested in a good cook who is accustomed to feeding two growing boys."

Mrs. Walker beamed. "'Twill be a blessing to have young lads about the place again. When I saw them, I swear for a moment I thought Master James had come back to us. I watched him grow up, I did, milady, and that Master Christopher is the spitting image of his father, I can tell you. Uncanny it is. Gave me quite a turn it did."

As they toured the house, Mathilda listened patiently to Mrs. Walker's seemingly endless stories of James's youthful pranks, interspersed by a growing list of repairs that required her attention. The housekeeper was evidently delighted to have the family back in residence, and promised to have the staff back to normal within the sennight.

Back in Bath in time for tea, Mathilda found Mr. Hampton ensconced in an easy chair, engaged in lively conversation with the ladies. He rose instantly as she entered the drawing room and raised her fingers in an elegant salute.

"The country air has put roses in your cheeks already, my dear lady," he murmured with a warm smile. "I daresay I shall have every single gentleman in Bath begging for an introduction when the word gets out that you have returned."

"I doubt that very much," Mathilda replied with a small shrug. "Besides, I really have no interest in such gentlemen, here or anywhere else," she added, thinking of a particular gentleman in London who had disturbed her peace of mind more than she had bargained for. "I have too much to do at Rose Park to be bothered with—"

"Mathilda!" her aunt interrupted sharply. "You will offend our dear Mr. Hampton with remarks of that nature. He will think you are lumping him together with all the idle bucks in Town who have nothing better to do than ogle all the ladies."

Mathilda glanced at Mr. Hampton and was relieved to see his ready smile. "I think Mr. Hampton has more sense than to believe anything so ridiculous, Aunt." She bestowed one of her most enchanting smiles on the gentleman, who responded with a courtly inclination of his curly head.

"I trust you did not find Rose Park in need of too many repairs," he murmured, tactfully changing the subject as Mathilda settled herself on the green damask settee beside her mother.

"Yes, dear," her mother seconded, pausing in the act of mutilating a slice of seed cake, "do tell us if the place is too terribly run down."

"Oh, quite the contrary. There are many things that need attention, of course, but once I have hired a full staff, which should be completed within a sennight, I shall be able to move in with the boys. They were quite insistent that we stay there today, but I want to give Mrs. Walker time to engage a cook. The poor woman is quite unprepared to cook meals for two growing boys."

"Speaking of which," Hampton said, accepting a delicate cucumber sandwich from his hostess, "I have sent for two ponies from my estates in Devon. I am convinced they will do nicely for Christopher and Brian. My nephews have outgrown them, and the animals are in dire need of exercise. They should be arriving at the Grange any day now."

"The Grange?" Mathilda echoed, turning startled eyes in his direction. Visions of daily visits to the Southmoor stables and the inevitability of running into the earl caused her heart to accelerate alarmingly.

"Yes. Southmoor will be arriving in a day or two, and I shall be staying with him for most of the summer. I was not sure if you had room for horses at Rose Park."

Pulling herself together, Mathilda replied with more confidence than she felt. "I believe the stables are in fairly good condition. But you must be the judge of that yourself, Mr. Hampton. You are welcome to inspect them at any time you choose."

Shortly thereafter, Mr. Hampton took his leave, promising to ride out to Rose Park the following afternoon. No sooner was the door closed behind him than Lady Denton expressed her satisfaction at the way things were progressing.

"Not only do you have London's most coveted bachelor dancing attendance on you, my dear, but you have evidently lured Southmoor into the country before the end of the Season. You will have only yourself to blame if we do not see you wed by Christmas. Would you not agree, Angela?"

Mathilda met her mother's eyes over the tea-tray and was alarmed at the calculating look she encountered there. The last thing she needed in her life was two officious matrons playing Cupid. If she were to find the peaceful life she had intended for herself and the boys, she realised she must nip this idiotish conspiracy in the bud before it blossomed into a full-blown invasion of her life.

"I hate to disappoint you, Aunt," she said coolly, "but I have not lured the Earl of Southmoor into anything. And as for Hampton dancing attendance, he is only being civil to us all because of your long-standing friendship with his aunt, Lady Bedford."

Mathilda spoke with a nonchalance she was far from feeling. Neither of the two elder ladies made any attempt to refute her, but Mathilda caught a sly smile on her aunt's face as she exchanged a glance with Lady Heath that told her more clearly than words that the subject was not closed.

SEVEN

Summer Flirtation

The closer his curricle and four matched greys came to his family estate near Bath, the more the Earl of Southmoor questioned the sanity of his precipitous removal into the country. The London Season still had several weeks to run, and his friends—those he had bothered to serve notice of his departure—had protested his desertion before the last dregs of enjoyment might be wrung from those final frenetic days.

Miles also questioned his own motives. Was he or was he not justified in carrying out his devious plan for retribution against Mathilda for the wrong he had suffered at her hands so long ago? He had done nothing to deserve the public jilting that still rankled when he allowed himself to dwell upon it. He had offered her everything a female might conceivably wish for—his name, his rank, his fortune. Even his heart—although he had never admitted it in so many words. It had seemed unmanly to confess to such tender emotions, and Miles had always shrunk from exposing his feelings. Unlike James, he had never been able to express himself in matters of the heart.

He had not realised just how deeply he felt about his lovely betrothed until after she had gone. Losing her had left scars that time had not healed.

It was all very well to claim that time cured all things, Miles thought morosely, weaving his team around a large hay wagon that blocked the lane, while the driver exchanged gossip with a boy in charge of a flock of noisy geese. But Miles knew he was living proof that time was not so kind. His heart had constricted most painfully at the mere sight of Mathilda getting into her carriage on Piccadilly Street. And when he came face-to-face with her in the dim aisle at Hatchard's, he had felt the full impact of his loss. No denying it.

Turning under the imposing stone entrance to the Grange, Miles experienced—as he always did when returning home after a lengthy absence—a sharp pang of loneliness. He had chided himself for this foolishness many times, but he could not shake the feeling that, had his life unfolded as he had once imagined it would, Mathilda would have been at the Grange to welcome him home.

Shaking off these maudlin thoughts, the earl drove up the long tree-shaded driveway at a spanking pace. He pulled up before his front door with a flourish and threw the reins to a groom who stepped forward to receive them.

"Welcome home, milord," Jackson, the under-butler, greeted him at the open door. "I trust your lordship enjoyed a pleasant journey."

"Fair enough, Jackson, thank you," Miles responded absent-mindedly. "Are my sisters still at the tea-table?"

"Indeed they are, milord. The ladies Sarah and Rose are on the back terrace with Mrs. Braithwaite. The weather has been so fine, they ordered tea outside this afternoon."

"Then I shall join them," Miles said impulsively. "Send up a fresh pot, will you, Jackson?"

Without waiting for a response, Miles strode through the house to the glass conservatory, which gave onto the wide terrace overlooking the extensive rose-gardens.

His arrival was greeted with shrieks of delight from his sisters and a cordial greeting from Mrs. Braithwaite, a distant cousin on his mother's side of the family. In exchange for a generous stipend and a roof over her head, Maud Braithwaite had for years first been governess and then companion to the Stephens twins. Miles considered it money well spent when his hoydenish sisters began to take on the demeanour of young ladies of quality, a feat Lady Southmoor had despaired of achieving.

"Miles," exclaimed Lady Sarah, the more rambunctious of the two, "what a lovely surprise. We did not expect to see you for another three or four weeks. What happened? Did they blackball you at White's, or something equally nefarious? Do tell, Miles, we are all agog."

"Lady Sarah!" Mrs. Braithwaite said sharply. "That is no way to address his lordship. Whatever will he think of you, child?"

"Pooh! What do I care," Sarah retorted, casting a saucy smile in her brother's direction. "We heard that you did not offer for Celia Pritchard after all, Miles. And applaud your good sense. The girl is scramble-witted and has a lisp. Not at all the sort of female we want to see installed as mistress of the Grange."

"Sarah, that is unkind of you," Mrs. Braithwaite said reproachfully. "One should never speak ill of the less fortunate."

"It is true, nevertheless," Sarah insisted, reaching for a damson tart, while Rose, more conscious of social niceties than her sister, poured the earl a cup of tea. Her hand paused in midair, and she glanced at him, a speculative gleam in her blue eyes.

"You will never guess who is back in town, Miles."

Miles schooled his features, maintaining a bland expression, although it was not hard to guess whom his sister meant.

"Well?" Sarah added impatiently. "Cannot you guess, Miles? Someone you used to know well," she added with a sly smile. "Very well indeed, actually."

Miles refused to rise to the bait. He raised his cup and took a long drink of tea.

"Do not be a tease, Sarah," Mrs. Braithwaite chided. Turning to the earl, she added, "We happened to run into Lady Denton yesterday, and she had her niece with her—Lady Parmenter and her two boys."

"We were invited to tea," Sarah added, regarding her brother with a calculating gleam in her eyes. "Delightful creatures those boys, I can assure you. She must be very proud of them. And we cannot wait for you to see Mathilda Parmenter again. She is absolutely gorgeous. Would you not agree, Cousin Maud?"

"No one can deny that Lady Parmenter is indeed a diamond of the first water, dear, but it is doubtful that his lordship is desirous of seeing her again," she added tactfully.

"And why not, I would like to—"

"I have already seen the lady," Miles interrupted mildly, anxious to deflect his sister's overzealous interrogation. "In London, naturally. At Hatchard's to be more precise." He returned his attention to the slice of pound cake Mrs. Braithwaite had placed on his plate.

"You have met Mathilda already?" Sarah exclaimed, sounding rather disappointed. "Why ever did you not say so, Miles? Lady Parmenter did not mention anything to us, and you can be sure we queried her."

Miles made no reply to this, hoping his sister would drop the subject.

"Do not tease your brother, dear. His lordship has barely arrived home. Let him have his tea in peace."

Miles silently applauded Mrs. Braithwaite for her good sense, but doubted it would curb Lady Sarah's curiosity.

"Well, perhaps you can tell us what your friend Mr. Hampton is doing trailing around after Mathilda like a sick dog. We thought he was supposed to come down with you for the summer. Can it be that the Honourable Willy is finally contemplating giving up his wild ways?"

"Sarah," their elderly cousin admonished, "that is no way to speak of a gentleman. Sick dog, indeed! Wherever did you learn to be so ill-mannered? Lady Denton made it quite clear that Mr. Hampton offered his escort to her and Lady Heath. It was pure coincidence that Lady Parmenter was travelling to Bath at the same time."

"Yes, Cousin, and if you believe that whisker, you must certainly believe that babies are born in cabbages."

"Sarah!" Miles's voice cracked like thunder in the quiet afternoon. "That was unspeakably rude of you. You will apologise to your cousin immediately."

His wayward sister was instantly contrite. "I did not mean to be rude, Cousin; you know what a rattle I can be. I apologise most sincerely. Please say you will overlook my rudeness."

Mrs. Braithwaite quickly assured Sarah that she was forgiven, but Miles was not so easily convinced.

"If I hear any more thoughtless rudeness from you, Miss Rattle, I shall veto our mother's plans to bring you out next Season. I will not have my own sister behaving like a hoyden. Count on it."

"I am sure Sarah meant no harm, my lord," Mrs. Braithwaite ventured after an awkward pause. "She is a little highspirited, that is all."

"And it did seem to me that Hampton was overzealous in his attentions to Mathilda," Sarah added, apparently unrepentant. "And if you doubt me, you should escort us to tea at Lady Denton's tomorrow afternoon."

"That is quite enough on that subject," Miles said dismissively. Obedient for once, Sarah launched into a detailed list of the purchases she simply had to make if she were to attend the many festivities planned for the summer months.

Miles listened with only half an ear. The confirmation that Hampton might well have set his sights on Mathilda caused mixed emotions. His first impulse was to dismiss the idea as ludicrous. On the other hand, might it not be possible that his friend, confirmed bachelor that he had always claimed to be, might have fallen prey to Cupid's arrow?

The notion alarmed him. His plan had made no allowance for the presence of a rival for Mathilda's affections. Its success depended entirely on winning the lady's undivided attention and convincing her that they might rebuild a relationship that had been sundered ten years before. He could not risk allowing Hampton to divert the lady with a second option.

* * *

"When will you send the ponies over to Rose Park, sir?" Mathilda heard her youngest demand no sooner had Mr. Hampton reported that the horses he had ordered sent up from his estate in Devon had arrived at the Grange.

"May we go over there tomorrow to see them?" Christopher wanted to know.

"We might even try out their paces," Brian cried excitedly. "What do you think, sir? May we ride them back home?"

"Do not pester Mr. Hampton while he is having his tea, boys," Mathilda scolded, marvelling once again at the seemingly endless patience their visitor displayed with the children. "If you make a nuisance of yourselves, there will be no riding at all."

"But, Mama," Brian protested loudly, "Mr. Hampton promised to teach us the finer points of horsemanship. He cannot do so if we have no horses."

"I am sure that when he made that rash promise, Mr. Hampton did not anticipate being pestered over the tea-table, Brian. You might at least wait until he has tasted some of Cook's raspberry tarts." She turned to Mr. Hampton, who lounged at his ease next to his hostess on an elegant claw-footed settee in the Chinese style.

"Please bear with this unseemly enthusiasm, sir," she said with a warm smile. "The boys have talked of nothing else but horses since you permitted them to ride your grey in London. I am quite at a loss to understand this sudden enthusiasm."

"If we are to be proper gentlemen, we must have light hands and a good seat, Mama. Everybody knows that a true gentleman excels on the hunting field and drives a team of Welsh-breds like Mr. Hampton's," Christopher explained in a tone so like his father that Mathilda felt a lump form in her throat.

"I see," she said softly, trying not to smile. She caught Hampton's eye and was startled to see him wink. There was no denying that this particular gentleman was like no other she had ever met. While not handsome in the strictly classical sense, as his friend the earl definitely was, Hampton's expression was invariably cheerful, and his disposition good-natured and kind. His fondness for children was certainly genuine— she had no doubt of that—and his generosity with her sons touched her as few things ever had. Not many wealthy gentlemen of fashion could be counted on to spend their time entertaining two small boys, initiating them into the mysteries of horsemanship, or providing suitable mounts for them from his own stables.

Mathilda wondered—not for the first time—whether her Aunt Agatha might not be correct in believing that the gentleman's interest went beyond the children to include her. Hampton was reputed to be richer than Golden Ball, but wealth had never mattered to Mathilda. She had chosen to marry Sir James without once considering if he could support her in the style Miles obviously could. She had been young and entirely irresponsible, motivated solely by the love in his eyes, the fervour of his kisses, and the magical promises he had made.

The memory of the thoughtless, romantical girl she had been caused Mathilda to shudder. It had been pure coincidence that James had lived up to her youthful dreams of love. He had kept all his promises, been a loyal and devoted husband, and provided her with a lovely home and a tidy fortune. She had trusted him implicitly from the moment she had set foot in his carriage that eve of her eighteenth birthday. James had not betrayed her trust, and it was not until months later that Mathilda fully realised the pain and disgrace he might have caused had he taken advantage of her innocence, had he betrayed her as she had betrayed Miles.

The guilt had diminished over the years, but had never disappeared. The sight of Miles's broad shoulders in Hampton's curricle and his disturbing presence in Hatchard's had brought the past flooding back. The encounter with him had not been unexpected, although Mathilda had never expected he would approach her so openly. What had disturbed her was the way her heart had jumped into her throat at the sight of him standing there in the dim aisle at Hatchard's, his eyes full of emotions she had never expected to see in them.

The sudden opening of the drawing room door distracted Mathilda from these uneasy thoughts, but when Harris announced the visitors, her heart jumped again, as it had in the bookshop. They had been expecting Ladies Sarah and Rose Stephens, with their companion, Mrs. Braithwaite. But as Benson intoned the names of the visitors, Mathilda's gaze flew to the gentleman standing in the doorway behind them. It was *him*.

For the briefest moment their eyes met, and Mathilda swore she detected a glimmer of something threatening in those grey eyes. Something predatory. Vaguely frightening, yet exciting, too. It was gone before she could be sure, but it left an odd sensation in her heart that his smooth greeting and the kiss he bestowed on her gloved fingers did not erase.

Miles was unprepared for the full impact of his former betrothed in the bright afternoon sunshine slanting through the bow windows of Lady Denton's drawing room. In the dimness of Hatchard's musty aisles, she had appeared slim, elegant, and lovely—what little he could see of her face framed by that fetching bonnet. Here, in the unforgiving light of day, she took his breath away.

He saw at once that his presence had shocked her. The slight widening of her dark eyes and the falling away of her gaze after that initial startled glance told Miles that he made Mathilda uneasy. He smiled to himself as he greeted the two elder ladies. When he came to Mathilda, he took her proffered hand and made sure that his lips pressed firmly enough on her gloved fingers to leave the warm imprint of his mouth through the thin cotton. Her repressed shudder gave him a powerful sense of satisfaction. She was not indifferent to him.

Conscious that he was the centre of attention, Miles smiled

blandly at his friend Hampton and turned to the boys, standing beside their grandmother.

"So these are the lads I have heard so much about, are they?" he remarked, bringing up the quizzing-glass he rarely wore. They were certainly two fine strapping lads, and Miles was again overcome by rage that they were not his.

"Yes, these are my grandsons, Christopher and Brian," Lady Heath acknowledged with obvious pride. "Make your bows to the Earl of Southmoor, boys. He is a close neighbour of yours, so you should be on your best behaviour."

"What is *that*, sir?" Brian queried with his usual bluntness, pointing at the quizzing-glass. "Did you know it makes you look like a horse?"

"Brian!" his mother and grandmother exclaimed in unison.

Hampton burst into raucous laughter, choking on the piece of seed cake he was eating. "By gad, you may be right, Brian," he added between suppressed gurgles of mirth. "But it is not always a good thing to tell a gentleman he looks like a horse, lad. Might set his back up, if you know what I mean. And if he were a fighting man, you might not like what happens to you."

"Would he darken my daylights for me?" the culprit asked with obvious relish, staring eagerly at the earl. "Are you a fighting man, sir?"

"Mr. Hampton!" Mathilda exclaimed reproachfully. "I beg you will not encourage the boy in these impudent starts. And Brian, how many times must I tell you not to use cant expressions in the drawing room? I want to hear you apologise to his lordship this instant."

"I only meant his eye, Mama. His eye looks just like Horatio's. And you should know, sir—your lordship—that I like horses." Brian accompanied this revelation with a sunny smile. "In fact, I intend to become a smashing rider and ride a prime goer like Horatio."

Miles had a hard time keeping a straight face. The lad had the kind of spirit he admired. It might be amusing to teach the boy to box, he mused, watching the enthusiasm reflected on

Brian's face as he talked of his ambitions. He had the right blend of eagerness and fearlessness required by most manly sports, and undoubtedly would do well in anything he undertook. But he obviously needed a man in the house to counteract his mother's overprotective ways. *A man in the house?* The idea struck Miles as incongruous. Such a notion did not fit into his plans for Mathilda at all. He did not count on becoming more than superficially acquainted with her boys. Their future welfare was none of his concern. None at all.

"That is not an apology, Brian," his mother was saying sternly.

"There is really no need for one." Miles glanced at Mathilda as he spoke and was charmed by the delicate flush on her cheeks.

"Nevertheless, I insist that he do so."

So Brian apologised, grudgingly, but with a certain boyish charm that enchanted Miles and seriously weakened his resolution to ignore the boys in his assault upon their mother. What really sealed his fate was the roguish gleam in the boy's eyes, which seemed to imply a conspiracy between them to humour his mother in her restricting demands.

"Well? Are you a fighting man, my lord?" Brian insisted once Miles was seated with a tea-cup balanced in one hand and a plate of tarts on the table beside him.

"Have no doubts on that score, lad," Hampton put in unexpectedly to Miles's embarrassment. "His lordship is a prime Follower of the Fancy. Sparred with Gentleman Jackson in his saloon for years. Quite top-o-the trees, he is. Not many of our friends will venture into the ring with him, and that is a fact."

"Really?" Brian's blue eyes fixed on Miles with open admiration. "I have never met a Follower of the Fancy before. Does it hurt to plant someone a facer?"

"It can if done incorrectly," Miles was drawn into responding. Even before the lad reacted, he realised he had made a tactical mistake.

"Will you teach me how to do it right, then? I have always

wanted to plant a facer. How do you hold your fist? Like this?"

The lad held up a small fist and adopted an awkward, belli-cose stance.

"Brian, let his lordship have his tea in peace. If you cannot behave, I shall ask Mrs. Grey to take you up to the school-room."

The boy appeared not to have heard a word of his mother's admonition. He stared fixedly at Miles and turned on a charm-ing, dimpled smile. "Please say you will, my lord. You will change my whole life, I swear it."

The idea of changing a young boy's life appealed to Miles, and before he could consider the ramifications of his action, or the effects on his carefully laid plans, he found himself oddly flattered by this novel request.

"Boxing is an art," he said, "not to be taken lightly. It re-quires hours and hours of practice."

"My lord," Mathilda interrupted, for the first time address-ing him directly. "Please pay no attention to this outrageous request. It is unforgivable of Brian to impose upon you in this fashion."

Miles glanced at her. An anxious frown marred her brow, and her eyes were wary, but her mouth seemed infinitely soft and kissable. Miles suddenly remembered that he had never once kissed her.

"There is no imposition, my dear," he replied, relishing the flush his endearment brought to her face. He glanced at Brian and read the yearning in the boy's eyes.

The moment was sweet, and Miles responded instinctively. "If you can spare the time from your riding lessons with Mr. Hampton here, I shall be glad to show you how to plant a facer."

Later, as he drove back to the Grange with Willy Hampton, Miles congratulated himself on a successful step forward in his campaign to teach his former betrothed that there was a price to pay for jilting a gentleman without apparent cause—and breaking his heart.

A stiff price, if his campaign proceeded as planned. Miles deliberately chose to disregard the added complication of her son Brian and his promised boxing lessons.

EIGHT

Friends or Rivals?

Mathilda arose the following morning with the uneasy sensation that her life was becoming unnecessarily complicated. The appearance of the Earl of Southmoor in her aunt's drawing room the day before had shaken her more than she liked to admit. It had also called into question her naïve assumption that she could retire to the Parmenter estate with her boys and lead a quiet, inconspicuous existence, watching them grow into manhood.

She might have known better, she thought, accepting the cup of steaming chocolate offered by Maggie, her aunt's plump-faced maid she shared with her mother. How had she even for a moment imagined that her boys—particularly Brian—were capable of leading a quiet life? Within a week of arriving in London, they had struck up an acquaintance with one of the most eligible gentlemen in England and inveigled him not only into teaching them to ride, but into providing them with ponies from his own stables.

And this was only the beginning. Evidently the soul of generosity, Mr. Hampton had sent to his estate in Devon for the ponies, which were even now stabled at the Grange. Mathilda shuddered. The Grange, no less. She had sworn never to set foot in that place again. How could she, after what she had done to Miles ten years before?

In contrast to what she had expected of him—aloofness and disdain—the earl had thoroughly confused her by actively seeking her out. Their encounter in Hatchard's might have been coincidence, Mathilda would admit that much, but his appearance yesterday with his sisters could only be deliberate. He had *wished* to take tea at her aunt's. And then had allowed himself to be enlisted as a pugilistic instructor to a precocious boy he had just met.

Mathilda could find no reasonable explanation for the earl's odd behaviour. He had been disconcertingly pleasant—although once or twice a certain hardness in his eyes had alarmed her. And vastly handsome. She had forgotten just how handsome he had been in those days when she had naïvely imagined he loved her. Captivated by his dark, classical beauty and impressive stature, she had let herself believe that theirs would be a love match. It was not until the betrothal was official that Mathilda had noticed the cool grey eyes never warmed when they regarded her, and that tantalising mouth she had longed to kiss rarely smiled.

She had expected him to ignore her yesterday afternoon, or address her with that cold condescension she remembered so well from their brief betrothal. But the warmth in his eyes had brought colour to her cheeks and confusion to her heart. Was this the same man she had known? Would the Miles Stephens of the past have allowed himself to be cajoled into tutoring a small boy in the art of boxing? Mathilda could not imagine it for a moment. Yet he had indeed done so, and Brian still had stars in his eyes when she tucked him into bed last night. She hoped he would not be disappointed.

As for her own peace of mind, Mathilda found herself in a quandary. Mr. Hampton had graciously offered to drive her and the boys to the Grange that morning to see their ponies. How could she refuse? She could hardly explain that she was loath to go near the earl's estate, especially since he was now in residence. On the other hand, she was equally loath to allow the boys to go alone.

With rare perspicacity, Mr. Hampton had seemed to guess the cause of her hesitation, for he hastened to assure her that they would not disturb the countess, who was still in London.

They would pick up the ponies and her mare at the stables and ride back to Rose Park. It was not the countess Mathilda wished to avoid, and she suspected Hampton had guessed it, but she appreciated his tact.

When Hampton's landau bowled into the stable-yard at the Grange later that morning, Mathilda had reason to regret venturing onto the earl's estate. The first person she saw as she stepped out of the carriage was Southmoor himself, standing beside a magnificent chestnut gelding that one of the grooms was saddling. Though his back was towards her, Mathilda would have known the set of those broad shoulders anywhere.

Both boys jumped out of the carriage and rushed over to talk to the earl, leaving Mr. Hampton to escort their mother. As Mathilda approached, she heard her youngest telling the earl with all the aplomb of a connoisseur that the chestnut was a bang-up piece of horseflesh.

Miles appeared bemused by this youthful enthusiasm, but made no protest when Brian stroked the gelding's silky nose. There was a smile on his face as he turned to greet Mathilda, but anything he might have said was interrupted by Brian's usual string of questions.

"What is his name, my lord? Do you race him? He looks as though he could give Horatio a run for his money."

"I call him Thunder," the earl replied when Brian paused for breath. "And no, I prefer to hunt, although I would be willing to wager he could run Horatio into the ground."

"You would be wasting your blunt, old man," Hampton replied jovially. "Your Thunder may have the same sire as my Horatio, but that does not make him a better horse by a long shot."

"They are brothers?" Brian demanded, eyeing the earl dubiously.

"If they have the same sire, of course they are, silly," cut in Christopher, eager to show his superior knowledge of breeding.

"Nobody asked you."

"Boys," Mathilda warned, sensing that the discussion might deteriorate into a shouting match at any moment.

Hampton came to the rescue. "Thunder was born on my stud farm in Devon, as was Horatio. Southmoor purchased him, what is it, two years ago?"

"Three, I believe."

"And you have never raced him?" Brian's voice held all the scorn of a seven-year-old faced with the incomprehensible behaviour of adults. "Why not?"

"Brian, I thought you were interested in seeing the ponies Mr. Hampton has so kindly provided for you." Mathilda interrupted, hoping to bring this exchange with his lordship to an end.

Brian glanced contritely at Hampton. "Oh, yes, please, sir. But I still think you should race Thunder," he threw over his shoulder at the earl before disappearing into the stable behind Hampton.

Mathilda found herself suddenly alone with the earl in the stable-yard. She avoided his eyes, but was uncomfortably aware of his gaze fixed upon her.

Before the silence could become awkward, the earl cleared his throat. "I regret you did not approach me about the ponies, Mathilda. I could have easily provided you with suitable mounts."

How could he imagine she would approach him about anything? Mathilda thought crossly. The last thing she wanted was to revive a relationship that had ended so abruptly and—if what her aunt had told her was true—quite painfully for Miles years ago. She had not wanted to see him again at all, much less come uninvited to his estate and stand about trying to make polite conversation with a man she had cast off so publicly.

Mathilda glanced at him, and found him regarding her quizzically. She would have to speak to him, she realised, suppressing a flicker of panic. There was no getting out of it, and he seemed to expect it, quite as though she were here at his invitation and not Hampton's.

"I did not approach Mr. Hampton, either," she said finally. "In truth, I have only recently met the gentleman, but he seemed to be genuinely interested in the boys, so when he offered to lend them the ponies and teach them the finer points of horsemanship, I found it difficult to refuse."

Mathilda glanced anxiously towards the stable doors, but there was no sign of the boys. She should have accompanied them, she chided herself. Instead, here she was standing about, making stilted conversation and revealing more than she intended about her acquaintance with Mr. Hampton. Miles's offer to provide her with mounts for the boys had to be facetious, she decided. Why would he care if they had ponies to ride or not? It was none of his concern—or should not be.

He smiled then, and Mathilda's heart did funny things in her chest. "Our Willy is hard to refuse," the earl murmured. "He has the proverbial heart of gold and is quite capable of giving away the last shilling in his pocket if he thinks you need it. He collects stray dogs and penniless orphans, besides keeping track of a score of nephews and nieces who adore him. Old Willy is a confirmed bachelor and will doubtless become their favourite uncle in his old age, for he can be counted upon to keep secrets, get them out of scrapes, and open his purse at the slightest hint of an emergency."

"Mr. Hampton sounds thoroughly delightful," Mathilda remarked at the end of this surprising speech. She could not fathom why Miles was telling her all this, unless, of course, he wished to warn her away from his friend. Suddenly, she recalled her aunt's sly description of Hampton as an excellent match. Mathilda had paid little mind to these speculations at the time, since she was not on the catch for a second husband. If she had been, Mr. Hampton would naturally make an ideal candidate. But she was definitely not. Was she? Despite his reputation for eschewing marriage, Mr. Hampton had shown more than ordinary civility towards her. Or was this her imagination again?

Mathilda wondered what Hampton's thoughts were on this matter, and why the earl wished to give the impression that his friend was a confirmed bachelor. Her speculations were cut short when the gentleman himself emerged from the stable, followed by the boys, each leading a pony. A groom trailed in their wake, holding a spirited bay mare by the bridle.

"Mama, look!" Brian shouted excitedly, startling the earl's gelding and causing the little mare to sidle playfully. His own pony paid no noticeable attention to the commotion. "His name is Bernard, and Mr. Hampton says he is older than I am. I gave him some sugar lumps, and he nibbled my hand. Is he not beautiful, Mama?"

Mathilda duly admired Bernard, who was apparently infinitely bored by the proceedings, and watched while a groom lifted Brian into the saddle and led the pony around the yard.

"Mr. Hampton says we may take a turn in the pasture before we ride back home," her eldest son explained, climbing onto his own pony, a placid-looking beast with white markings on his face. "This is Blaze, and he runs faster than Bernard. Mr. Hampton said so." This last comment was accompanied by a condescending glance in his brother's direction.

"No, he cannot," Brian retorted hotly. "Mr. Hampton says it depends who is riding him. I know I can get Bernard to beat that old slug any day of the week."

"Since we are not going to do any racing, it hardly matters, does it now?" Hampton said mildly. "Jones"—he turned to one of the grooms—"you and Tom take the lads into the pasture while I introduce her ladyship to Buttercup. And Tom, you can bring out Horatio if you will."

As Mathilda settled herself in her saddle with Mr. Hampton's help, she wondered if perhaps she should have worn her new scarlet riding habit instead of her serviceable green one. On second thought, she realised the scarlet was rather flashy for an informal outing with the boys and Mr. Hampton. And she could not imagine wishing to impress Miles. Especially since she had not expected to see him. Something in this reasoning rang hollow, but Mathilda brushed it aside and smiled down at Mr. Hampton, who was adjusting her stirrup. It might be rather pleasant to have a gentleman in her life again, she mused, to take care of those little attentions gentlemen were so good at. The thought startled her, and she quickly pushed it aside.

"She is *so* beautiful," Mathilda murmured, stroking the mare's silky neck. "I have rarely seen such a handsome animal. I cannot thank you enough, Mr. Hampton—"

He grinned up at her with evident pleasure. "Everyone calls me Willy, and I wish you would, too."

"Actually, we call him *Sweet* Willy, and you can see why," the earl interjected, throwing a buckskin-clad leg over his mount and controlling the chestnut with a firm hand, as the horse pranced impatiently and tossed his head.

"And as for Buttercup," Hampton continued as if his friend had not spoken, "I am glad you like her. She looks a little high-spirited, but I assure you she is really a docile little thing."

Mathilda had deliberately ignored the earl during this exchange, but as she moved over to watch the boys in the pasture, she felt him at her side. "You can always depend on Willy's cattle to behave well," he remarked. "Breeds the best hunting stock in the country, does Willy. Does the Regent still have that big black you sold him five or six years ago, old man?"

"Yes, indeed. Prinny was good enough to mention him to me just the other day at Almack's. It seems the horse has lived up to my predictions. In fact, the Prince appears keen to obtain another mount from me."

An excited yell cut short this exchange, and Mathilda glanced anxiously at Brian, who had managed to urge Bernard into a canter. The lad was hugely delighted by this show of speed and taunted his brother, who was circling the arena at a sedate trot.

"Brian," she called out as the boy cantered past, a look of pure glee on his face, "you must not race, and you are not to torment your brother. If you cannot behave, I shall have to send you home in the carriage."

"Oh, Mama, only see how he runs," Brian yelled back, undaunted by the threat.

"Your mother is right, Brian. It is never wise to race a new horse until you know his temperament. To misjudge one's mount is to risk ending up in a ditch." Although Hampton spoke mildly, the effect was immediate. Brian pulled up and walked the pony over to the fence.

"But trotting is so uncomfortable," he complained.

"Not if you do it properly," Hampton said calmly. "Did Jones not show you how it is done?"

"Yes, but I want *you* to show me."

Mathilda watched in amazement as Hampton entered the arena and patiently guided Brian through the intricacies of correct posture. Not once did she hear a word of protest from her rambunctious son.

"It appears the lad needs the authority of a man's guidance," she heard the earl murmur beside her.

She glanced at him, conscious of a pang of guilt. He was right, of course, but if Reginald refused to acknowledge her, she could think of only one other solution—one she was loath to embrace under those circumstances.

"Their uncle will eventually fill that role, I trust," she responded without much conviction.

"Your brother is not exactly the authority figure I would choose in your place," Miles remarked. "There are other, far more pleasant alternatives available to you, my dear. As I am sure you are well aware," he added in a low voice that made Mathilda's spine tingle.

Mathilda refused to dignify this impertinent suggestion with an answer. She fixed her gaze on the instruction taking place in the paddock, and wondered, not for the first time, what kind of a husband Mr. Hampton would make. That was what Miles was suggesting, was it not? The only other possibility was that Miles himself . . . But no, that was unthinkable. It was simply inconceivable that the earl would contemplate an alliance with a female who had disgraced him and made him the laughing-stock of London.

Neither her mother nor Lady Denton appeared to consider it impossible, a little voice whispered inside her head. But Mathilda knew better. She had firsthand experience with Miles's temperament. He had always been intransigent in matters of honour. It was true, of course, that he was acting unlike the old Miles of ten years before, but that did not necessarily mean . . .

She let these confusing thoughts slide away into the recesses of her mind, determined to ignore them. This resolution turned out to be harder to keep than Mathilda had imagined. It was almost as though something in her heart did not want to believe it.

Miles listened with half an ear to Willy's lighthearted chatter as they rode back to the Grange after a vigorous morning spent trying to keep pace with two small boys intent on riding their ponies into the ground. To his surprise, Miles had discovered in himself a hidden aptitude for keeping the young lads in line and had derived a good deal of satisfaction from sharing his considerable expertise on horsemanship with two eager minds. Having no younger brothers or nephews himself, he had never experienced the informal rough and tumble of boys at play. Much as he doted on his two sisters, Miles had never been called upon to pluck them out of muddy ditches by the seat of their pants, pick burrs and stickers out of their hair, or swab minor scratches with his pristine handkerchief until it resembled a soggy rag.

He had thoroughly enjoyed himself, in spite of an inner voice that warned him of the dangers of such intimacies.

"I had no idea you were so good with children, Miles," Hampton remarked with a laugh, interrupting Miles's ruminations. "It is high time you settled down and started your own nursery, old man. Pity to let all that talent go to waste."

"Not a chance," Miles responded promptly.

"Of course, children, especially boys, can be hazardous to one's clothes. Perhaps that is why so many of London's most prominent rakes are reluctant to tie the knot. Double their tailors' bills in an instant."

Miles stared in surprise. "I am *not* a rake, Willy, so speak for yourself. We all know you are one of the Seven Corinthians, whose exploits have been the *on dit* in every London saloon for years, and still give marriage-minded mamas the vapours."

"Nonsense!" Hampton's expression became abruptly serious. "When Robert Stilton succumbed to parson's mousetrap last summer with Melrose's daughter, the Corinthians gave up the ghost. They are no more. No more rakes in London worthy of the name. Monroyal was the last true rake in England, and if he could fall, none of us is safe."

"What about you, Willy? Do not try to convince me you were not one of them."

His friend cast him a doleful glance that sat oddly on his round face. "'Tis true, I enjoyed their company, and have many fond memories of the adventures we indulged in. But shocking the *ton* has lost some of its piquancy now that I am getting on in years."

Miles looked at him in astonishment. "Never say you are in your dotage, old man. That is pure balderdash."

Hampton smiled, and his face resumed its jovial expression. "Perhaps not my dotage, Miles. But you have no idea the pressure my mother is putting on me to take a wife. I can understand why the most unlikely men will suddenly shoot off notices to the *Gazette*. Desperation, old man. Pure and simple. They will do anything—even take a wife—to stop that infernal blathering on about duty and family and all that bunk."

A fleeting apprehension caused Miles's fingers to tighten convulsively on the reins. Thunder tossed his head nervously and pranced sideways until Miles regained his composure. He glanced briefly at his companion. When he spoke, his voice revealed none of his inner trepidation.

"Are you perchance considering taking a wife?"

Hampton let out a crack of laughter. It struck Miles that there was little amusement in his friend's mirth. Could it be that Willy had fallen prey to Mathilda's charms as he had suspected? The thought chilled him.

"If you are asking whether I intend to offer for our fair Mathilda, as I suspect you are, old friend," he remarked bluntly, shooting Miles an enigmatic glance, "let me assure you that the wind does not blow from that direction."

"It appears to me that the lady shows a distinct partiality towards you," Miles felt impelled to remark, although he wished he could cut off his tongue as he spoke.

Hampton chuckled. "Ah, my dear Miles, there is a vast difference between what you call partiality and the encouragement I would have to see in a lady's eyes before taking such a momentous leap into the abyss of matrimony." Willy's tone was jocular, but Miles recognised that his friend was deadly serious.

"I had no idea you were such a romantic, old man."

"Then you know little about me, Miles. I have ever been a devotee of Aphrodite, as were all the Corinthians, but my ideal has always been a delicate balance between Aphrodite and her elusive woodland sister Artemis, the goddess of purity and restraint. An impossible combination, you will say, and indeed I have found it to be so. Hence, my long career as a bachelor."

Miles stared at his friend in amazement. This was a side to Sweet Willy he had never suspected. "Have you never come close to this female perfection you seek?"

Hampton grinned, but with his new insight into his friend's heart, Miles detected a glimmer of sadness on that merry face.

"Rarely—only *very* rarely—I come across a glimpse of

those qualities I look for in a woman. Unfortunately, they often appear in creatures with buck teeth and squints, which would not be fatal detriments—a sweet nature can compensate for many physical blemishes—did they not all too often hide a deplorable lust for my fortune."

"Which is obscenely large, you have to admit," Miles cut in bluntly. "Would you have a female ignore it, or pretend to?"

"No, of course not. But I do prefer to rank above mere possessions in a lady's estimation. Quaint of me, I admit, but there you have it."

Miles stared at Hampton for a moment before an uncomfortable thought struck him. "Have you perchance glimpsed these stringent qualities in Mathilda?"

Hampton grinned. "As it happens, I have," he said ruefully.

"Then make her an offer and be done with it, man," Miles exclaimed, angry at himself for bringing up the subject at all. He was forced to recognise that for Willy, he would be willing—reluctantly—to abandon his plans to humiliate his former betrothed.

"Unfortunately, the lady's interest lies elsewhere, my dear boy," his friend responded matter-of-factly. "And I have a strange aversion for casting my heart upon the rocks."

No more was said as they cut through the South Meadow and made for the stables. Miles longed to ask what Hampton had meant by his remark about Mathilda's interest. He tried to find the words to prod Willy into revealing his thoughts on the subject without appearing too anxious. But he could think of none.

By the time they reached the stable-yard and dismounted, his mind was still so unsettled at Hampton's admission that he found Mathilda desirable that Miles could think of nothing except the next time he would see her.

NINE

Sir Reginald Intervenes

Several days later, Mathilda was startled to hear a familiar female voice in the hall below. She had spent most of the morning going through the linen closets with Mrs. Walker, the housekeeper, making a long list of all the linens that needed to be mended or replaced. It was a tiring task, and Mathilda was glad when the butler appeared to inform her that Lady Southmoor awaited her in the morning room.

"Have the kitchen send up a pot of tea, Walker," Mathilda commanded, removing the apron she wore over her plain morning gown. "And tell Cook that we can expect another guest for nuncheon."

After a quick stop in her chamber to tidy her hair, Mathilda ran down to the first floor, where Walker was waiting to show her into the morning room.

"My dear girl," the countess exclaimed after embracing her hostess warmly, "country air certainly agrees with you. You are looking absolutely charming. Miles warned me that I would not recognise you, and he was right. Now do tell me I am forgiven for calling upon you at such an early hour. I arrived yesterday and could not wait to hear how you and the boys are settling in. Miles tells me the place was in sad need of a woman's hand. One can never depend on servants—no matter how well trained—to take care of every little detail. Would you not agree, dear?"

The countess had seated herself on the newly upholstered green brocade settee, causing a momentary halt in this flow of words. Mathilda took advantage of the pause to remark on her neighbour's early return from London. "We did not expect you for another two or three weeks, my lady. I fear the house is still in a state of chaos. The drawing room, morning room, my own suite upstairs, and the nursery wing have been refurbished, but there is still so much to do—"

"Do not fret yourself, child," the countess interrupted. "I shall send you a dozen or so housemaids from the Grange to help set things aright here. I daresay you have not been able to find trained girls in the village to fill your staffing needs."

"How very kind of you, my lady, but—" Mathilda began, but her protest was cut short.

"Do not give it a second thought, dear. I have no doubt your housekeeper—Mrs. Walker, is it?—will be glad of the help. Of course, Rose Park is not nearly as large as the Grange, but that is an advantage when one is refurbishing an entire house." The countess glanced around the room critically. "If this is a sample of your taste, my dear"—she waved a gloved hand languidly—"then I must congratulate you, Mathilda. It is quite charming."

Lady Southmoor paused briefly when Walker brought in refreshments, but no sooner had the butler closed the door behind him than she brought up the purpose of her visit.

"The truth of the matter is I have a favour to beg, Mathilda," she said, taking small sips from the dainty tea-cup.

"You have but to name it, my lady," Mathilda replied, her curiosity aroused. "I shall do everything in my power to oblige you."

Her ladyship's beautiful face broke into a satisfied smile. "Then that is settled, my dear. You have taken a load off my mind. Miles did warn me that you might be reluctant to involve yourself in our affairs, but I told him I knew you better than that."

Mathilda stared at her guest, conscious of a flicker of apprehension. What had she unwittingly let herself in for? she wondered. "Exactly what does this favour entail, my lady?" she asked cautiously.

Lady Southmoor's smile broadened. "You remember the traditional Bazaar and Public Day we hold every year on the estate grounds? Your mother and Lady Denton have both promised to help me again this year, as they always do, but the festivities would not be complete unless you agree to help me with the arrangements, too. There is always so much to do, and I vow I can no longer keep track of all the details the way I used to. Miles tells me I am nearing my dotage, the unfeeling oaf. But he may be right, much as I dislike admitting it."

The woebegone expression on her guest's lovely face looked so comical that Mathilda could not repress a smile. "Fiddle! You are nowhere near your dotage, my lady. Unfeeling oaf is right. Your son must be bird-witted to suggest such a thing." She took particular pleasure in disparaging the earl, and it felt so satisfying that she was impelled to elaborate. "Dotage, indeed! If he is not careful, his lordship will arrive at that dreaded milestone long before you, my lady."

It was only after the countess had left that Mathilda realised she had been cleverly distracted from her original intention of avoiding any involvement in the Southmoor festivities. Throughout the light nuncheon they had enjoyed together, the countess had talked incessantly about the various booths, side-shows, exhibits, baking contests, musical entertainment, jugglers, fortune tellers, pony rides and races for the children, feats of dexterity for the tenants, judging of vegetables and poultry, and so many other festivities that Mathilda's head began to whirl.

In the end, she felt it would be churlish indeed to decline the countess's plea for help. By the time she discovered that the earl himself had suggested his mother apply to Mathilda for assistance, it was too late to draw back.

At one point during the avalanche of words, Mathilda had plucked up enough courage to mention her reluctance to inflict her presence upon his lordship. "It cannot be pleasant to encounter me at every turn," she murmured self-consciously. "After all, I did treat him rather shabbily all those years ago."

"Oh, nonsense, child!" the countess exclaimed amid a gale of tinkling laughter. "You sadly misjudge my son if you believe him capable of such pettiness. Quite the opposite is true if you want my candid opinion. Miles was full of your praise over the breakfast table this morning, and appears quite delighted with the boys. He distinctly told me that Brian has all the makings of a fine little pugilist, and that if his enthusiasm does not flag, by the time he is old enough to go to Eton, he should be ready to take on any bully who crosses his path."

Mathilda was so taken aback by this information that she nearly choked on her cold chicken. "I daresay it will be some time before the boys go away to school," she murmured. "I intend to find them a reliable tutor to start them on regular lessons this summer. Mr. Hampton has been kind enough to recommend one to me. A Mr. Baker, who tutored his nephews before they went off to Harrow."

Lady Southmoor regarded her speculatively. "Willy is certainly a godsend," she remarked. "So generous with his time and money. He appears to have quite taken you and the boys under his wing, my dear. Miles tells me Willy has provided ponies from his own stable for them to ride and has even undertaken the role of instructor to them. You are fortunate, indeed, my dear. Willy has an enviable reputation with horses, and I am sure you are also aware that he is London's most eligible bachelor."

The countess smiled slyly at this last remark, which was uttered in a suggestive undertone.

Mathilda felt the blood rush to her cheeks. "I have heard that he is much sought after, but it is his sweet nature and kindness to my boys that I find most appealing about Mr. Hampton."

"Yes, of course, dear," the countess responded airily. "But Miles tells me that Willy has also provided you with a mount from his stables. I should tell you that Willy has a high regard for his cattle and does not lend them out indiscriminately. I believe you have made quite an impression on the gentleman, and perhaps with a little more encouragement—"

Mathilda interrupted before her guest could say what was obviously on her mind. "I have not encouraged Mr. Hampton in any way, my lady," she said with an edge to her voice, "and do not intend to do so. He has been the kindest of friends, and that is all there is to it."

Lady Southmoor's smile indicated clearly that she did not believe a word of this. Mathilda wished people would not automatically assume that a widow was on the hunt for a second husband. Had James left her penniless, it might have been a different story, but that was far from the case. She would be untruthful if she claimed that the thought of marriage had not crossed her mind. After all, her mother and aunt had mentioned the possibility as soon as they discovered the identity of the mysterious stranger she had met in the park. But Mathilda herself had mixed feelings on the subject.

"I trust that Lady Rose has recovered from the slight fever she had the last time we met," she continued, anxious to change the subject.

"Rose has recovered nicely, thank you. But now Sarah is complaining of the same ailment. I am always amazed how the twins are identical even down to the indispositions they suffer. Which reminds me, dear, Sarah asked me to invite you and the boys to tea tomorrow. They are having a small celebration for Mrs. Braithwaite's birthday."

Mathilda was not to be caught twice with the same trick, however. "I am promised to my aunt's for the afternoon tomorrow, so I shall have to decline," she murmured, making a mental note to drive over to Bath to make good her excuse. "Perhaps the girls would like to take tea with us later this week. The garden is beginning to look quite lovely."

"Oh, that sounds delightful," the countess exclaimed, finally rising to take her congé. "I am sure Miles can be persuaded to drive them over," she added carelessly. "He is so attached to his sisters, you know."

Mathilda's heart sank at this tactless remark. She had deliberately omitted the gentlemen from the invitation, but now it seemed she would be saddled with them anyway. As she accompanied the countess to her carriage, it occurred to her that Lady Southmoor had—perhaps quite unconsciously, but then again perhaps not—peppered her conversation with references to her son until Mathilda had grown quite tired of hearing what Miles had said, or suggested, or thought, or mentioned.

And now he had been thrust upon her for tea at Rose Park, she thought disgustedly, as the countess's carriage disappeared beneath the spreading chestnut trees that bordered the driveway.

Perhaps he would not come. Perhaps he would be otherwise engaged as gentlemen so often were. Perhaps he simply would not wish to spend the afternoon in her company.

Even as Mathilda considered these possibilities, she knew in her heart that he would come. She could not explain the feeling, but it was so strong that she could almost visualise the earl sitting at the tea-table on the brick terrace in the shade of the old oak tree that had witnessed such family tea-parties at Rose Park for more years than she cared to consider. She could even imagine his dark eyes fixed upon her and that faint enigmatic smile softening his well-shaped lips.

She sighed and turned to reenter the house, her thoughts not on the many tasks that remained to be done in the house, but on the new sprig muslin gown she would wear when the earl came to tea.

Two days after her encounter with the countess, Mathilda was again interrupted as she worked with Mrs. Walker in one of the many guest bedchambers on the second floor. The faded, mildewed curtains, in a dull shade of maroon, which looked as though they dated from the days of the Conqueror,

had been removed from the windows the day before by two
footmen, who stood ready to hang the new ones.

When the butler appeared at the doorway in the middle of
the afternoon to announce two gentlemen callers, Mrs. Walker
was supervising the washing of the tall windows by two
housemaids in mob-caps. Mathilda looked up from the lace
doily she was mending, wondering if she dared to send down a
message that she was not receiving today.

"Oh, dear," she grumbled, putting away her needle. "Please
tell the gentlemen I shall be down in a few minutes, Walker."

Mathilda was not in the mood for visitors. Much as she enjoyed the company of Mr. Hampton, the prospect of enduring
the scrutiny of the Earl of Southmoor for the duration of the
visit unnerved her. In Town such calls were strictly limited to
the prescribed half hour, but here in the country, the rules were
not so closely adhered to. What if he stayed for a whole hour?
What would she say to him? Of course, Willy would be there
with his amusing chatter. She could depend on him.

Pausing before the mirror on the landing to check her appearance, Mathilda was glad that she had chosen to wear one
of the morning gowns she had ordered in London. The pale
yellow muslin set off her auburn hair, which she had arranged
in a simple chignon that morning, and made her appear years
younger.

It would have to do, she thought, wondering what had
brought the earl and Mr. Hampton to Rose Park that afternoon.

When she stepped into the drawing room, Mathilda saw at
once that neither of the gentlemen who rose to greet her was
the earl or Mr. Hampton. For a fleeting moment she thought
they were both unknown to her. But when the shortest one
stepped forward to greet her, she felt herself tense as unpleasant memories flooded back.

"My dear Mathilda," Sir Reginald Heath began, a tight
smile pasted on his bovine face. "I see you are in fine fettle,
although that gown would be more fitting on a girl at her
come-out than on a matron of your years."

Her brother had not mellowed in the ten years since they had last met, Mathilda realised with a pang of regret. His very first words confirmed that he was still the same opinionated, odiously small-minded tyrant she remembered from her childhood. In spite of his overbearing ways, she had loved him dearly as a young girl. He could often be wheedled into escorting her on the long rides she loved to take through the countryside. Although he scoffed at the many ruins she was so eager to sketch, he would settle himself comfortably on a rug in the shade and doze off while Mathilda rambled through the ruins of abbeys, castles, and ancient chapels with her sketch-pad.

Those relatively happy days ended abruptly when the future Earl of Southmoor had called upon their father with his unexpected and highly advantageous offer. Once that offer was made and accepted, Mathilda's carefree rambles with her brother were over. Reginald changed, too. Suddenly, he had become bosom bows with Miles, hanging on his every word and basking in the glamour of being the future brother-in-law to a future earl.

Mathilda's elopement with James Parmenter had burst Reginald's bubble of complacency. He had never forgiven her. According to her mother, Reginald had considered himself the injured party as much as the earl and had disowned her very publicly. The aborted connexion with the Southmoors had been a major blow to his consequence, for which he held his sister entirely responsible.

These unhappy memories flashed through Mathilda's mind as she listened to Reginald's double-edged compliment. Nothing had changed. Her brother's sudden appearance could have nothing to do with his pleasure in her safe return from India, or interest in his two nephews. When he did not deign to ask after the boys, Mathilda felt her heart harden against him.

"What brings you to Rose Park, Reginald?" she demanded, without giving the slightest gesture of greeting.

"I have been most concerned for your welfare, my dear sister," he responded affably. "Only this morning, Margery reminded me at the breakfast table that it was high time I assumed my duty to you."

"Duty?" Mathilda stared at him in disbelief. The Margery she remembered from her childhood—daughter to the vicar and a shy creature who dared not utter a syllable without approval—would not have ventured to criticise her husband openly. "I am at a loss to understand what you mean by duty, Reginald. The boys and I have been back in England for weeks and were not aware of this *concern* you speak of."

Sir Reginald appeared slightly taken aback by her forceful response, but Mathilda transferred her attention to the other gentleman, who had remained silent during this exchange. There was something familiar about him, but she could not place him.

"Are you not going to present your friend, Reginald?"

Before her brother could respond, the gentleman stepped forward, an ingratiating smile on his handsome face. As soon as he spoke, Mathilda recognised him, and her heart sank for the second time that afternoon.

"I am devastated that you have forgotten me so soon, my dear lady," he murmured obsequiously, a calculating glance belying the sincerity of his words. "And here I have been harbouring the illusion that we enjoyed a warm friendship in India not so long ago. George Bennett at your service, my dear." He bowed gracefully over her hand, but there was a licentiousness to his smile that Mathilda remembered all too well.

"Lord George, of course," she replied, drawing her hand away as abruptly as politeness allowed. "Now I *do* recall you, sir, although I confess I do not share your illusions of India," she added with a calculated set-down. "All that stands out clearly in my mind is the unconscionable number of animals you slaughtered during your stay. I presume you have those unfortunate creatures hanging from your walls like so many trophies."

She had spoken with increasing scorn as the unhappy memory of the dead tigers and other victims of Lord George's hunting frenzy came flooding back. The man had been a veritable monster with an insatiable appetite for killing and plundering. Wanton destruction—of animals or women—had seemed to be his sole source of amusement, and Mathilda was appalled that he had washed up on her doorstep.

"Mathilda!" her brother blustered, evidently offended by her tone. "That is no way to welcome his lordship, who has graciously condescended to spend a few weeks rusticating at Heath Hall. He expressed a flattering interest in renewing his acquaintance with you, my dear, so I invited him to accompany me this afternoon."

It was all Mathilda could do to repress a snort of disgust. Reginald was being particularly pedantic, a circumstance that increased her irritation. And she could not help speculating on the real reason for the sudden appearance of these two disagreeable callers in her drawing room. Reginald's claims of concern for her welfare were pure balderdash, and Lord George's presence at Heath Hall could only mean that he had outstayed his welcome elsewhere and was on the hunt for fresh amusement.

A shiver snaked up her spine at the notion that she might once again become the object of his lecherous attentions.

"Then I must certainly thank his lordship for his condescension," she murmured stiffly. "Now, why do you not sit down, Reginald, and tell me the real reason for your visit." She gestured halfheartedly at the settee while seating herself in a stiff-backed chair.

"As I have already said, my dear," Sir Reginald began, lowering his considerable girth onto the settee, which sagged noticeably under the weight, "my concern for your welfare—"

"And I have told *you,* Brother, that my boys and I can rub along well enough without your concern. We have done so splendidly for nearly two months already, so put your mind at rest. Your sudden interest is appreciated, but not essential to our well-being, so you might have saved yourself the trouble of riding over here."

"You always were a stubborn lass, Mathilda," her brother responded, impervious as always to any attempt to thwart his wishes. "But it will not do, you know. It simply will not do for a female alone in the world to be saddled with the management of an estate this size. And if this extensive refurbishment you have embarked upon is any indication"—he waved a pudgy arm around the room—"you are squandering your fortune on fripperies."

Mathilda frowned. How did this pompous rattle know the extent of her fortune? A lucky guess, perhaps? But since she herself had not known that James possessed such a large fortune, how could it be public knowledge? They had always lived comfortably in India, but neither of them had hankered after the ostentatious displays of wealth that many of their countrymen affected. Why should this be of interest to her brother? she wondered.

A glimmer of suspicion began to take shape in her mind. "I fail to see what concern it is of yours how much I spend and on what," she said sharply.

"Your brother is to be commended for his desire to protect your interests, my dear lady," Lord George cut in smoothly. "You cannot deny that females, delightful creatures that they are, of course, are not suited for the rigours of managing large sums of money or running an estate. It is quite beyond their powers of—"

"Balderdash!" Mathilda interrupted briskly. "You must associate with an inferior class of bird-witted females, my lord. I can assure you that I have no trouble whatsoever in running Rose Park."

She was gratified to see Lord George's countenance cloud in anger at this second set-down, and was not surprised when Reginald came to his defence.

"It is churlish of you to chastise his lordship for expressing what any right-thinking gentleman would say under the circumstances, Mathilda. But let me assure you that you will not be burdened with such unfeminine tasks for much longer. I have already written to Mr. McIntyre in London to instruct him to transfer the management of the property to me. It is only right that, as head of the family, I should take care of everything until you see fit to marry again."

Mathilda could not believe what she was hearing. When the monstrosity of her brother's arrogance finally sank in, she stood up abruptly, her face set in anger.

"Since when are you head of the Parmenter family?" she demanded. "You are presumptuous to pretend that you have any right to dictate to me or to my sons. I am convinced that Mr. McIntyre will tell you so himself as soon as he gets over your temerity in suggesting such a thing."

The two gentlemen had also risen, and Mathilda took the opportunity to excuse herself.

"I must beg your indulgence for not receiving you with more fanfare, gentlemen. You caught me in the process of squandering money in refurbishing the guest chambers upstairs."

She rang the bell and stood stiffly until Woods appeared.

"Show these gentlemen out, Woods," she told the butler. "I wish you both good-day, sirs."

"You have not heard the last of this foolishness, Mathilda." Reginald warned as he turned to leave. "I shall return as soon as I have made the appropriate arrangements with McIntyre. In the meantime, try not to do anything you will regret."

Mathilda ignored him. She had spoken her mind on the subject, rather more forcefully than was her wont, but she did not regret her bluntness.

As she went along the hall to the library, her thoughts were on the letter she would send off to Mr. McIntyre that very afternoon.

TEN

Bath Assembly

Sir Reginald did not repeat his visit, and after receiving a comforting response to her letter to Mr. McIntyre, Mathilda felt vastly relieved about the future of Rose Park. The London solicitor assured her categorically that there was no legal way her brother could take control of her fortune by insisting on becoming her trustee. Sir James's will was quite clear. He left the bulk of his fortune to Lady Mathilda Parmenter without restrictions. Any income from the estate, legally belonging to his heir, Christopher, should be used for improvements and upkeep until such time as his son came of age under the joint guardianship of his solicitor, Mr. McIntyre, and his wife, Lady Parmenter.

The solicitor acknowledged receiving instructions from Sir Reginald Heath to instate him, as Lady Parmenter's only brother, as one of the trustees of the estate and to render an accounting of all past expenditures and refer all future ones to him for approval.

One morning a week later, Mathilda smiled as she perused a copy of Mr. McIntyre's reply to her brother. The letter was couched in legal terms, but it was clear to Mathilda that the solicitor was unimpressed by Reginald's blustering demands. He was polite yet firm. What Sir Reginald requested was not legally possible. In his letter to Mathilda, Mr. McIntyre had clarified that the only way control of her fortune could pass into the hands of another was if Lady Parmenter were to take a second husband. According to the will, however, the trusteeship for the underaged heir would remain unchanged.

This knowledge lifted a weight from her shoulders, and Mathilda was able to show a degree of civility if not warmth towards her brother and his guest when she encountered them leaving Lady Denton's town house on Regina Court one afternoon that same week.

"You will never guess who was just here, Mathilda," her mother remarked with barely suppressed excitement as soon as the group was seated in the Blue Saloon, and Benson despatched to bring up the tea-tray.

Mathilda grimaced. "We had the misfortune to run into the gentlemen as they were leaving, Mama. If I had only taken the time to change my bonnet before leaving the Park, we would have missed them. I had a strong premonition that I should have worn the new blue straw with the yellow bows, but Mrs. Grey insisted that this green felt with the feather looked better with my striped silk gown."

"You look absolutely charming, dear," her mother murmured approvingly. "But you missed meeting Reginald's dashing friend, Lord George Bennett, who is staying at Heath Hall for a month or two this summer. He had some very complimentary things to say about you, dear. Apparently you made quite an impression on him in India."

Mathilda grimaced in distaste. "Do not believe a word that scoundrel utters, Mama. He is nothing but a spendthrift and wastrel of the worst kind. No doubt he is rusticating here in Bath to escape his creditors."

"You are too unkind to the poor gentleman, Mathilda," her mother said, accepting a slice of pound cake and cutting it into bite-sized morsels. "Lord George is both charming and handsome, besides being the son of a duke. Such eligible partis do not come along every day, dear, especially in the country. Reginald is to be commended for bringing him to your notice."

"My brother was ever unduly impressed by titles," Mathilda replied snappishly, "and he has not changed a bit since he

made a spectacle of himself over Southmoor. What he sees in
Lord George I cannot imagine, but—"

"They were at Oxford together," her mother interrupted
gently. "They must have any number of things in common,
dear."

"You are an innocent, Angela," her sister put in bluntly.
"The man is obviously an adventurer and philanderer. A
charming one, 'tis true, but a rogue nonetheless. I would advise you to stay clear of him, Mathilda. Men like that are always on the lookout for a wealthy female to frank their
extravagances."

"Oh, I intend to, Aunt. But enough about that jackstraw. I
am more interested in what you intend to wear at the Bath Assembly next week. I have not been to a local assembly in so
long that I shall require your expert advice on what to wear."

As Mathilda well knew, nothing pleased her aunt more than
to be called upon for advice on all matters of style and fashion.
All thoughts of gentlemen were suspended for the next hour,
during which Mathilda learned more about current Bath fash-
ions than she really wanted to know.

During a lull in a lively argument between her mother and
Lady Denton on the advantages of a ball gown of watered silk
worn under spider-gauze strewn with silver spangles, or an
Italian crepe trimmed with blond lace and floss-silk, Mathilda
heard the unwelcome news that Lord George had offered to
escort the ladies to the Assembly himself.

"I trust you declined his kind offer, Aunt," she said sharply.
"I would rather stay at home than be seen driving around with
that gazetted fortune-hunter."

"Fortunately, Mr. Hampton had already offered his escort,
my dear. But do not think you will escape his lordship so easily. Lord George is determined to obtain the first waltz with
you. He told me so himself."

"Well, he is out of luck, Aunt. I have promised that waltz to
Mr. Hampton."

"And which dance have you saved for Miles?" her mother

wanted to know. "He is escorting the countess and his sisters, but I am sure he will join our party. He appears to be under your spell again, Mathilda. I trust you will treat him with more consideration this time."

"You are mistaking the matter as usual, Mama," Mathilda retorted crossly. "Miles was never under my spell, as you call it. Ours was an arranged match if you recall. I was never consulted, and I seriously doubt that poor Miles had much say in it either. The countess was set on the match and must have nagged her son into making his offer, which was lukewarm at best. Did you ever think to ask me if such a match was to my liking, Mama?"

Lady Heath looked at her in genuine surprise. "We all knew you doted on Miles, dear, so we assumed you would be in alt at the prospect. Besides, your dear papa was only looking out for your interests when he accepted Miles's obliging offer. He saw you as mistress of Southmoor Grange. His little girl a countess. Can you blame him for wanting the best for you, dear? Only consider what you might have—"

Mathilda was about to interrupt with some bitterness, but Lady Denton intervened. "Do not recriminate the poor child, Angela. What is done is beyond repair, and it does no good to repine upon what might have been. Our dear Mathilda is no longer a romantical chit of seventeen, and will no doubt see Miles and what he has to offer in quite a different light today."

Mathilda closed her eyes and took a deep breath. "You are putting the cart before the horse, ladies. Miles is not offering anything. And besides, I do believe Mr. Hampton is the better choice," she added impulsively. "He is kind and generous and absolutely charming."

But Sweet Willy, dear as he was to her, did not make her heart flutter wildly in her breast as Miles's slightest smile always did. Yet could she trust the earl? His attentions were flattering, but she could not understand his motives. And beneath his amiability she sensed a core of hardness in him that frightened her.

What was his game? she asked herself, listening with half
an ear to her aunt extol the wonders of apricot satin cut with a
Russian bodice, and embellished with rows of little seed
pearls. How deeply must she enter into it before he showed his
hand?

Mathilda was intrigued in spite of herself. Had Miles
changed at all from the cool, aloof gentleman she had aban-
doned years before? At times she was convinced of it. At others, she feared that she was allowing her heart to spin a web of
fantasy around him that had little to do with the real Miles.
Only time would tell.

With a sigh of frustration, Mathilda turned her attention
back to the conversation flowing around her.

With Lady Denton and her mother leading the way,
Mathilda trod up the stairs to the Assembly Rooms on the arm
of Mr. Hampton. She felt a little giddy with excitement. It had
been over a year since she had attended a formal ball, and
even longer since she had enjoyed the luxury of a new ball
gown, which her aunt had assured her was all the crack. Mr.
Hampton had also given his unstinting approval of the bronze
satin under a diaphanous gauze spangled with tiny seed pearls,
and if his gaze had lingered overlong on the plunging neckline
set off with a flirtatious ruff, Mathilda could hardly fault him
when he complimented her so prettily.

"You will be the envy of every lady present, my dear," he
murmured in her ear as they reached the top of the stair. "And
the despair of every gentleman not fortunate enough to have
obtained a place on your card."

"You flatter me, sir," she responded rather breathlessly, unaccustomed to such heady praise. "You have no cause to despair, however, since you have already secured the first waltz
with me." She smiled at Hampton as he guided her towards
the brightly lit ballroom already milling with guests. "Perhaps
I should not say so," she continued as they stood looking out

at the crush of people who had evidently just completed a country dance, "but I am so glad you did."

"Oh?" He glanced at her quizzically, amusement twinkling in his coffee-coloured eyes.

She blushed, realising that her words might have sounded too intimate. "You rescued me from a very tiresome gentleman," she clarified hastily. "One who insisted that nothing but a waltz would do for him. I had to invent a partner for the second waltz before he would settle for a cotillion. Very naughty of me, I know, but—"

"I know exactly what you mean, my dear. Some gentlemen cannot seem to see when their presence is *de trop*. One must invent excuses to be rid of them. I must confess that I have done the same myself a time or two. But never fear, I am sure Miles will be more than ready to stand up with you for a waltz. And speaking of the devil, here he comes. Let us ask him."

Mathilda glanced towards the entrance, where the earl, darkly handsome in a deep blue coat and silver pantaloons, had just arrived with his mother and two sisters. The latter were looking around eagerly as if searching for a familiar face. She felt herself grow rigid with panic at the thought of accosting Miles and demanding he waltz with her.

"Oh, no, no!" she exclaimed weakly. "I am sure his lordship has already chosen partners for all his dances. I cannot impose—"

"Nonsense!" Mr. Hampton began to edge through the crowd towards the Southmoor party. "I personally know that Miles fully intended to request a dance from you."

Mathilda wished she could escape into the potted palms in the corner of the room and hide there for the rest of the evening. She was saved from this drastic measure by the orchestra, which chose that moment to strike up the opening bars of a waltz.

Hampton responded instantly, slipping an arm round Mathilda's waist and gently guiding her onto the dance floor.

He was an accomplished dancer, and she was soon swept up into the intoxicating cadence of the music. Her partner's eyes sparkled with admiration, and before long, his merry conversation had put her completely at ease.

Mathilda loved to dance, and as a young girl had indulged in elaborate fantasies about dancing with Miles on a moonlit terrace at midnight. After their betrothal, she had been impatient to make those fantasies come true. But they never had. She had waited in vain for him to shower her with those intimate attentions that she had dreamed of; but none of this came to pass, and finally she had come to accept the unpalatable truth. Miles might have been persuaded to offer her his name, but he would never surrender his heart.

This painful discovery had driven her into the willing arms of Sir James Parmenter—a circumstance she had never regretted— and now Mathilda wondered if perhaps she was again being driven into another man's arms by the very gentleman around whom she had begun to elaborate a new set of fantasies.

Of their own accord, her eyes sought him out, this new Miles who had again captured her imagination. He was not dancing. Standing alone to one side of the entrance, he appeared to be staring right at her, and Mathilda quickly lowered her gaze. She was being quite foolish, of course. The earl might be interested in any one of the attractive ladies on the dance floor. There was no particular reason for him to look at her. Was there? Her heart fluttered briefly at the notion, but she quelled it ruthlessly.

Then abruptly the music ended, and with a flourish, Hampton brought her to a standstill beside the entrance. Although she had her back to him, Mathilda knew that the earl was still there, elegantly lounging against one of the Grecian-styled columns. When Hampton's eyes flickered over her shoulder, she was sure of it, and was not surprised to hear his voice at her elbow.

"Trust you to get a head start on the rest of us, Willy," the earl drawled after bowing over Mathilda's gloved fingers.

"Dare I hope that you have another waltz unspoken for this evening, my dear?"

Miles was looking at her so intently that Mathilda imagined the dance floor swayed beneath her feet. His eyes were dark and full of emotions she had never seen in them before. Or had she lost her senses like some naïve girl suffering her first infatuation? Flustered, she glanced down at her dance card, although she knew perfectly well there was no name opposite the second waltz. She smiled at how narrowly she had escaped having to give it to that odious Lord George.

"You are in luck, my lord." She handed him the card and watched while he scrawled his name on it. He paused for a moment, then wrote his name opposite a cotillion later in the evening.

"My mother has been asking for you," he murmured, handing back the card. "She specifically requested that I bring you to her when the dance ended."

Mathilda glanced around the crowded room and saw the countess standing with her mother and Lady Denton, apparently deep in conversation. Ladies Rose and Sarah, resplendent in frothy white gowns, had their heads together with a group of other young ladies, probably comparing dance cards, Mathilda thought, remembering her own days as a very young girl.

"There she is," she said, wondering what the shrewd countess had up her sleeve this time. She moved to push through the milling dancers, but instantly felt a guiding hand on her elbow.

"Here," drawled the earl, "allow me to get you through this crush, my dear. Hampton can make himself useful and procure us some punch. What do you say, Willy?"

"What *can* I say?" Hampton smiled ruefully at Mathilda and shrugged his elegant shoulders. "I seem to have been outmaneuvered by an expert here."

"You are far too modest, sir," Mathilda responded, throwing him a teasing smile before allowing herself to be led off through the crowd. The warmth of the earl's hand on her elbow brought back bittersweet memories of those first heady days of her betrothal to him. She had been ecstatic at the thought of becoming the object of those little intimacies she had imagined would be *de rigueur* between two people recently betrothed. She glanced up at him and was startled to catch him looking at her with an enigmatic smile.

"Have I said something to amuse you, my lord?"

One corner of his mouth quirked upwards. "I merely wondered at the thoughts going through that pretty head of yours, Mathilda."

She wished he would not use her given name or call her his *dear* as he did far too often for comfort. They had come to a standstill, and as she gazed at him, trying to decipher the odd glint in his eyes, Mathilda experienced a wild urge to tell him exactly what thoughts were flashing through her head. How would he react if she were to confess her improper urge to feel his arms crushing her against his immaculate blue coat until the breath was quite squeezed out of her? Would he be shocked or disgusted? And worse yet, what would Miles say if she were to rip off that neatly starched cravat of his and place her lips in the hollow of his throat where she could feel the beat of his heart?

The notion was so outrageous that Mathilda felt quite giddy. She closed her eyes for a moment, hoping the erotic vision would vanish, but when she opened them Miles was standing before her, shirtless, his broad chest quite taking her breath away, inviting her touch, tapering down in a cascade of dark hair to the top of his silver pantaloons.

She gasped in horror and instantly shut her eyes again, squeezing them to erase the erotic vision her heated thoughts had conjured up. This could not be happening. Not in the middle of the Bath Assembly Rooms with half of Bath's social set as witness. She must be losing her mind.

She felt both his hands on her arms and fought to keep from letting herself sink against that tantalisingly bare chest.

"Let me escort you to a seat, Mathilda," he murmured, urging her through the throng towards the chairs set against the wall. "You almost swooned, my dear. I shall call Hampton out for tiring you with his waltz."

Not hearing any shocked comments at their passage, Mathilda opened her eyes again and saw that Miles was regarding her with genuine concern. To her disappointment, his chest was covered with his conventional clothing and he did not appear the least shocked. Evidently she had not made an absolute fool of herself in front of everyone.

"Ah, here he is now with your punch," Miles continued, settling her in a chair next to the countess, who was regarding her anxiously.

"Whatever have you done to Mathilda, Miles?" she scolded. "The poor girl looks as though she has seen a ghost. Sit here and drink your punch, my dear," she continued, addressing a trembling Mathilda.

Her aunt sat down beside her and plied her vigorously with her fan. "You must not exert yourself to the point of exhaustion, my girl. You are not a schoolroom chit any more, you know. It is foolhardy to imagine otherwise."

"I did not imagine anything so nonsensical," Mathilda hissed under her breath, more than a little mortified at her aunt's unfair remark. "I am barely eight-and-twenty, Aunt. The truth is I have not danced since . . . in over a year," she corrected hastily. She had been about to say since James had left her, but Miles was standing within earshot, and she was reluctant to mention James to him.

"Well, we can easily remedy that oversight, my lady," Hampton's cheery voice interrupted as he appeared with her glass of punch in time to hear her remark. "My Aunt Bess— Lady Bedford, you know—is already planning her summer ball, which I claim the privilege of escorting you to. She is a bit of a dragon, but has always been one of my favourite aunts."

"I did not know you had an aunt in Bath, Mr. Hampton," Mathilda said, wondering where these pleasantries would lead.

"I have aunts all over the south of England, my dear, and not a few in the north as far as Edinburgh. Two more in Wales, and even one in Ireland. She was disowned by the family until we discovered that her new husband, Lord Stanthorp, raises some of the best hunting stock in the country. All sins are forgiven by the Hampton clan if one is a connoisseur of horseflesh."

"Lady Bedford is well known to me, Willy," the countess remarked. "She is reputed to be somewhat eccentric, like all the Hamptons," she added sotto voce to Mathilda with a teasing glance at Willy, "but her summer ball is not to be missed. I insist you join our party, dear."

"And do not forget the ball you are also planning, Mother," the earl remarked laconically, sipping his punch and gazing pointedly at the countess. "There should be enough dancing there to please everyone."

Mathilda could not say for sure, but she had the fleeting impression that the countess was not expecting this announcement. Lady Southmoor recovered with admirable aplomb, however, and it was not long before she had added details of her own and promised to send invitations to everyone present.

"There is always dancing at the Bazaar, too, if I remember from previous years," Hampton added, and was immediately seconded by Lady Denton, who reminded Mathilda that there would be two groups of musicians at the Grange for the festivities, one up at the house for the gentry, and another in the stable-yard for the tenants and farm workers. Mathilda had vivid memories of escaping from the formal ballroom and sneaking off to dance country jigs with the housemaids and stable-lads, who always seemed to have more fun.

"Oh, yes," she exclaimed nostalgically, "I remember how we used to escape to dance with the tenants, until Reginald, always the stickler for propriety, would notice our absence and drag us back to the Great Hall."

She glanced at Miles, wondering if he recalled those heady days of their youth when he and James were as close as brothers, and Reginald the eternal hanger-on followed them around like a shadow. Days of innocent happiness and uncomplicated dreams that had somehow dissipated after that momentous afternoon when Miles had presented himself at Heath Hall to make the offer that would change her life forever.

"Speaking of your brother, dear," the countess remarked, bringing her ornate lorgnette up to stare off towards the entrance, "there he is in the flesh. And what a revolting coat. Did he deliberately smother himself with rhubarb sauce, I wonder? Oh, botheration," she exclaimed, turning away with a moue of annoyance on her lovely face. "He has that Town Tulip Bennett with him. If it is true that one may tell a man by his friends," she continued acerbically, "it pains me to report that your brother has turned into a coxcomb, dear."

"Surely you remember that Reginald never did have any sense, my lady," Mathilda replied lightly. "So it should not surprise you to see him toadying up to a pretentious rogue like Lord George Bennett. I trust that my brother does not intend to attach himself to our party."

"Mathilda, darling," her mother broke in plaintively, "do not be so harsh on poor Reginald. I suspect he wishes to make his peace with you. Do be nice to him, dear, for my sake."

Mathilda glanced at her mother pityingly. Although the Dowager Lady Heath officially resided with her son and his pasty-faced wife, Margery, at Heath Hall, she spent most of her days with her sister, Agatha, in Bath. Neither of the two widowed ladies had much sympathy for the colourless creature her brother had wed, principally—Mathilda had always suspected—because of her obscure connexions with the Duke of Cambourne in Cornwall.

"He is ten years too late, Mama. I have no use for a man who disowned me, so he is wasting his time."

She sighed as she watched Sir Reginald approaching through the crowd, Lord George in tow. Did his lordship think so little of her intellect that he imagined she would overlook the obnoxious insinuations he had made to her in India? She had, for the sake of politeness, granted him one dance this evening, but that was as far as she was prepared to go.

She looked away, not wishing to appear curious, and found Miles staring at her, a fierce expression in his dark eyes. Oh, no. Surely he would not think she welcomed Bennett's attentions. Mathilda was surprised at the depth of her distress at the thought, and vowed to keep Bennett at arm's length.

ELEVEN

Unwelcome Suitor

Caught up in one of Willy's amusing stories, Miles was only vaguely aware of the conversation among the ladies. He did catch his mother's unflattering remarks about George Bennett, who was making his way across the room towards them in the wake of the all-too-familiar portly figure in a dull red coat. Some comment from Lady Heath made Mathilda bristle, and Miles felt a stir of pleasure at the sight of her tossing head and flashing eyes. His Mathilda had developed into a woman of unexpected spirit, and he looked forward to dashing that spirit as his own had been long ago.

"I suspect that shabster Bennett is the jackstraw who has our Mathilda in a pother," Willy said sotto voce as the gentleman in question bowed obsequiously over the ladies' hands. "That brother of hers seems too lackwitted to see the kind of man he is throwing at his sister."

Our Mathilda? Miles thought to himself, torn between annoyance and amusement. "In what way is Bennett bothering her?" he drawled. The thought of the Duke of Milford's wastrel son playing off his libertine tricks on *his* Mathilda gave Miles a nasty turn.

Lord George Bennett was well known in social circles as a man to be avoided. A reckless gamester, Bennett had a vicious temper when the cards were going against him, and Miles had heard the arrogant lordling was not above resorting to underhand tricks to win. He could be excessively charming when he chose, and was a great favourite with the ladies, but there was not a mother in Town with a marriageable daughter who would allow the man to cross her threshold.

Hampton glanced at him curiously. "She would not say exactly, but I gather they met when Bennett was shipped off to India after that scandal with Lord Huxley's wife. The blighter wounded poor Huxley rather badly, remember. Of course, the old man never had a chance against Bennett, who is the very devil with a pistol. But like most husbands, he felt he had no choice but to call the scoundrel out. 'Tis a wonder he is not dead, we all said at the time. Rumour has it that the duke has told Georgie boy to get himself a rich wife—"

Hampton broke off abruptly as Sir Reginald moved towards them. "Well met, Heath," he remarked blandly. "Come to kick up your heels, have you?"

It was all Miles could do to suppress a grin at the notion of the portly gentleman in dull red coat and pink pantaloons coming anywhere close to the sprightly activity implied in Willy's words.

He acknowledged Sir Reginald's effusive salutation with a brief nod, trying to avoid staring too closely at the ugly red coat and the botched attempt at a Mathematical the baronet sported round his neck. He could not recall the number of times in their younger days he had attempted to educate Reginald in the art of tying his cravat. Miles had given up finally when his pupil failed to grasp even the rudiments of the skill.

"Delighted to see you again, Hampton," the baronet brayed loudly, as though he wished to impress everyone in the room with his close acquaintance with men like the Honourable Willoughby Hampton. "I understand you are spending the summer at the Grange with our good friend Southmoor here." He inclined his ponderous form in Miles's direction, an obsequious smile pasted on his round face. "How jolly for all of us who will enjoy the privilege of basking in the rays of your wit, sir." His smile grew broader at this supposed piece of witticism.

Miles exchanged a pained glance with Willy, who appeared to be strangling on a fishbone.

"You are both well acquainted with Lord George Bennett, I am sure," Heath continued in his unctuous voice. "His lordship has done me the honour of accepting my invitation to spend a few weeks this summer at Heath Hall. We were up at Oxford together," he explained self-importantly, "and met again quite by accident in London last month. When I mentioned that my sister was back at Rose Park with her two boys, his lordship reminded me that he had met Mathilda in India. One thing led to another, and now here he is enjoying the salubrious airs of Bath."

Miles did not have to be told what things had led to the arrival of Bennett in Bath. It was quite apparent from the covetous glances the man was throwing in Mathilda's direction that he was on the hunt again. There had been rumours of a dust-up between Bennett and the brothers of one of that Season's beauties who had made her come-out that year. The affair had not reached the proportions of a full-blown scandal, but it was evident that Bennett had been forced to retire to the country to prevent the escalation of the incident into a vulgar brawl.

Miles could barely restrain a grimace of distaste. He envied Willy his sangfroid and the innate courtliness that allowed him to greet the licentious dandy with some degree of civility.

"Welcome to Bath," Miles heard Hampton say conversationally. "I suspect you will find us rather tame here, Bennett, especially after the delights of the London social whirl."

Bennett smiled. "Oh, I believe you underestimate your local beauties, Hampton," he said, sweeping his arm around the room. "I have seen any number of lovelies since setting foot in the hall. I am depending on my good friend Reggie here to introduce me. He tells me he has known them all since the cradle. Right, old boy?"

Miles saw Heath's heavy jowls swell under this fulsome praise. "Indeed, indeed," he simpered, his already high colour mounting to a hue closer to the rhubarb of his coat. "Happy to oblige in any way I can." His face contorted into what Miles recognised as Reginald's sycophantic smile. He had endured many such grimaces back in the days when Mathilda's brother had considered himself the earl's bosom-bow and hung on his coat-tails until Miles had despaired of ever getting free of his leach-like future brother-in-law. Mathilda's defection had dampened Reginald's enthusiasm, but every time they met, Miles was careful not to encourage the connexion.

It seemed clear to the earl that Mathilda was deliberately avoiding conversation with both her brother and Lord George. She kept her eyes lowered and absentmindedly furled and un-furled the delicately painted fan in her lap as she listened to the animated discussion that his mother was conducting with Lady Denton. Their topic was the countess's summer Bazaar and Miles caught snatches of his mother's lamentations regarding the unreliability of the crabmeat she always ordered from the coast for the elaborate dinner that had been a central feature of the festivities since the second countess had started the tradition in Tudor times.

"I simply cannot find a reliable supplier anymore," Miles heard her complain. "It used to be that old Mr. Cooper from the Cooper Fishmongers in Bath could be trusted to send me fresh crabs, but since the old man died, I have had at least two deliveries that were spoiled. Cook tells me that the young Cooper is not the man his grandfather was by any means, and I am sure that—"

Luckily this tirade against fish in general and crab-mongers in particular—which Miles had heard numerous times before—was cut short when the orchestra struck up the opening bars of a quadrille. As he had anticipated, Bennett's attention strayed from Sir Reginald's long-winded peroration about the dangers of purchasing sheep from a certain breeder in north Somerset whose flocks were vastly overrated. His eyes flickered towards Mathilda, whose gaze had that very moment rested briefly on his own.

Miles was quick to respond to this silent reminder. He strolled over and offered his arm. "Our dance, I believe, my dear."

"I was under the impression it was *mine,* Southmoor." Bennett stood beside him, his smile clearly less than amiable.

One hand resting on the earl's sleeve, Mathilda had risen and now cast a cursory glance at her dance card. She smiled briefly. "Yours is the fifth, my lord. A cotillion if you remember."

Bennett scowled, but had the grace to step back while Miles led Mathilda to join a set already forming on the floor.

"A nasty piece of work, that," he offered as they took their places in the set. "I am surprised your brother encourages him to dangle after you, my dear."

"Lord George is not dangling after me," Mathilda protested, but Miles noticed that her cheeks were tinged with pink. "I had the misfortune of meeting him in India when he was there—rusticating after some disgrace or other as I understand it. He presumes on that brief acquaintance, I am afraid."

Miles looked down at her as they waited their turn to dance. She had been lovely as a young girl ten years before, her crown of auburn curls framing a delicate face, her curiously pale amber eyes always wide with astonishment or delight at the world unfolding around her. Life had been kind to her. In the full bloom of her maturity, Mathilda took his breath away. The auburn hair was dressed with more sophistication, but her skin had kept that flawless porcelain quality of a schoolgirl. Her form, though still girlish in its elegant slimness, had filled out to stimulate the erotic fantasies he had been plagued with in those awkward days of his youth. Those perfect breasts, so tender and tantalising in his memories, had blossomed into a creamy expanse of inviting softness into which he yearned to bury his heated face.

With an inward groan, Miles tore his gaze away and pretended interest in the couple working their way down the row of dancers. If he was not careful, he would find himself infatuated with the wench again, and that would not do at all. No, that would not do. What would become of the dream of retribution he had nourished so carefully for so many years? He would not love again. Love had no part in the game he was playing. How could he love when his heart had been destroyed by the thoughtless cruelty of this same woman? The innocence she radiated was a lie. He of all men should know that.

Of their own accord, his eyes sought Mathilda's, and he found her regarding him. Those amber eyes were as beautiful as ever, but they had grown wary over the years. The naïve innocence he had treasured in the young girl had been tempered with caution in the woman.

When he was finished with her, Miles thought, conscious of a surge of rage rising from deep within him, she would learn that caution alone could not save her from paying for her sins against him. Paying dearly, he thought, allowing his lips to relax their grim lines into a slight smile.

The evening proved an uneasy combination of joy and frustration. Mathilda was flattered by the attention she garnered from the gentlemen, young and old, who flocked to demand introductions from the Countess of Southmoor or Lady Denton. The younger ones were blissfully unaware of her former disgrace, but the occasional oblique reference to her elopement by some of her elder partners threw a pall on her enjoyment.

Her first dance with the earl had not been the success Mathilda had hoped for either. He had been attentive and entirely correct, too much so, although she had clearly discerned the admiration in the depths of his slate-coloured eyes. Or what she had taken for admiration. But perhaps she had only wanted to find it there, she chided herself, marvelling at her own perversity.

She automatically went through the motions of the quadrille with the venerable Colonel Sir George Hilton, retired these many years but still carrying the army around with him like a chronic case of indigestion. His interminable conversations were so peppered with military expressions as to be virtually unintelligible, and Mathilda had soon lost the thread of his account of a heated battle charge the colonel had led fifty years ago.

She smiled at him as they made their way, slowly and with a good deal of creaking on the colonel's part, up the line of couples and back down again to the bottom to await their next turn.

The old colonel took out a large white handkerchief and mopped his brow. "Not as lively as I used to be, lass," he wheezed, neatly folding the linen and thrusting it back into his pocket. "Time was when Jumping George, as they used to call me in those days, could outlast the best of them on the dance floor, m'dear." He accompanied this piece of ancient history with a loud cackle of raucous laughter that drew several disapproving glances.

"I wager you could still give the best a run for their money, Colonel," Mathilda said politely.

After repeating this compliment three times until the old gentleman grasped her meaning and burst out into a great guffaw of delighted laughter that brought on another fit of coughing, Mathilda lapsed into silence.

Her dance with Lord George, by this time considerably into his cups and overtly amorous, began badly and quickly slipped towards disaster. After adamantly refusing Bennett's whispered suggestion that they take a stroll on the terrace in lieu of jostling an alarming number of ancients who had taken to the floor for the cotillion, Mathilda had to support his veiled hints that she was playing the temptress again.

"Again, my lord?" she exclaimed sharply, ignoring her aunt's advice to turn a deaf ear to the lascivious undertones in Bennett's light banter. "Surely you mistake me for another?"

"Are you telling me you did not play coy with me in India, my dear Mathilda?" he whispered close to her ear. "I seem to recall you were eager enough for my attentions when that dull husband of yours was not looking."

It was all Mathilda could do not to slap the smirk off his handsome face. "You have most definitely mistaken me for one of your flirts, my lord," she said stiffly. "No doubt you have so many it is difficult to remember which is which. I can assure you, however, that I have never played coy in my life, and do not intend to do so now. So you may disabuse yourself—"

"My dear lady," he interrupted rather abruptly with a crack of laughter, "you cannot imagine how deliciously your protestations titillate my ear. All in vain, I should warn you. I am well up to snuff in the tricks females play to ensnare our poor hearts . . ."

Tired of sparring with him, Mathilda turned away to take up her place in the set. Luckily, the lady standing next to her was known to her aunt, so she was able to exchange a few pleasantries to cover her annoyance. When next she glanced across at Bennett, she saw he had taken affront at her curt dismissal. His pale blue eyes had lost their flirtatious glitter and regarded her fixedly as a mastiff might glare at a kitten daring to defy him. It took all her fortitude to place her hand in his when it came their turn to dance.

As the cotillion progressed, her partner continued to murmur flirtatious nonsense in her ear, causing not a few knowing glances from other couples in the set. Mathilda tried to ignore Bennett's whispered comments, but as they grew increasingly bawdy and offensive, she did her best to appear oblivious to his attempts to scandalise her.

When the music drew to a close, Mathilda glanced around the room, anxious to remove herself from Bennett's odious presence as quickly as possible. To her relief, she saw the earl approaching, a grim expression on his countenance.

He stopped beside her and offered his arm, which Mathilda accepted gratefully. "I believe the next dance is mine, my dear lady," he said firmly, glancing around as if daring anyone to gainsay him. "But let me suggest that we repair to the refreshment room first. No doubt you are thirsty after all that dancing."

"I am afraid you will have to wait your turn, Southmoor," Bennett cut in with a smile so ferocious a tiger might have envied it. "I am about to escort the lady to the punch table myself. My lady," he said, offering his arm to Mathilda with an elaborate flourish that caused him to sway unsteadily.

Mathilda repressed a shudder. "I must point out to you, my lord, that this *is* Lord Southmoor's dance." She forced a smile. "You are such an admirable dancer, my lord, that the time has gone by wondrously fast. I look forward to dancing with you again."

She smiled with as much grace as she could muster and turned away, grasping the earl's sleeve with nervous fingers. He patted her hand as they made their way across the floor still milling with couples. When there was no roar of rage behind them, Mathilda glanced up and found Miles smiling at her.

"Bravo, my dear. But there is no need to be alarmed. He cannot eat you. Not the thing at all, I assure you. I think you were very brave to put the wretch in his place so smoothly. I feared for a moment there I would be forced to plant him a facer, which to tell the truth I was loath to do in the middle of an Assembly. Willy's Aunt Bess would have disowned me had I done anything so crude as to engage in fisticuffs in front of her friends, believe me."

"Anything the matter, Miles?"

Mathilda jumped at the sound of Hampton's voice at her elbow.

"Nothing to signify, old man," Miles responded easily. "Our friend Bennett is somewhat in his cups, I fear. As we both know, he tends to forget his manners when he is castaway."

"That toad never had any manners." Mathilda spoke up, her voice wavering slightly at the emotions that raged through her.

Although Mathilda had not meant to sound missish, both

gentlemen responded instantly, ushering her off the dance floor with gratifying attention. Gratefully, she allowed herself to be led back to her aunt, who glanced at her sharply.

"Do not allow that ill-bred jackanapes to spoil your evening, my dear," Lady Denton remarked. "I could not help observing that you did not appear to enjoy your dance with him."

"Indeed, I did not, Aunt. Bennett is odious beyond bearing. I trust he will have enough sense not to approach me again this evening."

"If he should have the audacity to do so, rest assured that Hampton or I will rearrange his pretty face for him."

Alarmed at the violence implicit in this calmly spoken threat, Mathilda raised her eyes and found Miles's dark gaze fixed upon her face. The intensity of it sent a tremor through her. How many times in her salad days had she longed for the unwavering attention he now focused upon her?

She had never received it, Mathilda reminded herself ruthlessly. At least not from Miles. When James had given it to her so freely, and his heart along with it, Mathilda's life had been changed forever. She had reached out to grasp the love she yearned for, from the man who offered it unconditionally. Once she had taken that irrevocable step, once she had climbed into James's carriage in the mews behind Aunt Agatha's house, she had rarely wasted time thinking on what might have been. Life with James had been too full of love and laughter and adventure . . . and the boys. She had had no time for regrets, no time to look back, no time to remember Miles.

As she gazed at him now, Mathilda was struck by the irony of it all. Here she was, back where she had started, with the man who might have been her husband—who *would* have been her husband had he given her *then* half the attention he lavished upon her *now*.

Life was indeed a topsy-turvy affair. Had it taken him ten years to discover that he wanted her after all? Was that the explanation for his assiduous cultivation of her attention? But the question that disturbed her even more was whether, after ten years of happiness with another man, Mathilda wanted the Earl of Southmoor in her life again.

A subtle change in his expression brought Mathilda out of her daydreaming. She had been staring. Conscious of a pause in the flow of chatter, she glanced around and noticed that the countess was regarding her with a surreptitious smile. Aunt Agatha gazed at her with open calculation. Her mother was, as ever, oblivious of the undercurrents swirling around her, and plucked at a loose thread in the sequin-studded band that encircled her high-waisted gown. Lord Snowburn stood beside her chair, his myopic gaze fixed upon her adoringly.

Feeling herself pressured by forces she was afraid to acknowledge, Mathilda looked up at Mr. Hampton. With a start, she saw she was still grasping his sleeve with rigid fingers. She snatched her hand away, her face flushing with embarrassment.

"Oh, dear, look what I have done," she stammered, reaching out to smooth away the wrinkles on the pale blue superfine. A slight shift in the earl's stance reminded her that such a gesture might appear too intimate to be seemly. But why should she care what Miles thought? Deliberately, Mathilda smoothed out another wrinkle, feeling that the whole room was following her every move, ready to find fault.

"I really am sorry about your beautiful coat, Mr. Hampton," she said softly, giving him one of her sweetest smiles. "I seem to have clung to you like a waif in a snowstorm. Please forgive me."

Hampton chuckled. "There is nothing to forgive, my dear lady. You had an unpleasant experience, and I am happy to have been of assistance. And I do wish you would call me Willy," he added with a cherubic smile that lit up his coffee-coloured eyes. "Everyone else does so."

Mathilda could not resist that smile. "Perhaps it would be

appropriate," she murmured. "Although you must agree our acquaintance is relatively short."

"I am working on that, my dear," he responded quickly.

Mathilda wondered what the rest of the party made of this rather intimate exchange. Not that she cared what Miles thought of her. She felt comfortable with Willy, moreso than with any man since James. She could do a lot worse than encourage him as a suitor if that was what he had in mind. Aunt Agatha had plainly told her so. And what if her heart was not engaged? She was no longer a romantical schoolgirl to be swayed by illusions of love, was she?

Conscious of Miles's stern gaze boring into her, Mathilda laid her fingers lightly on Hampton's sleeve when the orchestra struck up the first bars of their cotillion. "This is our dance, I believe."

Mathilda kept her smile firmly in place as she allowed Hampton to lead her onto the floor, ignoring the uneasy prickle of the earl's gaze on the back of her neck.

TWELVE

Willy's Advice

Looking back on that first public appearance at the Bath Assembly, Mathilda realised that the events of that evening presaged the weeks to follow. She was constantly in demand at neighbouring houses. She lost track of the invitations to garden parties, fêtes champêtres, card-parties, riding excursions to sketch indifferent renditions of picturesque ruins, picnics and croquett games, formal dinners and informal dances that cluttered her hall table every week.

Mathilda suspected that her Aunt Agatha and the Countess of Southmoor had more than a little to do with her newfangled popularity. She was not averse to mingling with the local gentry, but she favoured those entertainments that included children, for Mathilda was loath to be separated from her boys for any length of time. She particularly enjoyed their morning rides together, almost invariably in the company of Willy Hampton and the ever attentive earl.

So gratifying did she find this daily association with her former betrothed and his friend that she looked forward to the sound of small boots racing down the stairs as Brian inevitably beat his brother to the breakfast room every morning.

"Mama," her youngest greeted her one morning as she joined the boys in the breakfast parlour, "Uncle Willy says I stand a good chance of winning the blue ribbon with Bertram at the Bazaar next month. He says the competition will be fierce because the Milton boys have had a lot of experience racing their ponies, but—"

"But I cannot recall giving you permission to race at all, Brian," Mathilda interrupted quietly. "Only consider how short a time you have been riding. The Miltons have been riding for ages. Besides, I would not wish you to hurt yourself, dear."

"Oh, Mama!" Brian protested vigorously, as she knew he would. "Uncle Willy says the Miltons are overconfident, and that Bertram is a better jumper. He says if I practice hard, I can do it. Chris could, too," he added as an afterthought, "if he got his nose out of those musty old books he is always reading long enough to practice his jumps."

His brother gave him a withering look and continued to pick fastidiously at his smoked kipper. Mathilda regarded her first-born with affection. Christopher was so different from his rambunctious brother, and the two were constantly at odds about something. But he was fiercely loyal to his little brother, and if pressed, Brian had been heard to admit that his bookish brother was a good egg.

That morning, as usual, the boys finished their breakfast quickly and begged to be excused to go down to the stables. Mr. Hampton had insisted that a gentleman always knew how to saddle and tend to his own horses, so Brian in particular had thrown himself into animal husbandry with a fervour that spoke volumes of his admiration for the jolly gentleman from Devon.

By the time Mathilda arrived in the stable-yard, both Hampton and the earl were there, and Brian had insisted not only on saddling Bertram, but also brushing down Buttercup for his mother. He was as yet too short to throw up her saddle on the mare, but was quick to fasten the girth. He had also learned to walk the mare up and down a few times before allowing Hampton to give the girth a final tightening.

"She fills herself with air to avoid the girth, Mama," Brian explained for perhaps the fourth time since he had learned that many horses played this trick to fool their grooms. "Uncle Willy says you can come a cropper at the first hedge if you are not up to snuff."

Mathilda exchanged a smile with Hampton as he threw her up into the saddle. "Then I am lucky to have you to watch out for me, dear. I certainly do not wish to come a cropper, whatever that is."

"You have nothing to worry about, Mama," her youngest assured her confidently. "I doubt you will fall off. But if you should be tossed into a puddle, Uncle Miles will pick you out in a trice. He did so with me several times before I got the hang of Bertram's gait."

"Oh, how comforting, dear," Mathilda said faintly, wondering how it might feel to be plucked out of the mud by an earl. She was hard put to imagine such an inelegant predicament. She glanced over at him, already mounted on his chestnut gelding. He smiled when he caught her eye, and Mathilda wondered if he had read her mind.

"Uncle Willy says I must practice my jumps today," Brian was saying, happily ignorant that her attention had wandered. "And you should too, Mama, if you intend to enter any of the events."

This casual remark startled her. "But I do not aspire to anything so daring, dear, so I shall merely be a spectator today." She paused, then added, "And what is all this *uncle* business, Brian? Neither Hampton nor the earl are even remotely related to us, as far as I recall."

Brian looked surprised. "They insisted upon it, Mama. And besides, did you not almost wed Uncle Miles years ago, before you—"

"That is *quite* enough, young man," Mathilda cut in rather sharply. Her son's casual reference to that period of her life, even his knowledge of what had happened ten years before, was unexpectedly disturbing. "You have been listening to vulgar gossip, Brian, and you know what I think of that."

Her son looked so abashed by this outburst that Mathilda immediately felt guilty. After all, it was inevitable that rumours of her previous connexion with Miles would leak out sooner or later.

At that moment the earl appeared at her side, and Mathilda was unable to say more. If he had overheard Brian's incautious remark or her response to it, he gave no sign, but engaged the boy in a spirited discussion on the chances of the Challenger from the Colonies lasting more than three rounds with the current Champion, Tom Cribb, trained by Captain Barklay himself. Mathilda learned to her dismay that the match was to take place the following Thursday on the fairgrounds of a neighbouring village.

One look at her son's radiant face warned her what was coming.

"Oh, Mama," Brian pleaded, eyes glowing with feverish anticipation, "may I go to the fight? I have never seen a real live fight, and now we have one right here in Rawley."

Mathilda shook her head. "You are much too young to witness such rough sports, dear. Besides, you cannot expect me to—"

"Oh, I can go with Uncle Miles. May I go with you, sir?" he added, fixing his gaze longingly on the earl's face. "Please say I may go with you."

"Do not make a pest of yourself, Brian," Mathilda said sternly.

"What has me lad done now to get himself in the briars?" Hampton wanted to know, having drawn Horatio up beside the earl. "What have I told you about teasing your mother, Brian? 'T'aint something a gentleman does to a lady."

"I was not teasing, Uncle Willy," Brian responded plaintively. "All I want is to go to the prizefight with you and Uncle Miles." He paused for a moment. "You are going, are you not? Please tell Mama that no harm can come to me in your company."

"And if you believe that, sir, you will surely believe the moon is made of cheese," Christopher broke in quellingly.

"Nobody asked you, so keep out of it."

"Now, lad," Willy remonstrated gently, "that is no way to talk to your brother. We have much to do this morning if you are still planning to race Bertram against the Miltons, Brian. Did you speak to your mother as I told you to?"

"Yes, he did," Christopher answered quickly. "And made a mull of it, too, as I knew he would."

Brian retorted belligerently. "That is a bouncer if you like. Mama did not say I could not race—"

"No, she merely said she had not given her permission to do so, which seems to me to be pretty much the same thing. And as for going to the mill, she said you are still too young, which is true."

"It is *not*!"

Mathilda saw her youngest son's face pucker up as though he were trying hard not to burst into tears. That he would risk embarrassing himself with what he referred to as baby stuff warned Mathilda that she should change her tactics.

"If I hear one more word out of either of you, I shall send you back to the nursery and ask Mr. Baker to drill you on your multiplication tables." She hoped the mention of their zealous tutor would divert them, and she was right.

"If you wish to spend the day with dreary sums and Latin verbs, that is your choice," Hampton said smoothly in the uneasy silence that followed these words. "But if you expect to beat the Milton brothers next month, I suggest you let me see you put those ponies through their paces."

Both boys looked ready to dispute this order. Brian went so far as to mumble under his breath. "What is the point, if Mama will not—"

"Now!" Hampton said in a no-nonsense tone, pointing one elegantly clad arm towards the arena where the grooms had set up a series of low jumps for the ponies.

Without another word, the boys trotted away and were soon vying with each other over whose pony could jump highest, their recent spat forgotten.

"Boys will be boys, my dear," Willy remarked as the three riders moved over to the fence to observe the exercises. "Take note, my dear Miles, for the day will inevitably come when the twins will present you with a flock of nephews, not to mention the sons you will have yourself in the not too distant future."

Ignoring Mathilda's astonished stare, and Miles's frown, Willy continued gently, "Yes, boys will be boys, and in my experience—five-and-twenty nevies at last count—it is better to let them make their mistakes sooner, while one can keep an eye on them, rather than later, when one cannot."

"I shall endeavour to keep those wise words in mind for future reference," the earl remarked dryly.

"Am I to understand that you would allow them to race next month, even at the risk of breaking their necks, and to attend that brutal pugilistic event on Thursday?" Mathilda enquired, wondering if she had read Hampton's words correctly.

Hampton chuckled. "The boys will come to no great harm, my dear, since Miles and I will be there to make sure of it. What do you say, Miles? Do you feel up to fielding a nonstop barrage of questions from young Brian on the finer points of prizefighting?"

"I cannot ask you to play nursemaids to those two scamps," Mathilda protested, amazed that Miles would even contemplate the role Willy was suggesting. The Miles of long ago had never shown the least interest in children, or in anything else concerning her and their future together. She was hard put to believe he had changed so radically, despite the ample evidence of the past weeks.

His lazy smile dispelled her doubts. "I look forward to Brian's reaction to the realities of the sport," he drawled. "At present he harbours a rather romantical view that needs to be shocked out of him. It will do him good to see the bloody reality of it."

So Mathilda gave the boys permission to see the prizefight after all, and they came home so full of cant expressions that she felt she was listening to a foreign language. To her surprise, Christopher developed a taste for the sport and spent several hours every day sparring with his brother in a makeshift ring set up in the stable-yard.

She was fairly certain their frenzied pursuit of the sport would wane with time, so took the black eyes and bloodied noses they collected in stride. What haunted her more than she cared to admit, even to herself, was the earl's philosophy that Brian's romantical view should be shocked out of him.

Might those words not be said of her own growing attraction to the gentleman from her past? she wondered.

Might there not be a shock in store for her if her romantical fantasies, which seemed to grow stronger every time she encountered Miles's dark eyes assessing her, did not fit the reality of his intentions?

Miles stood on the raised terrace at the back of the house and surveyed the frenzied activities on the south lawn, stretching from the rose-gardens all the way down to the small stream that marked the southern boundary of the Park. Across the stream in the South Meadow, the sheep had been banished, the grass neatly scythed, and gaily-coloured booths set up in orderly rows at right angles to the stream.

·On the lawn itself, an army of Southmoor retainers were busy setting up the huge canvas marquees destined to provide shade for the local gentry and the select group of noble house-guests who descended upon the Grange every summer to enjoy the lavish entertainment for which the countess's Bazaar was famous. At one time or another, Miles recalled, watching two laughing maids making their way across the lawn, leaving footprints in the dew-covered grass, everyone with any social standing at all had vied with one another to obtain the coveted invitation from the countess. Prinny himself had appeared quite unexpectedly one year, driving his own curricle and charming all the ladies with his bluff humour.

As Miles watched, the sun pushed the tip of its orange nose over the low hills in the distance, confirming the general prediction among the estate gardeners, who were rarely wrong about such things, that the day would be a fine one indeed. The sky took on a brighter shade of blue, and the last shreds of mist hovering over the stream gradually thinned out to non-existence. The bustle among the booths across the stream increased as more villagers and tenants arrived with baskets and bundles of goods and vegetables they were offering for sale. The local housewives had prepared for months for this event and vied with one another for the cherished awards distributed by the countess herself during the day.

Miles glanced at the long driveway shrouded by dense oak trees planted, it was recorded in the history of his family, by his great-great-great-grandfather in the days of Henry VIII. The sight of these massive monuments to the passage of time always reminded Miles of the ephemeral nature of his own existence. It was a sobering thought to know that these same oaks would undoubtedly witness the triumphs and follies of his own great-great-great-grandsons.

The thought of his role in the inevitable unravelling of Southmoor history reminded Miles of Willy's recent comments. Like most of his contemporaries, Miles had been hounded since coming of age by the need to propagate his bloodlines. During his most obsessive infatuation with Mathilda Heath, he had concealed his passion for the girl, fearful that he was losing himself in a morass of sensuality. Was not duty, rather than self-gratification, the primary reason for marriage? he constantly reminded himself. After their betrothal, it scared him that all he could think of was the wayward auburn curl that lay against her delicate neck, begging to be kissed. He convinced himself that it was unmanly, unworthy of a Stephens heir to succumb to romantical fantasies more at home in a Minerva Press novel than in the mind of a gentleman.

The consequences of that excessively punctilious concern for duty had been catastrophic. He had lost the woman he loved.

The woman he still loved, a perverse whisper echoed in his heart.

Miles shrugged the thought away. How could he have any

tender feelings for a female he intended to humiliate in front of the whole world? It was best not to dwell upon it.

His eyes flickered towards the driveway again. She had promised to come early. Miles chided himself for his impatience. She had been there most of the day yesterday, with her mother and aunt, helping the countess with final preparations for the Bazaar. How his mother had overcome Mathilda's reluctance to set foot on his estate, Miles could not imagine. But she had, and he had watched his former betrothed sitting in the Blue Saloon, walking down the Grand staircase, taking tea on the terrace. He had himself escorted her around the grounds arm-in-arm with his mother, stopping to talk to his tenants, most of whom knew her from the days when they had expected her to be their mistress. Mistress of Southmoor Grange. The Countess of Southmoor. His wife. The mother of his children.

None of this had happened, of course. Miles felt the familiar stab of bitterness tinged with regret. His eyes were drawn to the oak-covered drive again, although he knew she would not come so early. Why should she? Miles had sensed her discomfort at being in his house. She had come under duress, and Miles had done his best to make her feel at home. The success of his plan depended upon it. When he had finally taken his mother's gentle hint and gone off to oversee the accommodation of the livestock he was to judge that afternoon, he knew Mathilda's guard was weakening.

Today he would try harder. Willy had no trouble at all teasing her into a smile. Why would she smile for Willy and not for him? Miles backed off from the question he had asked himself before, perhaps unwilling to know the answer.

The glass doors opened behind him, and Miles turned to find the butler wheeling out a trolley piled high with breakfast plates, cups and saucers, two large tea-pots, and enough covered dishes of meat, fish, and eggs to feed an army. It was one of the traditions Miles most enjoyed, started by his grandmother he believed, that during a house party at the Grange, breakfast would be served outside on the terrace if the weather allowed.

"Good morning, milord," Harris greeted him cheerfully, motioning to the footmen who had followed him to wipe off the long wrought iron table that served as an al fresco sideboard. "Seems her ladyship will be lucky again this year with the weather. No rain in the forecast, or so old Wiggins assured me last night."

Miles glanced up at the cloudless sky, now taking on that special brilliance that only English skies in the early summer mornings seemed to possess. "Wiggins has been predicting fair weather for years, Harris. I always thought he did it to humour my mother, but perhaps there is more to it than that."

"Oh, indeed, milord. Nobody in these parts plans an outing without consulting old Wiggins. Quite a hand he is to be sure. Will you have your coffee now, milord?"

Miles settled himself at one of the round tables now covered with a pristine cloth and accepted a steaming cup of coffee from his butler.

"Any of the guests up and about yet, Harris?"

"Mr. Hampton walked down to the stables ten minutes ago, milord. The marquess's valet came down for shaving water, and Colonel Sheldon sent for his an hour ago. None of the ladies is astir as far as I know." He paused to refill his master's cup. "May I serve you some breakfast, milord?"

"I shall wait for Hampton—"

"Aha! Who is taking my name in vain?" Hampton himself came round the side of the house and mounted the steps to the terrace. "Breakfast!" he exclaimed with obvious relish. "Just what I need after a brisk walk. Coffee, if you please, Harris," he added, settling himself at Miles's table.

Miles laughed. "You call a stroll down to the stables a brisk walk, lad? Nothing amiss there, I trust?"

"Nothing to signify. Horatio got into a kicking match with that ugly brute Jason Ransome rides. Vicious and unpredictable, he is. Poor excuse for a horse," Hampton mumbled indignantly. "But then we should not expect a mere sailor to know anything about horseflesh, and so I told him yesterday when he rode in on the nag."

Hampton accepted his coffee from Harris and settled back to view the activities on the lawn and the meadow across the stream. After a brief pause, he murmured, "Looks as though your mother will be able to chalk up another success to her record." Abruptly, he turned to look at Miles, a frown marring his sunny features.

"Something on your mind, Willy?"

"Actually there is. I want to talk to you about Mathilda, Miles."

The earl's cup clattered as he placed it on the table.

"What exactly is there to discuss?" His voice was expressionless.

"Now I forbid you to poker up with me, laddie. You will hear me out whether you like it or not."

A cold knot had formed in the pit of Miles's stomach, and he found it difficult to breath. What he had suspected ever since Willy had encountered Mathilda in London beside the Serpentine was about to be confirmed. Miles did not think he could bear it. He could not be losing her to yet another close friend.

"What about Mathilda?" His voice had turned bleak.

When Willy did not answer immediately, Miles knew his suspicions were correct, and the knot in his stomach became a giant rock that expanded till it threatened his breathing.

"You have decided to abandon your frivolous ways and settle down with a wife?"

Hampton grinned. "I will admit the thought did occur to me." He stared off into the distance, and Miles felt the urge to grind him into dust. "It is not every day that a man meets a female as perfect in every way as our Mathilda."

Miles let out his breath slowly. So, it was happening again. At least this time he had not made a fool of himself over a treacherous baggage. Yes, he may have paid her special attention, but no more than that. He had not declared himself; nor would he ever again to Mathilda. He would not give her another opportunity to trample on his feelings. With a great effort he pulled himself together. "Then I suggest you make your move before that jackstraw Bennett makes his."

Hampton had the audacity to laugh, and the sound cut deeply into Miles's heart. "Bennett is not in the running, old man. No fear of that."

"It must be gratifying to be so sure of the lady's affection." Miles heard the bitterness he had tried to hide seeping into his voice.

"Indeed it is, old man. Indeed it is." Hampton's smile faded. "But it is not my move we are talking about here, Miles. Nor Bennett's. Although believe me, if I thought there was a chance . . . But no, no sense even mentioning it."

Miles stared at Willy, wondering if his friend had suddenly run mad. "What move are we talking about then?"

Willy's face relaxed into the sweetest of smiles. "Why yours, of course, old man. And if you were not such a nodcock, you would have made it already, instead of trailing around after the lady like a love-sick puppy."

The Bazaar

Mathilda gripped the railing erected to mark the course for the pony races. Butterflies fluttered in her stomach, and she ceased to hear the clamouring of the crowd around her.

"Nervous, my sweet?"

The question, whispered directly into her ear, caused her to gasp. A shiver ran down her spine as the warm breath teased her hair. There was no mistaking the mellifluous insincerity or the flirtatious undertones of Lord George's comment.

Mathilda turned her head to find him standing far too close, smiling down at her as though she had uttered something suggestive or indecent. She stepped away without responding, fixing her gaze on the ragged group of ponies lined up at the starting point.

Brian was the second from the inside rail, and Mathilda prayed he would not be jostled too roughly by the eldest Milton boy when the ponies took off.

She heard Lord George chuckle beside her. He had stepped close to her again, and Mathilda felt his fingers trace a lazy path from her wrist to her elbow. The pressure of his hot fingers through the thin muslin of her buttercup-yellow gown gave her goose pimples. Removing her arm with as much decorum as she could muster, Mathilda glanced around, but found herself separated from her aunt and mother by a group of squealing children with their harried nursemaid.

"No one to rescue little Mathilda from the big bad wolf?" Mathilda could have sworn that the grin accompanying this facetious remark was more bestial than human. She edged away.

"No need for alarm, my sweet," he purred. "This wolf is putty in your beautiful hands." He reached for her elbow, but she evaded his grasp. "Allow me to escort you back to your mother, my lady." The words were edged with sarcasm, and Mathilda knew he was taunting her.

"I am trying to watch my son race his pony, my lord," she said tersely. "If you will permit it, that is."

Lord George inclined his handsome head and grinned. "Anything you want, my dear. Anything at all."

There was a flurry of activity at the starting post, and Mathilda did not listen to the rest of his words. She wished she could have been there with Brian, but he had absolutely balked at this suggestion.

"I do not need anyone to hold my hand, Mama," he had said scornfully when she sought him out in the paddock before the race was called. "Uncle Willy will be there, anyway, so . . ."

She had not heard the rest of her son's words, for at that moment the contestants were called in and Brian dashed off with several other small lads, all chattering and shouting at once. Mathilda had felt a brief but sharp sense of loss. She had known that inevitably the boys would outgrow her mothering as they turned into men. She had not realised the extent of hurt involved in this gradual separation. Brian in particular had never taken a step without his small hand firmly wedged in hers. Now he was off with boys his own age, without a backward glance, his thoughts on the race, on his pony, on winning, on all those things that were so important to the man he was becoming.

And he had been right. Willy was beside him at the starting post, checking Bertram's girth, settling Brian's feet more firmly in the stirrups, correcting his posture, patting his knee and smiling encouragement as any loving father would to a favoured son.

Mathilda felt a lump in her throat and a suspicious dampness in her eyes. This is what her boys were lacking; what she could not give them—a father's touch. Had Willy made her an offer at that precise moment, she wondered, giddy with emotion, would she not have accepted him without a second thought? The irrationality of this notion made her smile. Much as she valued Willy as a friend, she did not love him the way a wife ought to. Her heart was set—she might as well admit it to herself—on quite another man who might or might not . . .

Her train of thought was interrupted by the start of the race. The ponies leapt forward, small riders squealed encouragement, and the crowd roared enthusiastically. The eight entries rushed past in a drumming of small hooves on the grass track, and Mathilda's heart contracted as she caught a glimpse of Brian's face, flushed and exultant with the promise of victory.

By the second lap, the Milton boy was leading with Brian glued to his tail. Four others followed in a pack some way back; one little boy on a fat, dappled-grey pony cantered along in the rear as though he had all the time in the world. The eighth rider had disappeared, and Mathilda saw a groom on the other side of the track leading his pony off while the lad, smaller than the others, brushed off his clothes and pretended that he had intended to fall off from the start.

On the third and last lap, Milton's chestnut pony was showing signs of tiring, but Brian's Bertram was edging up alongside with little effort.

"Go for it, Brian," she heard her aunt yell inelegantly as the two raced past. As if in response to the shouts from the spectators, Brian urged his pony forward, and by the time they reached the finishing post, Bertram was almost a full length ahead of the chestnut.

Mathilda was ecstatic. She turned to join her mother and aunt, but found herself blocked by the broad chest of a gentleman who had evidently stood beside her unnoticed during the race.

The earl smiled and put out a steadying hand. Mathilda felt her heart lurch. Lord George had mercifully disappeared.

"Did you see Brian win his first race?" she bubbled happily, unable to contain her pride, and a little breathless at the earl's closeness. "He will be impossible to live with for weeks now. Have you seen Christopher? I do hope he wins, too."

"His race is not until this afternoon," Miles responded, his smile bordering on a grin. "That young Brian is a true hellion. I never imagined he would beat that Milton brat so handily. If you can tear yourself away, my mother sends for you. She says it will soon be time to judge the cabbages."

Mathilda could not resist his infectious grin. "I have no idea how I got talked into judging cabbages," she replied ruefully. "I know nothing at all about them. Do you, my lord?"

His mouth quirked up at one corner. "Whatever happened to Miles?" he asked softly.

She stared. "Never in my life have I called you that, my lord."

"Not even in your dreams?"

Of course she had called him Miles in her dreams—and many other endearments, but she was not about to admit it. She shook her head. "The countess is waiting for me," she murmured, turning away.

"Let me escort you, Mathilda."

"Only if you promise to help me tell a good cabbage from a mediocre one, my lord. That would be very useful."

"Only if you promise to use my given name," he countered with a grin.

Mathilda laughed. She was enjoying the new Miles who was emerging from beneath the staid old Miles she had once known.

"We shall have to see about that," she demurred playfully, taking his arm anyway. This teasing Miles was a stranger to her, and she found him much to her liking.

Miles would never have guessed that judging cabbages with Mathilda could turn into such a sensuous experience. Somehow this new Mathilda did not fit into his plan as neatly as he had imagined. Willy's comment about making his move had made Miles question his motivations, made him unsure of his own heart.

The truth be told, he had never given cabbages much thought at all until he found himself standing beside his ex-betrothed at the row of booths exhibiting a bewildering assortment of fruits and vegetables of every shape, size, and colour. He had seen them many times in his tenants' gardens and on his mother's dinner table, but the experience of observing a beautiful woman gently squeezing the rock-hard head of a monstrous cabbage stimulated his imagination and quickened his senses in ways he had never thought possible.

"What do you think of this one, my lord?" she enquired, indicating the grandfather of all cabbages, squatting—almost voluptuously he thought—in its bed of straw.

"I thought we had agreed—"

"Very well, Miles it is." She smiled delightfully and indicated the fat cabbage. "Is it not a cabbage worthy of a king?" She had removed her gloves to grapple with the squeezing, touching, and patting of the exhibits more intimately. Miles felt himself tingle as he watched the white fingers curl around the enormous head and bestow one final, loving squeeze on the lucky vegetable.

"I cannot find the least fault with your reasoning," he said, noting the gratified smirk that spread over old Mr. Weston's wrinkled face at this praise for his prized possession.

Miles hoped that no one had noticed his quickened breathing.

Mathilda shook the old man's hand, placed a blue ribbon on the smug-looking cabbage, and moved on to the next booth, where the process was repeated. By the time they reached the last booth, Miles's brow was damp, and he wondered if his cravat looked as wilted as he felt.

During the leisurely nuncheon under one of the gaily-coloured marquees set up on the lawn for the convenience of the house guests and other local gentry, Miles made sure

Mathilda met his particular friends. As he had guessed, Nicholas Morley, Earl of Longueville, and his wife, Lady Sylvia, found immediate favour with Mathilda, and it was not long before the conversation turned to India, where the earl had resided for many years following his first wife's death. The dowager countess had chosen to reside at Farnaby Hall in Bath with the earl's aunt, Mrs. Lydia Hargate, after Morley's second marriage. As prominent members of Bath society, and well known to Miles's mother, both ladies had been recruited to judge needlework.

"I understand the climate in India is unforgiving," the young countess remarked to Mathilda, who had taken a seat beside her. "I have never been there myself, but from what the dowager reports, the heat is unbearably intense when it is not pouring with rain. She had serious reservations about the cows running loose in the streets and the snakes popping up in baskets."

Mathilda laughed, and Miles's heart constricted at the sweetness of her expression. "Much that is reported about India is exaggerated," she replied. "True, the summer is scorching compared to our English weather, but there is so much to admire there one soon becomes accustomed to the exotic differences. I imagine that as an artist you would be enchanted by the abundance of colour in the landscape."

"I have often thought so myself," Lady Longueville said. "I have hinted that I would enjoy painting a series of Indian portraits, but Nicholas never . . ." Miles missed hearing what the earl would never do because at that moment Mathilda's two boys came racing up to their mother, Christopher dragging his sopping wet brother by the hand.

"Brian fell into the pond, Mama," he announced as if he were personally responsible for this mishap. "He was showing off again."

"I am sure we can do without your commentary, Christopher," his mother said before turning her attention to an unrepentant Brian. "Now what is your excuse for this disgraceful behaviour?"

"Tom Milton fell in, too," Brian exclaimed with a satisfied smirk. "He was upset about the race I won."

"You won a race, did you?" Lady Longueville asked. "You must have been good to beat one of the Milton boys. I hear they are excellent riders."

Brian preened himself and gave a lopsided grin. "Yes, I beat him fair and square," he said without a shade of modesty. "And he accused me of cheating. Not in front of the others, of course, but while I was punting on the pond with Sarah. He laughed at me, so I tipped him into the water with the ducks."

"And he pushed you in as well, I take it?"

Miles, who had been listening with the other gentlemen to this amusing account became suddenly alarmed at the mention of his hellion sister. "You were in a boat with Sarah?" he demanded. "I trust she did not end up with the ducks as well?"

Brian looked at him pityingly. "Oh, no, sir. Sarah is a great gun. She was teaching me to punt when Tom came up beside us and said something rude about Bertram. Bertram is my pony," he stopped to explain to Lady Longueville. "He has lots of bottom," he added with all the reverence of the initiated.

As he listened to this artless conversation, Miles was struck once again by the strange sense of loss he had experienced before while in the company of the Parmenter boys. By rights, and if things had gone as planned ten years before, these splendid lads would have been his sons. His and Mathilda's. If James had been the true friend Miles had thought him to be. If Mathilda had not betrayed him for the sake of . . . for the sake of . . .

Miles had never come up with a satisfactory explanation for her betrayal. In those first painful days he had believed—and had continued to believe even when the evidence emerged to the contrary—that his promised bride had been lured, perhaps even kidnapped and certainly seduced away from him against her will. It had taken him a long time to admit to himself that Mathilda had deliberately chosen another man over him. When it finally became clear that he had been set aside and humiliated by an eighteen-year-old girl in favour of a man Miles had considered his brother, his anger had hardened into a cold rage that he still carried deep in his inner self.

He had learned to dissemble—to cover his fury with a light gloss of civility that seemed to convince his friends and family that he no longer cared. Perhaps that he had even forgiven the unforgivable. But of course, they were wrong. He had not forgiven anything, and as he watched the tender scene between Mathilda and her sons, Miles felt his bitterness like a hard lump around his heart. Which was a good thing, he told himself, for thanks to Willy that same heart had shown alarming signs of softening towards the very female most deserving of his hatred. But he would not allow that.

He became aware of a sudden pause in the banter around him. Nicholas had a sly grin on his bronzed face, and Willy Hampton cocked an eyebrow enquiringly.

"Well, old man, what can you say for yourself?"

Miles glanced around and noticed that the ladies had left the table and were strolling down towards the stream, where his mother was berating a bedraggled Tom Milton.

"About what?"

"Hampton tells us you are seriously thinking of getting riveted, old man," Longueville drawled, his eyes following his wife's graceful figure. "I heartily recommend it. I applaud your choice, too. The widow is lovely enough to make any man walk willingly into the noose."

Miles smiled tightly, but said nothing.

His eyes strayed to the group of ladies beside the pond. Mathilda and the flame-haired countess stood together, evidently enjoying an intimate coze. The countess glanced towards the marquee and waved to her husband. Mathilda turned her elegant head, and their eyes met for a long moment. She dropped her gaze, and even from the distance, Miles could see a rosy blush stain her cheeks. The sight aroused him.

Yes, the prey appeared more than ready to fall into his trap. A heady rush of power drove him to his feet.

"Aha," Lady Longueville murmured, linking her arm with Mathilda's as the ladies strolled along the footpath towards the site of the next pony race. "Would I be speaking out of turn to congratulate you on your admirer, my dear Mathilda?"

Mathilda adopted an air of innocence. "Admirer?" she teased, for no reason at all feeling young and foolish again. "Which one do you mean?"

The young countess laughed delightedly. "It is unseemly to brag, you know; but I could not fail to notice several gentlemen with amorous gleams in their eyes. Come now," she added conspiratorially, "you can confide in me. Which one do you fancy? Is it that rogue Lord George? Or the peerless Willy? Or that poor Mr. Thornton who makes sheep's eyes at you at every turn? Or perhaps it is the enigmatic Miles himself? And now that Jason has caught a glimpse of you, there might be a pirate in your future? Which will it be?"

"Not Lord George, that is for sure."

Mathilda felt herself relax in the warm glow of the countess's friendly interest. She was delighted to confide in Lady Sylvia, whose sensibilities so closely paralleled her own. The light-hearted interrogation made her smile.

"I would not expect it of you, Mathilda. Nicholas calls him a jackstraw, and though I do not exactly know what this is, it cannot be pleasant, for Nicholas can barely bring himself to be civil to the lout."

"Yes, he is exceedingly unpleasant," Mathilda agreed. "To tell you the truth he makes my skin crawl."

The countess nodded. "Mine, too. A detestable villain, and so encroaching. I frankly do not think the admirable Mr. Thornton is your style at all, but what about Willy Hampton? A grand catch, of course, but he is also a sweet, generous gen-

tleman, and so-o-o very attentive." She rolled her eyes playfully, causing Mathilda to giggle.

"Or is it to be the dashing Miles? Again?"

Mathilda felt her laughter fade. Did the entire county know
of her long-ago indiscretion? No, it had been much more than
an indiscretion. She had betrayed Miles in the most con-
temptible way. She must be the world's worst ninny to imagine for a moment he might have forgiven her. Yet it seemed he
had done exactly that. She had begun dreaming of a reconciliation when common sense warned her that what she had done
to Miles was beyond forgiveness, beyond any hope of anything but contempt from him.

"Well, is it?" Her companion was waiting for an answer and
had come to a standstill beneath a chestnut tree, its branches
heavy with green nuts.

Mathilda shook her head, memories from the past rushing in
to steal the joy from her day. "Ten years ago Miles and I were
betrothed," she began softly. "Unwillingly on his part, I am
convinced of it. I was young and thoughtless. I wanted more
than a dutiful husband. So I . . . I ran away with another," she
finished with difficulty. "So you may remove Miles from your
list, Sylvia. He is no admirer of mine."

The countess stared at her in dismay for a moment. "I am so
sorry to have distressed you, my dear," she began as they resumed their walk. "I had heard the story, of course, but seeing
the two of you together, the way he follows you with his eyes,
I was convinced that . . . well, I thought that you and he—"

"Oh, no," Mathilda said firmly. "Nothing like that, I fear."

"But you would be willing, I take it?"

"There is not the slightest chance—"

"But if there were?" the countess insisted, her grey eyes
dancing.

Mathilda could not repress a small smile. "I would be de-
luding myself if I were to—"

"Then go ahead and delude yourself, my dear," the countess
exclaimed with an infectious laugh. "I deluded myself for

months about Nicholas, you must know. My reputation was destroyed beyond repair when I ran off with his cousin. At least your James married you. I was surprised that Nicholas would even speak to me, fallen woman that I was." She sighed theatrically. "But look at me now—the happiest woman alive." She squeezed Mathilda's arm encouragingly.

"Now, tell me truthfully. Would Miles be your choice? Supposing your delusions were to come true, of course."

For several moments Mathilda said nothing. She was sorely tempted to confide in this charming young countess with the flame-coloured hair and a spirit to match.

"As far as delusions go," she replied, finally plucking up the courage to speak her mind, "there is no doubt that Miles would be my choice. But I do not allow myself to dream about something that cannot come to pass. I have sworn to make a comfortable life for the boys at Rose Park, to help them become men their father would be proud of."

Her voice trailed off, and Mathilda knew that, much as she loved her boys, their welfare was not all she longed for. Try as she might, she could not stop her thoughts from circling round to Miles again. Sylvia was right. Her woman's heart cried out for the love of a man. She had just admitted as much to the countess.

And that man was Miles. No other would do.

FOURTEEN

Planned Seduction

Ruthlessly banishing all tender feelings from his heart, Miles threw himself into the seduction of Lady Mathilda Parmenter.

He set the stage carefully. No longer did he remain silent when his mother sang their beautiful neighbour's praises over the tea-table. Interspersed between cups of China brew dispensed in delicate Sèvres cups, Miles found it easy enough—and with only an occasional twinge of guilt—to add enthusiastic comments of his own to his mother's long list of advantages accruing from such an alliance.

"Besides the obvious happiness such a match would bring to all of us," the countess remarked with alarming regularity, "Mathilda is my goddaughter after all—you would present me with the grandchildren I have almost despaired of enjoying in my old age."

Here she would pause and gaze fondly upon her only son, who felt constrained to assure her that she was nowhere near her dotage.

"Of course not, you silly boy," the countess would invariably protest. "No one said anything about dotage, Miles. I am merely overjoyed that you are seriously considering filling this big house with little ones while I am still spry enough to keep up with their games."

Spry was not exactly the word Miles would have used to describe his mother, and he found it impossible to imagine her taking any but the most restrained interest in any of the children's games he had himself played as a child. Mathilda, on the other hand, had no such inhibitions. Only yesterday he had ridden over to Rose Park with Willy and found her playing blind-man's-bluff with her boys and half a dozen of the tenants' children. She had presented a delightfully dishevelled picture, and had soon persuaded both gentlemen to join in the game before sending the children off for their tea with Mrs. Grey and the young tutor, Mr. Baker.

The notion of his mother running barefoot through the grass with her hair in disarray made him smile.

"You can laugh all you like, Miles," the countess chided, reaching for his empty cup. "It is high time you did your duty to the family. And I must confess, I am glad you did not offer for the Pritchard chit after all, my dear. Mushrooms every one of them, the Pritchards."

Miles did not bother to remind his mother that she had chosen little Celia Pritchard herself and nagged him ceaselessly to take advantage of Sir Joseph Pritchard's house-party to make his intentions clear. He did agree, however, that it was fortunate he had not put his neck in that particular noose.

"I was not laughing at you, Mother," he assured her. "I was merely thinking how accurately the medieval notion of fortune as a wheel describes our lives. One moment we are on top of the world, the next we find ourselves at the bottom. Then, quite unexpectedly, we are on top again."

Lady Southmoor stared at him, her expression puzzled. "What an odd thing to say, Miles. I never did put much stock in the Middle Ages myself, but perhaps you are right. I trust you are not coming down with anything," she added half under her breath.

Casting the ancient times back into oblivion where they belonged, the countess returned to more immediate concerns. "Did you remind Mathilda that she is to accompany us on Lady Bedford's picnic tomorrow?"

Miles confirmed that indeed he had done so, and that the boys were unlikely to let her forget such an outing in any event.

"Hampton suggested the boys take their fishing rods. When he discovered they had never fished before, he raided our attic and brought down a whole assortment of rods and other tackle in case there are any other sportsmen in the group tomorrow. He tells me the Clayford Abbey ruins lie close to the Clay River, which is famous for its trout, he says."

"I suggest you leave Willy to entertain those delightful boys with his trout, Miles, and spend your time more profitably. As I recall, there are many pleasant—and secluded," she added slyly, "walks in and around the ruins. You would do well to make sure that Lord George or that dashing Captain Ransome do not make off with Mathilda when you are not looking, dear. Rumour has it that Ransome is ready to give up his roving and settle down, and that here-and-thereian coxcomb Bennett is always on the watch for a victim. I do not count poor Gerald Thornton, of course. Besotted with her he is, but too timid to make a push to win her. And then there is Willy, who is a dark horse in this race if ever I saw one."

Lounging in his favourite chair, long legs crossed at the ankles, Miles sipped his tea and listened to his mother's litany of advice on how to win Mathilda. It amused him to think that the countess had come so close to mirroring his own thoughts on the matter. He agreed with her evaluation of the competition, but the only one who gave him any cause for concern was Captain Ransome, a handsome devil who had displayed an alarming ability to make Mathilda laugh with his easy flow of chatter at the Bazaar the previous week.

"Willy would consider it an honour to be likened to a horse," he remarked dryly. "But he is not yet ready to cast off five-and-thirty years of freedom to shackle himself. He told me so himself. Ransome will be gone back to Cornwall in a few weeks with the Longuevilles, so—"

"A lot can happen in a few weeks, my dear," his mother warned.

Miles did not bother to tell her that she was absolutely correct. A lot was about to happen in the next few weeks, none of which had anything to do with the handsome captain, but at that moment the door opened and Harris announced the arrival of Lady Denton and her niece.

The sudden appearance of the female he was poised to ruin caused Miles a flutter of excitement. Suppressing the sensation of power that was almost sensual in its intensity, he rose to greet the ladies.

"Where are the boys today, my dear?" his mother demanded. It amused Miles to see the almost grandmotherly concern the countess had developed for the two Parmenter boys. She was more than ready to have grandchildren of her own, and it suddenly occurred to Miles that his plans for Mathilda—which did not include marriage or children or any of the other conventional trappings of family life—would inflict considerable emotional distress upon a woman who had done nothing to deserve such shabby treatment.

He brushed the uncomfortable thought aside. Once he had vindicated himself and shown Mathilda that she could not trample his heart into the ground with impunity, he would choose a wife—it hardly mattered who—and marry her posthaste, possibly before Christmas, and produce all the grandchildren his mother could possibly wish for.

Once his plan had played itself out, and Mathilda was history . . . This thought was arrested as the lady in question smiled up at him with such sweetness his heart lurched in his chest. He led her to a small settee beside the window and watched as she settled the pale green muslin of her afternoon gown around her knees.

How could Mathilda—his Mathilda—become history? he wondered. Somehow Miles had not considered the aftermath of his plan, other than to dismiss Willy's suggestion of a more permanent alliance. What a foolish oversight. His whole energy had been focused on the moment of victory when this woman from his past would learn what it was to be humiliated, spurned, rejected. What would happen afterwards had not interested him.

Now as she smiled at him, Miles felt a shadow of doubt twist around his heart. He was so close to attaining retribution that he could almost smell it. His eyes traced the delicate lines of her face, her elegant nose, sensuous mouth, small chin that would fit perfectly into his hand. His gaze slid down her graceful neck and settled on the gently rounded swell of breasts he had yet to touch. And he would touch her, Miles reminded himself. All of her. That was an essential part of his plan. Mathilda would come to him gladly, a rose begging to be plucked, faintly tarnished but still his flower of choice.

Always his flower of choice, a voice inside him whispered.

In the background he heard his mother and Lady Denton chattering on about the astounding success of the Bazaar, the latest escapades of the boys, and the last-minute arrangements for tomorrow's picnic.

"Miles, dear." He heard his mother's voice over the excited thumping of his heart. "If you have finished your tea, I am sure Mathilda would enjoy a stroll in the rose-garden. The new pink ones we put in this year are flowering. Such a glorious sight."

Miles smiled. "Of course, Mother, an excellent idea." He rose and placed his empty cup on the tea-tray. He offered his arm, and Mathilda came to him and allowed him to lead her out through the open French windows onto the terrace.

What a happy coincidence the boys had not accompanied her today. He would have her all to himself. The notion aroused him. Was it his imagination, or were those expressive amber eyes signalling her readiness to take the next step with him? The next step towards her downfall?

The day of the picnic dawned with the promise of sunshine, but much as she was looking forward to the outing, Mathilda dawdled in bed beyond her usual hour. Her sleep had been punctuated with semi-erotic dreams in which she ran through the ruins of an ancient castle in her night-rail. Behind her, never clearly seen except as a lurking shadow, a figure followed her down the crumbling halls, past glaring gargoyles and hideously distorted masques of Greek tragedy. Every time she plucked up the courage to turn and challenge it, the figure disappeared. When she ran on, she could clearly hear the footsteps on the flagstones behind her.

Someone was playing a dangerous game with her, Mathilda was certain of it. Someone from her past. In the dream she had felt it had to be a man. The length of the shadow, the breadth of the shoulders, the swirl of the long black cloak, and the heavy tread of boots all pointed to a male pursuer. The threat of danger hung heavy around her.

She was reluctant to open her eyes when Dolly brought in her hot chocolate and drew the heavy curtains to let in the sunlight.

Mathilda snuggled down under the covers. One moment longer, she kept telling herself, and she would turn to find the black figure within arms' reach. She would look into those hooded eyes and—

Her bedchamber door shook with the thumping of four small fists.

"Mama." Brian's high-pitched voice rang through the thick wood. "We will be late for the picnic if you do not hurry. Uncle Willy is coming for us at nine, and it is past eight already. Dolly says you are still abed."

Reluctantly, Mathilda threw back the covers and sat up. "Go down and have your breakfast, dear," she called out, resigned to the demands of small boys. She would have to leave the unveiling of the dark stranger for another time.

"We have already had our breakfast, Mama." Christopher sounded put out that their mother had not guessed this already.

Mathilda sighed and climbed out of bed. "Then go away and let me get dressed," she said, reaching for the bell-pull to summon Dolly.

She had chosen to wear one of her new London gowns to the picnic, a fetching green muslin creation, scattered with pink knots of rose-buds and a ruff of pink lace around the décolletage. It made her look like a girl again, and when she added the green embroidered slippers, the frivolous straw bonnet, and lace parasol, Mathilda felt ten years of her life fall away miraculously.

When the gentlemen from the Grange arrived to escort them, Mathilda found that the countess had taken it upon herself to arrange things to her own satisfaction.

"The boys will ride with Willy and me in the open landau," she announced as soon as the carriages assembled before the front door. "Miles will drive you in his curricle, Mathilda, and lead the way. The footmen will follow in the dogcart with the baskets of food Cook has prepared for us. Lady Bedford's notion of what small boys eat is not realistic, and I could have sworn that last year her devilled eggs were not as fresh as I like."

Mathilda glanced cautiously at the earl, but he appeared to accept his mother's arbitrary disposing of passengers with equanimity. Once seated in the sporting vehicle, she found the burgundy velvet cushion surprisingly comfortable though smaller than expected. It was a little disturbing to find herself wedged against a gentleman's firm thigh with no room to edge herself away.

"Comfortable?"

Mathilda glanced up at the earl from beneath the brim of her new straw bonnet, garnished with rose-buds and tied beneath her chin with a green ribbon matching her gown. He was smiling that enigmatic smile she had seen so often in recent weeks, but his grey eyes held unmistakable admiration.

"Oh, yes, indeed," she lied gamely. There was no way she could tell a gentleman, much less Miles, that she could feel every movement of his thigh muscles against her own. The prospect gave her the chills.

"I have always wanted to ride in a curricle and four," she babbled, trying to hide her suspicion that Miles was reading her mind and finding it intensely amusing.

"I wish you had told me long ago, my dear," he replied, evidently forgetting that she had hinted at least twice that she would enjoy being taken up in his curricle. To no avail, of course. With consummate skill Miles wheeled the fidgety team into the driveway after waving his groom away from the horses' heads.

"Oh, but I did, my lord," she could not stop herself from re-marking as the team raced smoothly down the drive and out into the lane. "It did not signify, of course, like so many other things that . . ."

She let the words fade away, hoping he had not heard. It was a mistake to break the silence of the past. Nothing could be gained by harping on what might have been. Mathilda had no desire to quarrel with him when he was behaving so gra-ciously. She wanted to enjoy the new Miles and discover how far he would pursue the flirtation she had seen in his eyes.

"What other things, Mathilda?" he asked after a long pause.

The hedgerows, filled with mauve and white foxgloves, and clusters of creamy hawthorn, and lacy wild parsley, flew past in a blur of green and colour. She could feel the tension in the length of his thigh and wished the subject had never come up.

"Oh, look, there is a yellow chaffinch," she said, pointing at a low-hanging branch that whipped by.

"What things, Mathilda?" he repeated, and his deep voice carried easily over the rush of the horses' hooves on the dirt road.

She sighed. "All the things that went wrong."

"Enlighten me. I seem to recall only one."

"I do not wish to talk about the past."

"Humour me, my dear."

Mathilda detected the hint of steel in his voice that made the words a command rather than a request. A hint of the old Miles she had left behind her. Instinctively, she stiffened her shoulders. His lordship had no right, no right at all to com-mand her. If things had gone as planned all those years ago, she would have been more than willing to be his loving and obedient wife. Being his wife would have fulfilled her heart's desire.

It had not happened. Her life had branched out on a different path that had brought her more happiness than most females dream of in a lifetime. James might not have been her first choice. But as she had soon discovered, he had been her best choice. And if Miles did not cease teasing her with questions that should remain unanswered, she would tell him so, and demand to be set down immediately.

He drew his team down to a sedate trot, and Mathilda marvelled at the controlled power in the horses' gleaming rumps and arching necks. They moved in perfect symmetry, their ears pointing forward as they approached a bend in the lane, then flicking back to catch the sounds from the man whose hand they obeyed without hesitation.

"Tell me about all the things that went wrong, Mathilda."

She shook her head, staring at the horses' ears to avoid his gaze, which she felt upon her. "There is no profit in looking back at what cannot be mended, my lord. I have learned to forgive and forget and move on with my life. It is the present and the future that matter now, for it is today we can adjust our perceptions of others and of ourselves to avoid making the same mistakes again. To hold on to grievances from the past is to harbour resentments that can destroy us. Life is so very brief in any case, it makes no sense to dwell on what goes wrong. Far better give thanks for the precious things that go right and bring us the happiness and joy my sons have brought me." She paused, wishing she had the courage to include James's name together with his sons, but fearing she had said too much already. "You will know what I mean when you have sons of your own, Miles," she added softly. "Believe me."

No more was said until they reached the crossroads with its faded sign indicating that Clayford Abbey lay nine miles to the west. Miles halted his team as another carriage rounded the bend on the Bath Road at a spanking pace. The Earl of

Longueville had also elected to drive his lady in his curricle, and as the carriage came abreast, Mathilda exchanged speaking glances with Lady Sylvia—they had become firm friends since the Bazaar—as the two men launched into a detailed examination of the finer points of horseflesh exhibited by the two teams.

Miles maintained his silence as they drove on towards Clayford, and Mathilda wondered if she had effectively dampened his interest in her with her plain speaking. The notion pained her, for she had begun to hope—cautiously and with many reservations—that she and Miles might bring to fruition the relationship that had foundered between them ten years before.

The silence was heavy and beginning to be uncomfortable when the curricle arrived at the Abbey, and the Tiger jumped down to take the horses' heads. To her surprise, Miles caught her by the waist and lifted her down. The warmth of his hands on her waist brought the colour to her cheeks, and she fiddled nervously to furl her parasol to avoid knocking off his tall beaver.

He held her close to him for a second or two longer than necessary, steadying her with one hand resting lightly on her hip. Mathilda had not been this intimate with a gentleman in a long time and was overwhelmed by his intoxicating masculine scent. His hand seemed to burn through the thin muslin of her gown, and with a sense of profound shock she fancied she felt his fingers burning into her flesh beneath in the most intimate of gestures.

Hastily, she stepped back, glad of the floppy brim of her bonnet and the parasol that she unfurled and held up to cover her flaming face. His fingers slipped away, and Mathilda felt a perverse sense of abandonment, as if his hand on her had promised the security and protection she yearned for without realising it.

She heard him murmur something about making things go right in the present, but her agitation prevented her from making any sense of it. She was saved from replying by Lady

Longueville, who came up with her husband and immediately claimed Mathilda's arm for the short stroll over to the expanse of greensward where the preparations for the picnic were well under way.

Lady Bedford was in her element. A rather full-figured woman, as were all the Hamptons, and well into her seventies, she nevertheless made a point of overseeing even the smallest aspect of the festivities. Followed by her long-standing companion, Mrs. Sloanes, the dowager marched about the picnic site, trumpeting out instructions to the army of servants she had brought with her from Bath quite as though these harried retainers had never heard it all before.

As the two ladies made their way up the slight rise to greet their hostess, Mathilda felt Lady Sylvia's eyes upon her face.

"Are you quite well, my dear?" she asked after her initial chatter about the weather and the delights of nature had gone unanswered. "You seem preoccupied, as though . . ." She paused and a smile lit up her face. "As though you have just had a very agreeable coze with a favoured admirer. Tell me, Mathilda, has Miles hinted at his feelings for you?"

Mathilda stared at her friend. "Feelings for me? Miles has no feelings for me, Sylvia. You are mistaken to suppose otherwise."

Lady Sylvia gurgled with laughter. "Why are you deliberately denying what is obvious to us all, my dear? Miles is besotted with you. He may not wish it to become generally known. In fact, Nicholas thinks he is on the horns of a dilemma given your previous history together. Frankly, I believe Miles is reluctant to abandon his role of martyr. Like most men, he enjoys being the centre of attention, and the role of jilted lover has become like a second nature to him. To pursue you, he must give it up, which might not be so easy after all these years."

Mathilda stared in astonishment. She had never thought of Miles in that light before. "That is quite ludicrous," she declared with some heat, unwilling to give any credit to Sylvia's words. "I will not believe that Miles still considers himself wronged by me. I doubt he has even given me a thought in years. He has certainly shown interest in other females."

"Aye, but he avoided marrying any of them, my dear," Lady Sylvia pointed out somewhat smugly. "It is almost as though he were waiting for you to come back to him."

"Now that *is* ridiculous," Mathilda cried. "Utter nonsense, if you will forgive me for saying so. Miles could not have known . . . indeed I did not know myself that James would be taken from me. You are making him sound rather sinister, Sylvia. I trust you are jesting." She shivered in spite of the warm sun shining down upon them.

Her companion must have sensed her distress, for she laughed and guided Mathilda to a bench set under one of the spreading oaks that surrounded the Abbey walls. "Perhaps I am," she confessed. "Nicholas says I let my imagination run away with me too often. Let us sit here and wait for the gentlemen to finish their endless perorations on the advantages of one team of bone-setters over another. All of it over my head, I am afraid."

Mathilda agreed, but if she imagined her companion had finished with the topic of Miles's supposed infatuation, she was mistaken. She allowed her eyes to wander to where Longueville and Miles, still deep in conversation, stood watching their grooms lead their horses away.

A chuckle brought her attention back to Lady Sylvia. "Miles is indeed a fine-looking man," the flame-haired countess remarked in her teasing voice. "He is quite good enough to paint. Almost as handsome as my Nicholas, I have to admit. And confess it, Mathilda"—she leaned forward to bring her face closer, her grey eyes dancing—"is it not thrilling to imagine a gentleman waiting all these years just for you? Even, as you say, if there was no hope of you ever being free again?"

Mathilda considered the idea more bizarre than anything else, so she said nothing. Her gaze rested on Miles again, and the memory of his hands came back to her so vividly, she caught her breath. What Sylvia was suggesting was outrageous, of course, but had she not herself indulged in fantasies about him that were both immodest and highly improbable?

"Perhaps you are right," she said, quite unable to lie to her new friend. "But fantasies are one thing, reality quite another. Besides, this conversation is highly improper."

When Lady Sylvia's tinkling laughter erupted around her, Mathilda found herself laughing, too. The young countess had given her much food for thought.

FIFTEEN

The Kiss

The sound of female laughter caused Miles to turn his head, his attention straying from his friend's account of a carriage mishap suffered on the way up from Cornwall.

"We were damned lucky not to land in the ditch," Longueville was saying, a rueful grin on his tanned face. "The biggest hare you have ever seen dashed in front of the team, and the foolish beasts spooked, tangled the traces, and had to be . . ." He stopped in mid-sentence and followed his friend's gaze up the rise to where the ladies sat in a huddle, their laughter sweet and clear in the morning air.

"Does a man's heart good to see them, would you not agree, old man?" Longueville said with feeling, his harsh features softening. As they watched, captivated by the beauty of the scene reminiscent of Constable's pastoral landscapes, the flame-haired countess glanced their way and waved at her husband with a gay insouciance that spoke volumes on the tenderness of their feelings for each other.

Miles felt a twinge of envy. What would it feel like to be loved so openly by a beautiful woman? He willed Mathilda to turn her head, and after a moment she did so, seeking his gaze, her amber eyes luminous with suppressed emotions. He stopped breathing for an instant, stunned by the invisible flash of current that passed between them. This must be one of those speaking glances poets were always referring to, he thought, his knees suddenly unsteady and his heart thumping uncomfortably.

Then it was over. The two ladies turned away to resume their confidences, and Miles was left teetering on the brink of an emotional chasm that threatened to engulf him in a warm sea of sensations he had never experienced before. He shook himself mentally to dispel the odd feeling of giddiness he could not explain. Glancing down at his highly polished boots, he confirmed they were firmly planted in the turf. He had not, as he had briefly imagined, levitated into the warm summer air.

Longueville was regarding him with amusement, his grey eyes full of speculation. "Have you asked her yet?" he asked, nodding towards the hill where the two ladies seemed to have lost themselves in their secret coze.

Miles pretended ignorance as to the earl's meaning. "I assume you refer to Mathilda, but I cannot imagine what I am supposed to ask her." He raised an eyebrow and returned his friend's gaze steadily.

Longueville laughed. "Do not play the flat with me, my friend. A blind man could not miss the languishing glances that pass between the two of you. My wife assures me that before the summer is out we shall read an interesting announcement in the *Gazette*. That is if my friend Jason or—Lord forbid—that execrable Bennett fellow do not edge you out of the running. My advice is to speak up before you lose her." Longueville did not say *as you did once before,* but Miles could hear the threat ringing in his head as the two men turned back to their discussion of horses.

The words clung to the back of his mind, taking up residence there, resounding when he least expected it. *Before you lose her.*

Miles had no intention of losing Mathilda a second time. And Longueville was right on the mark about the announcement in the *Gazette*. There would certainly be an announcement, but not exactly couched as his friend anticipated.

The notion of sending off a notice to the London papers had come to him fairly recently. The irony of it had seemed delicious at the time. What better way of confirming his intentions—or better said, his *supposed* intentions—and lulling the lady's suspicions—if there were any lingering in that lovely head by then—than by the time-honoured notice to the *Gazette*? Miles knew exactly what it would say. He had revised the wording in his mind until he had the exact text he wanted. The effect would be devastating on Mathilda, which was as it should be. Had her betrayal not been devastating upon his reputation, his heart, his very life?

His eyes wandered again to the slim figure in green seated beneath the oaks. She was still the most beautiful woman he had ever known. The admission startled him, for Miles had known many lovely women, most of them paraded before him by his mother as prospective countesses. Not one of them had made his heart race as Mathilda did. Even now, as he prepared to destroy her reputation utterly, humiliate her, and if possible break her heart as his had been broken, Miles felt a part of his secret self rebelling against what he was about to do.

And then the thing he had begun to fear happened. A voice he had ignored ever since his encounter with his lost love in the dusty aisles of Hatchard's, a voice he had studiously quashed and buried deep in his subconscious, asked the question he did not want to hear. Why not allow this travesty of a courtship to become what Mathilda would think it was? Resentment can destroy us, she had said. What if she was right? Would the destruction he had set in motion for her destroy him, too?

"I think it is time we rescued our ladies from predatory males," Longueville said, and Miles realised that while his thoughts had been wandering, Lord George and Captain Ransome had engaged the countess and Mathilda in conversation. "I shall suggest a stroll by the river. What do you say to that, old man? Those groves of willows offer excellent opportunities for privacy." There was no mistaking the salacious wink that accompanied this remark.

By the time the party had strolled along the tow-path beside the river, and spent some time watching Hampton instruct several young lads in the art of fly fishing, it was time to return to the picnic tables to sample Lady Bedford's scrumptious fare. Miles had stayed close to Mathilda during their stroll and was gratified to see her deftly parry the obsequious Lord George's attempts to capture her attention.

With the glaring exception of Lord George, the group gathered at the Longueville's table was convivial and in a festive mood. Hampton outdid himself with an endless stream of fish stories, each more outrageous than the last. Lady Sylvia was cajoled into talking about the portraits she had done recently, and amused the company with vivid descriptions of her husband's reluctance to appear as a highwayman.

"He objected to the horse I had chosen for him," the countess explained with a fond smile at her husband. "I cannot imagine why. Poor old Hercules was not the most handsome of horses, 'tis true, but he had a certain flair—"

"Oh, yes, indeed," the earl interrupted with a short laugh. "And now you will convince everyone that the ratty old cloak and feathered hat you insisted I wear gave me a *certain flair* to match that bag of bones."

Miles noticed that although his friend complained loudly, his eyes, resting on his flame-haired countess, were soft with affection.

"Speaking of painting," Miles remarked, "I hope you have your sketching pad with you, my lady, for the Abbey offers many prospects worthy of your skill."

This invitation to explore the ruins broke up the conversation as Miles intended it should. Hampton returned to the river with seven or eight lads in tow, while Lady Bedford retired to her chaise longue, set up by her servants in a shady spot under the oaks, to indulge herself with a nap, and a group of younger members of the entourage were already deep into a noisy game of croquet.

Miles caught Longueville's eyes and from the sly wink his friend gave him, knew the time had come to move into the next phase of his plan. He would separate Mathilda from her friend Lady Longueville, who strolled beside her, arms linked. And keep her away from other marauding males who might entertain similar thoughts.

The exploration of Clayford Abbey would challenge his predatory instincts, but Miles already felt the rush of excitement at the promise of victory.

The faintly giddy sensation that had kept her in a delicious state of euphoria since Miles had lifted her from his curricle gave Mathilda an acute awareness of the undercurrents swirling about her. She noticed the silent glance shared by Miles and Longueville and deduced that the former had shared a confidence with the Cornish earl. The satisfied smile that curled Miles's strong mouth confirmed that something was afoot, but she dared not speculate further.

What did gentlemen talk about when they were alone together? she wondered. Besides horses, and dogs, and card games, and their tailors, of course. And females of the kind Mathilda preferred not to think about. She had caught the Earl of Longueville's assessing glance upon her several times since the day of the Bazaar, and wondered if Miles had spoken to his friend of his intentions towards her.

Was Miles merely being polite? He had always prided himself on being the perfect host, and as his mother's guest, she might presumably rely on his attention to her comfort. But the warmth of his hands on her waist and the admiration in his eyes spoke of something far stronger then mere courtesy. She could still feel the imprint of him on her skin beneath the thin muslin of her summer gown. There was an intimacy about the thought that quickened her breath.

When she heard Miles enquire about Lady Sylvia's sketching pad, Mathilda knew an exploration of the ruined Abbey was imminent. She had looked forward to this moment with some apprehension. Her memories of the old ruins, which she knew well from her many visits there with her brother, were bittersweet. The greatest disappointment had occurred soon after her betrothal to Miles had been announced. They had all been there at Lady Bedford's annual picnic—her mother and Lady Denton, a smugly triumphant Reginald, Miles's parents, his young sisters, and of course, James.

There had been many other guests, but all Mathilda could remember was the moment she and Miles had found themselves inexplicably alone in the small chapel at the south end of the Abbey. She had innocently believed that Miles had engineered the moment alone with her, and her heart had swelled to bursting point.

Mathilda had been so sure of their love for each other that she would have done anything, given him anything—including her very innocence—to prove her devotion. In a moment of madness Mathilda had even wished he would demand that ultimate gift from her. What better place than an ancient holy shrine, she had reasoned feverishly, to forge that sacred bond between a man and a woman sworn to become one in the eyes of God and the world?

She repressed a shudder at the memory of this youthful foolishness. She had been willing to commit blasphemy for him. As it was, she had polluted the holy chapel with impure thoughts. It was a wonder she had not been struck down by the guardian spirits of the place.

Her distress and humiliation had been beyond belief when, instead of seizing the moment for lovers' dalliance, Miles had become rigid, his face turned to stone. Mathilda had stepped close to him, daring to lay a hand on his arm and smile up at him provocatively. He had flinched visibly and expressed an exaggerated concern for propriety rather than joy in the precious moment they were sharing. In fact, he had chided her in a voice that chilled her very soul for allowing herself to be drawn away from their party into a highly compromising situation.

It had been there in the dim chapel long ago that a corner of her heart had cooled towards him.

Mathilda repressed another shudder as the cluster of chattering guests passed under the immense stone arch leading into the ruined Abbey. The smell of the place, a mixture of damp leaves blown in through the open door, the musty odour of long-disintegrated woollen cowls, the silent echo of leather sandals on the flagstone floors, brought everything back with startling clarity.

"Cold?" a voice whispered in her ear.

Mathilda glanced up and found Miles regarding her with one of his enigmatic looks she could not decipher. "It can get chilly in here out of the sunlight."

She shook her head. The sound of his voice brought memories crowding thick and fast around her. Had it not been for his half-teasing smile, Mathilda might have imagined herself back on that dreadful afternoon she had discovered that her betrothed had no desire to steal a kiss in the dim chapel, as she had hoped he would.

Would he do so today? she wondered. Was she ready to allow it?

The notion made her blood race.

Most of the guests, including Captain Ransome and a cluster of young members of the party, chose to direct their steps down the wide stone steps to the lower regions of the Abbey. There the dank dungeons still held remnants of old bones and iron fetters, sad reminders of the days when the monasteries were taken over by the Crown and used to quarter troops and prisoners.

The Earl of Longueville and his lady made their way up towards the battlements where long-dead monks had indulged their interest in the study of the heavens.

An elderly couple in front of them turned towards the south hall, which Mathilda knew led to the chapel. Her heart raced faster when Miles guided her in the same direction, but she did not protest.

"The place seems to have changed little since I was here last," she murmured, wondering if he would remember exactly when that had been. "Has the chapel been restored at all? I remember there was talk of doing so, but the purists objected to tampering with history."

"The purists won that battle," he replied with a laugh. "The place has been gently mouldering away since King Henry's troops devastated it back in the fifteenth century."

Mathilda passed under the low stone archway into the tiny chapel. Someone had placed a bunch of wild iris from the neighbouring meadow on the altar, drawing the attention of the elderly couple, who stood admiring them. The splash of bright yellow picked up the shafts of sunlight filtering in through broken windows high up near the roof, and their faint fragrance sweetened the cool air. A pair of tom-tits had found the opening and were nesting up in a corner of the rafters. As Mathilda watched, the tiny female flew in and disappeared into her nest, setting off a high-throated chorus of cheeps from her young.

Stepping over to the west wall, Mathilda removed her glove and ran her fingers over the names chipped into the grey stone. In the old days, when she had visited the Abbey frequently, these names had been as familiar to her as her own family. These were the men who had lived their pious lives and died their little deaths, blessed with the promise of salvation, secure in their belief in heavenly rewards.

These were the lucky ones. There were many whose names were never recorded in this sacred place. Those whose lives had been shattered by violence. Dragged from their cells and stripped of their robes by the King's men, they had perished anonymously. Mathilda had always prayed for those unfortunate souls, hoping that they, too, had reaped their promised rewards.

She heard the voices of the elderly couple fade as they wandered out of the chapel. Mathilda was alone with Miles again, as she had been then, and the air was heavy with the same expectancy. In the ensuing silence, she felt a movement behind her. Miles laid his hand beside hers on the cool stone. She glanced over her shoulder and found his eyes full of emotions she had wanted to see there long ago.

The name she had been tracing was that of a young monk called Lucius. Mathilda gently touched the dates that recorded the space of his brief stay on earth.

"How young he was," she whispered. "Only seventeen. I used to wonder what took him so untimely from his chosen path. Scarlet fever perhaps? An accident of some sort?"

"We shall never know, my dear." He paused, and Mathilda felt his breath warm on her cheek. "I, on the other hand, always wonder what evil hobgoblin's spell turned me into a complete lackwit the last time we were here together."

So he did remember! Mathilda felt a glow spread through her limbs. What could she say? He was absolutely right, but her mind struggled with the impossibility of finding a civil response.

When she did not reply, he broke the silence. "Did you not think me a witless fool for not seizing the moment that afternoon?"

Her fingers were still on the dates of Lucius's death, but as she watched, Miles's hand covered hers lightly, lifting it away from the wall and cradling it in his. "Did you, my dear?"

Mathilda could not look at him, but she clearly heard the anxiety in his voice. There was but one truthful answer to his question.

"I did."

In the silence that followed, Mathilda was acutely aware of her fingers resting lightly in his. She had no wish to remove them.

He cleared his throat. "You wished me to kiss you, and I disappointed you?"

Again, she chose to be truthful. "Yes," she admitted quickly before her courage failed.

In the ensuing silence, Mathilda clearly heard the excited voices of the tom-tits' young squabbling over some luckless insect offered by one of the parents.

Miles brought her fingers to his lips and kissed them leisurely. "I trust I shall not disappoint you again, my love."

Mathilda closed her eyes as the import of these words sank in. She knew this would seem a tacit acceptance, but she did not care. She had wanted his kiss then; she wanted it now. Nothing could change that. The only thing that intrigued her was whether this sudden rekindling of interest from her former betrothed was serious or merely a summer flirtation.

Mathilda was not averse to flirting with Miles, but she hoped it was not mere flirtation he sought. They were more equally matched now than they had been ten years before. She was no longer the silly romantical chit who had thought the sun shone out of his eyes, while Miles seemed more worldly and relaxed, less obsessed with himself and his duty. Could it have been fate that had kept him safe from the marriage-minded girls who flooded the great London houses during the Season? Mathilda could not hazard a guess on the twists and turns of unknown forces, but she recognised that her return to England fit smoothly into the general scheme of things. Perhaps, as Lady Sylvia had suggested, Miles had deliberately avoided committing his heart to another. Almost as though he had known she would come back to him.

"Was that one of the things that went wrong?" His voice was low and husky, causing Mathilda's heart to flip-flop alarmingly.

She shook her head. "Let us not talk of the past, Miles."

"You prefer to live in the present?"

Mathilda had to laugh. "When you are the mother of two small boys, it is impossible to live anywhere else."

"Then we must focus on the present moment, and not let it get lumped with all those other things that went wrong."

Mathilda silently agreed, and when he lowered his head, she lifted her face for his kiss without coyness.

It was as she had always dreamed it would be, only more so, because Miles's first kiss was not a dream. Warm and gentle, his lips touched hers, tentatively at first, lulling her into a sweet stupor that invaded her limbs, causing her to lean into him as trustingly as a child. The strength of his arms around her promised the comfort and protection she had longed for without realising she needed it. She luxuriated in the lean hardness of him against her breasts and hips, and when she felt the heat of his tongue against her mouth, she opened her lips eagerly in response to his passion. Pressing herself against him, Mathilda heard him groan deep in his throat with pleasure. His kiss became more demanding, plundering her softness with increasing urgency.

Without knowing quite how they got there, Mathilda felt her arms tighten around his neck, the black curls soft against her fingers. She felt herself opening to him, physically and emotionally, in ways she had never imagined possible with the Miles she had once known.

In that delicious instant of surrender, Mathilda knew that her heart belonged to this man. She loved him. All over again, and stronger than ever before. Whether he returned her love or not.

No other man could satisfy her, she thought, feeling the heat of his desire burning all modesty away.

No, no other man would do.

SIXTEEN

Coup de Grace

In the days following their stolen kiss in the chapel, Mathilda walked around in a haze of happiness. Her whole world had taken on a golden glow, and she found it difficult to concentrate on her daily tasks. All too often she would find herself looking down at some object in her hand with no recollection of having picked it up. Or standing at the window of the sunny morning room gazing out at the riot of flowers in the garden below, her eyes dreamy and a soft smile on her lips.

Lady Denton came upon her in this abstracted state early one afternoon. Mathilda was sitting at her piano in the drawing room, her hands resting in her lap, her eyes unfocused. She was not aware of her visitor's arrival until she sensed her presence beside the piano.

She stared at her aunt without speaking until that lady became alarmed.

"Whatever ails you, Mathilda?" Lady Denton demanded in her forthright fashion. "I came to share some extraordinary news with you, and I find you moping around like some romantical heroine from the latest Minerva Press novel. Ring for the tea-tray, dearest, I am parched," she commanded, linking her arm through her niece's and guiding her out onto the small brick terrace overlooking a very agreeable prospect of lawn and ancient oaks. "And then I want you to tell me if there is any truth to the rumours about you and Miles," she added with a sly glance at her niece.

This mention of the earl aroused Mathilda's full attention.

She had been expecting something of the sort and was not surprised that her inquisitive aunt would be the one to broach the subject so openly.

"What is this extraordinary news you have to share with me, Aunt?" she countered, avoiding the issue.

"You remember Lord Snowburn? Constantly underfoot he is, although always perfectly civil, I must say. One of your Mama's most devoted cicebos."

Mathilda laughed. "How could I not remember him? Dear Lord Snowburn—or Uncle Aloysius as I used to call him—has been a fixture in our family since before I was born, Aunt. He was at Oxford with Papa and then best man at his wedding." She paused, her eyes widening. "Do not say that he has finally come up to scratch? Oh, I am so glad to hear it. Reginald will be livid. He cannot stand the notion of our mother taking a second husband."

"Your brother is a pompous coxcomb, dear," Lady Denton said dismissively. "I have not been able to wheedle the truth out of your mother as yet, but last night after Lord Snowburn took her for their usual stroll in the garden, she was all atwitter. I sensed that something was afoot. Now, tell me dear," she continued, changing the subject abruptly, "is there any truth to the rumours about you and Miles?"

Mathilda felt her face grow warm. Even a casual mention of Miles seemed to throw her into a fluster. "Since I do not know what rumours you speak of, Aunt, I really cannot say."

"Oh, fiddle!" the elder lady snorted. "Do not play the peagoose with me, child. Everyone knows you spent an inordinate amount of time with him at Lady Bedford's picnic. Exploring the ruins, were you? And it is no use denying it. Old Mrs. Fraser claims she saw the two of you cuddling in the chapel. Ever so shocked she was, or so she claims, the sanctimonious busybody."

"We were *not* cuddling," Mathilda protested instinctively, although the memory of what they had actually done together made her blush. "How very vulgar of her to spread false rumours. She and that crotchety old rumstick she is married to were in the chapel all right, but Miles and I were looking at the names of the monks on the wall—"

Lady Denton interrupted with a hoot of sarcastic laughter. "Come, my love, this is your old auntie you are talking to. What else happened in the chapel to cause that gabble-grinder's malicious remarks? Surely she saw something to set off her wagging tongue?"

"There was nothing to see, Aunt," Mathilda responded less than truthfully. Unless of course the old biddy had only pretended to leave and returned long enough to see Miles kissing her. The thought was disquieting, but Mathilda admitted that once Miles had pulled her into his arms, she would not have noticed if the Archbishop of Canterbury himself had walked into the chapel.

"He kissed you, did he not?"

Mathilda stared at her aunt, fearful that her expression would betray her. The memory of that kiss must be imprinted there for everyone to see. Perhaps not everyone. But certainly her aunt who knew her better than her own mother. "Of course not," she protested, determined to defend her secret with her last breath. "And Mrs. Fraser could not possibly have seen anything improper. She and Mr. Fraser left almost as soon as Miles and I came into the chapel."

"Oh, I see," her aunt said innocently. "So the old biddy was not even there when Miles kissed you?"

"No, she most certainly was not," Mathilda began, then stopped abruptly when she saw the complacent smile on her aunt's face. "That is to say," she hurried on, trying to correct her blunder, "she could not have seen what was not there to be seen, now could she?"

"Of course not, dear," Lady Denton said soothingly. "In any event, the old Tabby left before anything happened, so how could she know about the kiss?"

"There was no kiss," Mathilda lied stubbornly.

"Then why are you blushing like a schoolgirl, dear?"

Mathilda let her gaze wander over the beds of summer perennials that she had taken such pains to resurrect from their languishing state. The hardy lupines, foxgloves, and tall hollyhocks were flourishing against a neatly trimmed hedge of lilac bushes, while the more delicate pinks and nasturtiums and forget-me-nots formed gaily-coloured clusters in oranges, deep pinks, and pale blues.

"'Tis no sin to steal a kiss, Mathilda." Her aunt's voice was gentle. "Gentlemen do it all the time. You are still young and beautiful; I am not surprised Miles kissed you." She dropped her voice suggestively. "I fully expect to celebrate two happy events in our family this summer, my dear, so I expect you to inform me the moment Miles makes his declaration. There are always so many things to plan for a wedding. Promise me you will, dear. I insist on being the first to know."

Mathilda was thankful when her aunt's confidences were interrupted by the butler bringing out the tea-tray. There was no way she wanted to confess that all this talk of weddings had raised the specter of her own fears. Was Miles working up to making her an offer? Or was that secret kiss in the chapel a prelude to a summer dalliance?

She smiled at her aunt across the tea-table. "I promise."

"Steady there, Brian, steady. Science is what will carry you through, not brute force," the Earl of Southmoor remarked casually to the lad bouncing around him in the ring, fists flying in all directions. "It is laudable to plant your opponent a facer or darken his daylights, but if you have no grace and style—no *science,* that is—a fight becomes a brawl. And gentlemen do not brawl. Is that not so, Willy?"

"No argument there, old chap," Hampton responded promptly. He stood, leaning against the ropes of the professional-sized ring set up in the earl's private gymnasium, critically observing the progress of his friend's young pupil. "Brawls are vulgar and to be avoided by gentlemen of any sensibility."

"Will I never get to draw your cork, Uncle Miles?" Brian demanded belligerently.

"I most earnestly hope not, lad. I have no wish to have blood sprayed all over my shirt."

"But it has been more than a month since you started tutoring me, and I have yet to mill you down, sir."

Miles grinned. "I sincerely hope that never happens, lad. At least until you are much bigger. By then—if you are patient—you might well become an excellent boxer, and I shall probably stay out of your way."

Brian brightened immediately. "Good enough to stand a round with Gentleman Jackson?"

"I would not doubt it for a minute, lad."

The eagerness on the boy's face touched some vital part of Miles that had been dormant for too long. This is what fathers do with their sons, he thought nostalgically. This is what he should have been doing with his own sons, had not that traitorous hussy betrayed him. The thought of Mathilda distracted him, but the white-hot resentment that had sustained him throughout the years was slow to stir in his memories. All he could feel was a sweet yearning for more of those passionate moments they had shared in the chapel.

How very different his life would have been had he kissed Mathilda during their first visit to the chapel together. What other things had he failed to do with his betrothed that she had expected of him? She had openly confessed to being disappointed in him that afternoon long ago—in waiting for the kiss that he had denied her. Miles could no longer recall why he had not kissed her. Some misguided sense of prudery, he supposed. He had been young and inexperienced with females. But whatever the reason, it had not impaired his performance during their second visit.

A sudden intake of breath from Hampton made him duck instinctively and bring up his defense just in time to prevent Brian from tipping him a settler. He acknowledged the boy's near hit with a smile, and pulled off his gloves.

"If I do not have some sustenance soon, I might find myself milled down by a novice," he joked, rolling down his sleeves and drying his face with his towel.

"I nearly got him," Brian yelled, prancing around the ring, pleased as Punch. "Did you see, Uncle Willy? I nearly milled him down. I nearly milled him down."

"It is not sporting to gloat, Brian," Hampton pointed out, but Brain paid no heed.

"Did you see that, Chris?" he called to his brother, who was practicing on the punching bag. "I nearly milled Uncle Miles down."

"Hardly likely," his brother replied crushingly. "And do not gloat, Brian. You heard what Uncle Willy said."

Brian did not let the subject die, but carried it all the way down to the fanciful pergola erected by the earl's grandfather on the west side of the lake, where the countess and their mother were waiting. Only the sight of the platters of delicacies the footmen had laid out on the picnic table chased his near success out of the boy's mind.

"Do not make a pig of yourself, Brian," Mathilda chided gently before letting her son loose to get his plate filled at the table. "Mr. Hampton will be most disappointed if there are no pickled mushrooms and breaded prawns left. You know how much he enjoys them."

Miles saw the boy hesitate briefly before the heaping basket of prawns, then with a supreme effort signal the footman to serve him cold lamb chops instead. Christopher ate more sparingly, limiting himself to thin slices of broiled chicken with glazed onions and peas. Miles knew the boys' eating habits well enough to know that Mathilda's eldest son had a sweet tooth and would fill up on the profusion of pastries, jellies, creams, and baskets of strawberries his cook had prepared to appeal to his young guests.

The picnic was to be followed by an eagerly anticipated lesson in rowing on the artificial lake, constructed by one of Miles's earliest ancestors as a reservoir of water to combat

possible fires. As the years went by, fish were added, then
swans, punts and rowboats, and finally the fancy Grecian pergola for the comfort of the ladies who turned the utilitarian
lake into a place for picnics and pleasure.

Repeated admonitions from their mother to allow Uncle
Willy to rest for an hour after his substantial meal did not prevent the boys from running off to hunt for frogs and garter
snakes on the grassy banks.

Unlike his mother, who was able to doze peacefully through
the noise of two small boys playing with water, Miles found
himself impatient to be out on the lake with Mathilda. He was
relieved when—after a half hour of trying to fit his portly
frame into the delicate bamboo chairs designed for frailer
forms—his friend sighed and heaved to his feet.

"Must be cooler out on the water," Willy said, mopping his
cherubic face with a huge handkerchief. "And no doubt you
will be anxious to watch those boys of yours fall into the lake,
my dear," he added cheerily, turning to Mathilda, who sat up
in alarm at this flippancy.

"You assured me they would be safe, Willy."

"Safe as houses, m'dear," Hampton replied with an infectious grin. "I am an excellent swimmer, as is Miles here. And I
guarantee that the boys will come to no harm. A little water
never hurt any of my nephews, believe me. And they all swim
like ducks. Have since they were in shortcoats. Brian has already been ducked in the pond by that Milton hooligan at the
Bazaar, you will recall, and suffered no ill effects. It is time
Christopher got his feet wet, too."

Mathilda was on her feet by this time, and Miles escorted
her down to the small pier, where several punts, skiffs, and ca-
noes were moored. The boys had already commandeered a
skiff and were climbing around in it, trying to fit the oars into
the brass locks.

"You are putting it in backwards, silly," they heard Christopher chide his brother.

"There is no backwards or forwards for oars, is that not so,

Uncle Willy?" Brian retorted in his I-know-more-than-you voice.

Hampton clambered into the skiff, sat down on the cushioned seat, and launched into a practical explanation of how oars did indeed have a back and front, and could be swiveled around at will.

Miles drew Mathilda towards the punt.

At last he would have her all to himself again, and the possibilities made his blood race. This decisive step in his scheme for Mathilda's downfall had been planned long ago, but now that the moment was upon him, Miles could think of nothing but the velvety texture of her skin, the promise of surrender in her amber eyes, the seductive invitation of her soft mouth, already parted in anticipation of the inevitable kisses they would share.

This was what he had waited ten years for, he reminded himself to stem the rising euphoria of emotions. This was his moment of victory.

And then Mathilda smiled up at him, and Miles felt his bones melt and his heart take wings. A heart that had betrayed him.

"Are you certain the countess does not wish to accompany us?" Mathilda asked as Miles held out his hand to help her step into the punt. "There is plenty of room for three." She gestured around the comfortably appointed punt, which had been outfitted with all the luxury of a royal barge on the Nile. Anything to avoid the heat in his eyes.

Mathilda glanced back at Lady Southmoor and noticed with a tingle of apprehension that she had resumed her supine position in the malacca chaise-longue and placed a lacy handkerchief over her face. There would be no help from that quarter; Mathilda was destined to spend a lazy afternoon alone with Miles on the lake. A dangerous afternoon if his eyes were any gauge of his intentions. She could not decide whether the notion excited or terrified her.

He gave her a sensuous, caressing smile, leaving her in no doubt as to the entertainment he had planned for her. If she were prudent, she would claim a megrim and insist on joining the countess in the pergola for a quiet afternoon doze. But she was not prudent, Mathilda realised, and she refused to waste a summer afternoon sleeping and dreaming of this man who was offering her a most improper and imprudent alternative. No, she was not at all prudent, for she actually wanted to be se-duced here and now, by this man who had stolen her heart for the second time. There was a sense of inevitability about it, as though their union had been sanctioned by some benevolent fate that had chosen to smile at them.

Had she welcomed the lakeside picnic and boating lesson for the boys as an excuse to spend more time with Miles? she had asked herself several times without getting a satisfactory answer. Now she knew. The truth was staring her in the face. She was in love again, deeply and irrevocably, with a Miles she knew so well yet did not know at all. A man who held her future happiness in his hands.

The thought of his hands caused her skin to tingle, quite as though they were already inching their way across her body in a most familiar fashion. She wanted to close her eyes and enjoy the erotic fantasy, but his voice jerked her back to the present.

"I believe she prefers to rest," Miles replied, handing Mathilda into the punt. "Mother never was too enamoured of boats, and ever since her favourite sister Elizabeth drowned here when I was a lad, she has refused to set foot in one."

Mathilda settled among the gaily-coloured cushions and un-furled her parasol. She had never known the countess's sister, the tragedy of her death having happened before Mathilda was born. But her mother had often recounted how the countess went into such a deep decline that they had feared for her life. The birth of her twin girls had given the stricken countess a new lease on life, but the scars had remained.

"Your mother is probably right to fear the water," Mathilda

remarked hesitantly, letting her eyes stray to the recumbent figure of her hostess. "Perhaps it is unwise of me to venture out on the water myself, since I cannot swim." There was still time to stem this madness she felt roiling in her veins. If only she could summon the willpower to do so.

Miles let out a crack of laughter, as though he guessed her sudden qualms. "I seem to recall that you swam as a child, Mathilda. Did you not tag along with your brother and me and"—he hesitated over the unspoken name of James Parmenter—"when we came down here to swim, against my father's strict instructions I remember?"

"Oh, no," she responded quickly. "Reggie would never let me into the boat, remember? He made me sit on the shore with the dogs and watch you boys having all the fun. I disliked him intensely in those days," she added. And still do, she felt like saying, remembering her brother's unsuccessful attempt to take charge of her affairs. "I have always regretted not learning to swim." But at least she now had her own life well in hand, headed for happiness unless the fates turned against her again.

Mathilda leaned back into the cushions and trailed her fingers in the cool green water. The shrill call of a kingfisher drew her eyes to the north edge of the lake bordered by high rocky banks overgrown with blackberry vines and bushy hazelnuts. Suddenly, an electric blue flash skimmed low over the water as the bird darted back to its burrowed nest, a dragonfly clamped firmly in its dagger-shaped black beak.

"That is easily remedied, my dear." Miles stood in the stern, expertly poling the flat-bottomed boat through the placid water. "One afternoon after the boys learn to swim, we can all come down here, and I shall teach you. We might bring a picnic basket with us and make a holiday of it. Sarah and Rose both swim, you know, although I beg you not to tell Mother; she would certainly go into a decline were she to suspect it."

The surprising offer stunned Mathilda. As a child she had wished desperately to learn to swim, but her brother had refused to allow her to do more than paddle in the shallows with the tadpoles. But the notion of appearing before Miles in anything as revealing as the swimming costumes she had seen illustrated in *La Belle Assemblée* gave her palpitations.

"How kind of you," she said, wondering how to drop the subject. "Unfortunately, I have no appropriate clothes for swimming, and besides—"

"That does not signify in the least," Miles assured her. "I am sure the twins will lend you some."

Mathilda demurred, but her protests were swept aside, and she found herself committed to spend the very next hot afternoon on her first swimming lesson.

By this time, they had traversed the entire length of the lake, trailed by a pair of swans with their half-grown cygnets looking for scraps of bread. Behind them Mathilda could hear the excited whoops of the boys and a great deal of splashing and laughing. She glanced back nervously, but the moon-shaped lake curved gently, garlanded with a profusion of willows and a heavy stand of aspen still covered with their brown and green catkins that hid the other boaters from view.

"There is no cause for alarm, my dear," Miles said softly, again reading her mind. "Willy is more than a match for two small boys. You have no idea how many nephews and nieces he has scattered around the country. All of whom adore him, of course."

"Oh, it is easy to see why Willy is loved by everyone who knows him. And I know the boys are safe with him," she added, deriving unaccountable pleasure from the endearment as she always did. "I am just so used to having them with me, and I feel that since coming home, they are beginning to slip away from me."

Mathilda was surprised to find herself confessing these intimate thoughts to Miles, of all people. Had she not written him off as incapable of understanding the female sentiments she had once longed to share with him? Had he really changed that much while she had been in India? Mathilda knew that she herself had changed considerably. She was no longer the starry-eyed innocent who demanded that a gentleman be a Nonpareil, a model of classical beauty, gallant and charming beyond reason.

Miles had been none of these things, of course, and she had imagined her heart broken as her dream of love faded. Her disappointment, which she had blamed entirely upon him, had driven her into the arms of another man. Now she wondered if some of that blame should not have been laid at her doorstep. Now, when she suddenly found herself falling in love again, Mathilda asked herself whether she was merely seeing what she wished to see in this man from her past.

He was certainly worth looking at.

Miles had taken off his coat and rolled up his sleeves. As Mathilda observed him from beneath the shade of her parasol, she could not but admire the ease and grace with which he drew up the long pole and thrust it into the water again, leaning his weight against it as he propelled the boat through the water. The motion of his lithe body was mesmerizing. Muscles bunched under the thin linen of his shirt, and the buckskin breeches tautly outlined the strong thighs and narrow hips. Mathilda felt her palms grow moist at the memory of his hard length pressed against her in the shadowy chapel. There was a latent power there that she yearned to unleash. The overwhelming desire to explore that powerful body, to abandon modesty and cast herself recklessly upon the fires of passion brought on a sudden dizziness.

Briefly, she closed her eyes, opening them only when she felt the tickle of willow leaves across her face. The punt had passed under the overhanging branches, and they were suddenly plunged into a cool green world that closed around them, cutting off the outside. Mathilda heard the faint shrieks of her boys fading beyond the cocoon of silence that enveloped them.

Furling her parasol to avoid entangling it with the low branches, Mathilda glanced at Miles, who was mooring the punt to a low wooden wharf that gave access to the bank beneath the willows.

"I wager you do not remember this place, Mathilda," he said with a laugh, holding out his hand to steady her in the gently rocking boat.

Mathilda looked around nervously before placing her hand in his. "Could this be the secret hideaway where you boys held those mysterious meetings? The ones you never allowed me to attend? I could not discover it, although I tried hard enough."

Miles grinned, and Mathilda felt her heart lurch uncomfortably. Lowering her eyes, she allowed him to pull her up the bank. He did not release her immediately, and she found herself standing so close to him that the distinctive male scent of him assailed her senses. She breathed deeply, basking in the heady sensations that rushed wildly through her blood.

Then she raised her eyes and found him watching her with an intensely disturbing gaze.

He was so close that Mathilda could see the flecks of green in his grey orbs, the faint lines radiating from the corners, and the shadow the dark lashes cast upon his cheeks. Her gaze dropped to his mouth, and her heart contracted painfully. No man should have been born with a mouth like that, she thought. The bottom lip, full and lush as a ripe plum, begged to be tasted and nibbled, slowly and voluptuously, traced with uninhibited delight by a daring tongue longing to probe its promised sweetness.

Contrasting with this sensuous, forbidden feast, the finely drawn, classically-shaped upper lip reminded Mathilda that this man belonged to a long line of aristocrats, inheriting from the Greeks their physical beauty and godlike intellect. *Look but trespass at your peril* the mouth seemed to warn her, but she was in no mood to listen to warnings. Good sense seemed to have fled, and Mathilda felt her reason, modesty, and prudence crumble in the presence of the delights implicit in the man who held her enthralled in this secluded spot.

How vulnerable she was, a small voice warned; deliciously

so, another more aggressive voice countered. Even as she stared, unable to drag her eyes away, one corner of the mouth quirked up in secret amusement. Or was it triumph? Men had been predators since the dawn of time, she reminded herself. Women had always been their natural prey. Why should Miles be any different? And she had been such an easy victim. How trustingly she had walked into his trap, if indeed this hidden rendezvous was a trap.

The notion caused her thoughts to veer off in that direction. Had Miles brought her here to claim what should have been his long ago? To punish her, perhaps? Or did he wish to make love to her because he cared for her? The spot was ideally chosen for amorous dalliance—the greensward was soft and studded with violets, the willows sheltered them from the sun and prying eyes, the twittering song of a yellow wagtail, the bell-like trill of the male waxwing, and the warbling of a blue-throated thrush high up in the willows provided the musical counterpoint for seduction.

Feminine instinct warned her to retreat, but Mathilda was so lost to reason that she could only stand there, her hands clasped in his, her heart in her eyes, her whole body pliant and receptive to love. This was the man she wanted, the man she must have. Everything else faded into insignificance beside the warmth of his fingers, the desire in his eyes.

When Miles finally drew her into his arms and lowered his head, Mathilda could think of nothing but those tantalising lips on hers. Her whole world spiralled down to that focal point of surrender until nothing else mattered, no one else existed but the two of them caught up in the white-hot fire of passion.

When she felt his fingers fumble at the closing of her flimsy yellow muslin gown, her own instinctively came to his assistance—as women's fingers have for centuries in similar situations. Between them they removed her gown, leaving her standing in her lacy chemise. Then it was her turn to fumble at the buttons of his fine lawn shirt, damp across the shoulders with his sweat. Mathilda's mouth went dry at the sight of his well-muscled chest and the pad of dark hair tapering down to the top of his breeches.

She swallowed hard as he bent to retrieve a tartan rug from the punt and extended it with one swift movement beneath the nearest willow. He kicked off his short boots, and removed her yellow embroidered slippers, running his hands slowly up her calf to the top of her stockings. She could not repress a shudder of ecstasy as his warm fingers touched the inside of her thigh. Then, with a growl of pure animal pleasure, he swung her up in his arms and laid her down, sprawling his long length beside her.

Mathilda gave herself up to the pleasure of his hands roaming her body, his warm mouth on her breasts, his hips pressing hers into the sweet-scented grass. And when he impatiently pulled off his breeches and demanded her final surrender, she gave herself to him in the certainty that—no matter what had happened before or what might happen afterwards—at that precious moment of possession, not only his body but his heart belonged to her as surely as hers was his alone.

SEVENTEEN

The Announcement

The Earl of Southmoor was off his food that morning after his seduction of Mathilda at the lake, a rare occurrence that threw the entire kitchen staff into a frenzy of alarm.

The news spread throughout the house like smallpox. The upstairs maid carried it into the countess's boudoir with the silver pot of hot chocolate. Long before the countess was dragged from her rest by her personal dresser, agog with the news, the twins had heard it from Betty, the little maid who had taken care of them since she was thirteen. The twins, immediately thinking the worst, had burst into Mrs. Braithwaite's cosy chamber with a vastly exaggerated version of their brother's sudden, perhaps fatal languishing. It had taken all that lady's powers of persuasion to prevent a mass exodus to the breakfast room to confirm the alarming news of the earl's demise.

Fortunately for his peace of mind, Miles was unaware of the pandemonium occasioned in his household by his loss of appetite. He had too much else on his mind, mainly concerning his unfortunate reaction to a delicious female with amber eyes and an unexpected passion that matched his own. According to his carefully laid plans, he had achieved a major victory in that secret grove beside the lake. Why then, he asked himself for the umpteenth time, did he feel so vanquished? So overcome by a lethargic sense of well-being that he had lost interest in everything else, most notably his food.

Having refused Harris's efforts to tempt him with baked

ham and coddled eggs, kippers with *ouefs à la coque,* soused herrings, rare beef sirloin, and various other dishes he would normally have wolfed down with gusto, Miles finally settled, without much enthusiasm, for a small serving of buttered eggs and a muffin. He was not to enjoy even this modest collation in peace, however.

"What is this I hear, my dear boy?" his mother demanded, fluttering into the breakfast parlour like a demented butterfly, antennae on full alert, before he had time to finish his first cup of coffee. "Harris informs me you will not eat your breakfast, Miles. Are you coming down with something, I wonder?" She tripped down to the head of the table, where Miles sat morosely, asking himself that same question, and laid a pale hand on her son's brow.

"Oh, my gracious!" the countess exclaimed at her most theatrical, "you are burning up, Miles. I shall tell Harris to send for Dr. MacIntyre this very instant."

"No, you will not, Mother." Miles glared with distaste at the gaily-coloured apparition hovering beside him. If there was one thing about his mother—whom he otherwise adored—that set his teeth on edge, it was her propensity for melodrama early in the morning.

"What did you say, dear?"

"I said you will not bother the good doctor on my account. Now do sit down, Mother, and Harris will serve you a cup of tea to soothe your nerves. You must not excite yourself, you know." He rose and pulled out the chair next to his own. When she demurred, he took her gently by the shoulders and made her sit. Since the countess appeared genuinely distressed, Miles forced himself to smile.

"There is nothing wrong with me, I can assure you, Mother. It is all a hum." He paused to cast a quelling scowl at his sheepish butler. "A slight indigestion from that dressed lobster we had last night for dinner. It was not as fresh as it could have been." He regarded her affectionately. "That is a vastly fetching ensemble you are wearing, Mama," he added, changing the subject abruptly to divert her thoughts into less tiresome channels.

"Yes, indeed it is, my lady," a cheerful voice cut in as Hampton sailed into the breakfast parlour, looking as though he had just stepped out of the pages of a fashion magazine. "That forget-me-not blue brings out the colour of your lovely eyes."

"Oh, Willy, you outrageous flatterer you," the countess simpered, obviously pleased at the compliment. "I do not usually appear downstairs in my peignoir, but I heard some disturbing news and hurried down to . . ." She shot a glance at Miles, who responded laconically.

"My mother heard that I was on my deathbed, Willy, but whoever set that rumour about vastly exaggerated the matter, I fear." He glanced at his butler again, but Harris busied himself industriously with the chafing dishes.

"'Tis no joking matter, Miles," the countess protested, "but since you mention rumours," she added, changing course as easily as a cork in a maelstrom, "I wish to ask you if there is any truth to those involving you and our dear Mathilda in the Abbey chapel last week. That old biddy Amelia Fraser is spreading it about that there is a match in the making. After witnessing your highly indiscreet behaviour at the lake the other afternoon, Miles, I cannot help but wonder if there is something I should know about your future intentions with the girl."

Miles grinned sardonically. "Mathilda is no girl, Mother. And I do not hear you asking Willy here if his intentions are honest. He is in her company every bit as much as I am."

Willy's response was instantaneous and unequivocal. "Low blow, Miles. My interest in the fair Mathilda is strictly brotherly. Her own brother is a curst rum touch, if you ask me, not to be trusted to protect her reputation from lecherous fortune-hunters like Lord George and his ilk."

Harris set a large brown jug of ale on the table beside Mr. Hampton, who promptly filled his tankard to the brim.

"Well, I expect both of you to keep Mathilda's reputation spotless," the countess insisted. "Particularly you, Miles," she added with a faint emphasis that caused him to wonder if his featherbrained parent was more astute than he had given her credit for. "And now if you will excuse me, I must warn Cook not to use any of that lobster for the supper at your birthday ball, Miles. We cannot have you under the weather at your own ball."

"I am much too old to be celebrating birthday balls, Mother. I think next year we will have a shooting party up at the Lodge. Gentlemen only."

"What a wretched thing to say, dear. You will quite spoil all my fun. Besides, a shooting party is no place to make announcements of a delicate nature." With these enigmatic words, and a speaking glance at her son, she swept out of the parlour in a flurry of pale blue georgette and blond lace.

Miles followed his mother's exit with a worried expression. Could that unexpected parting shot mean that she suspected his time with Mathilda on the lake had not been spent entirely on polite conversation? Could she conceivably have any idea of what had occurred between them? He could never ask her, of course, but the comment on guarding Mathilda's reputation sounded ominous. Almost as though the countess were warning him that there were certain things a gentleman did not do without accepting the consequences.

And just what were the consequences of his seduction of his former betrothed? he thought grimly. Miles knew precisely what they were, and exactly what his honour demanded of him. Mathilda must have known it, too. Perhaps she had even expected him to speak out as they lay together on the rug under the willow. Admittedly, he had strongly resisted the urge to open his heart to her then and there. She had been so perfect. So beautiful. So vulnerable. So much the Mathilda of his most intimate dreams and desires. He had come close to abandoning his plan entirely, of making her the offer she must be expecting, of ending these ten years of misery and rage.

Something in him had rebelled against letting her off so easily. His dark angel, perhaps, had balked at giving up his vindication, the final payment for all the humiliations he had suffered. Besides, he had already dispatched the announcement to London. He could not turn back now, even if he wanted to. So he had held his peace, watching with mixed emotions the troubled expression in her eyes as he had punted back to the pergola, where tea was being served.

"Is there going to be a *delicate* announcement?" Willy demanded, dragging Miles sharply out of his reverie.

The earl turned his attention from his muffin to his friend, who had just accepted a gargantuan serving of baked ham, coddled eggs, and a piece of rare beef sirloin large enough to choke two men. The sight of so much food made Miles feel distinctly queasy.

"I notice that the over-ripe lobster last night did not affect your appetite today." His jaundiced gaze flinched noticeably when it alighted upon his friend's plate.

"I was careful not to eat any," Willy answered succinctly. "And you are not bamboozling me for a moment. It is not the lobster that has you off your oats, is it? So tell me, Miles, would it be premature to wish you happy, old friend?"

In a sudden flash of insight, Miles saw that his carefully laid plans for the downfall and humiliation of his former betrothed were riddled with hidden pitfalls. His mother was obviously counting on a renewal of his match with Mathilda, and here was Willy demanding point blank if his intentions were honest. Miles was fairly certain—through several oblique remarks they had made over the past weeks—that his sisters were also counting upon welcoming Mathilda into their family. To say nothing of Mathilda's mother and Lady Denton, both of whom had taken to treating him with unusual condescension and affection. Quite as one of the family, he thought with a surge of helplessness.

If his plan was successful—and there was no doubt in his mind, after the passionate interlude they had spent together on the lake, that Mathilda was ripe for the plucking—all these people, people he loved, would be hugely disappointed. Not only that, he realised with the cold clarity of reason, but they would all hold him responsible for unspeakable, ungentlemanly conduct to one of the fair sex. Not a single one would consider his actions justified, a fair retribution for the humiliation he had suffered at her hands for a similar affront as that he was poised to inflict upon the lady in question.

Not even Willy. Particularly not Willy.

Miles stared across the table into his friend's warm brown eyes and suffered a sting of regret. If anyone would guess at the ignoble motive—Miles was honest enough to admit his obsession with revenge was ignoble—behind his assiduous pursuit of Mathilda, it would be Willy. He had no doubt that Willy would advocate a forgive-and-forget strategy, as did Mathilda herself. The past is beyond repair she had said, or something to that effect. Only the present can be changed to rectify the mistakes of the past.

Thus had the lovely Mathilda revealed her innocent belief in human nature. It sounded reasonable, but highly impractical—as naïve as she was herself. Unlike Willy, Miles had always believed that past wrongs must be righted, at whatever cost. He had lived the past ten years fueled by this belief, waiting for the moment when he could settle his score with his former betrothed. And now that the moment was within his grasp, so close he could almost smell it, he was suddenly beset by misgivings that had no place in his plan.

Suddenly, Miles was not sure about what he wanted. Did he truly wish to see Mathilda broken, humiliated, her reputation in shreds? Or did he want her in quite another way? A way that had not been part of his original plan at all?

"Well?" Willy was smiling, his cheerful face gentle with sympathy. "Tell old Willy all about it, lad."

Miles longed to confide in him. He was confident Willy would understand what had driven him to waste ten years of his life pursuing a dream that had suddenly turned sour. But he also knew that Willy would tell him to put aside his rancour and follow his heart. Unfortunately, that advice presumed that Miles knew what was in his heart. He was not at all sure that he did. And would he be willing to follow it if it led him off on a tangent from his carefully laid plan?

Miles was not yet ready to answer that question.

He shrugged and spread orange marmalade on his muffin. "Perhaps. But then again perhaps not. It all depends."

"Depends on what?"

"On what happens at that confounded birthday ball, of course."

An unsatisfactory answer if ever there was one, Miles realised, but at least he had expressed some of the uncertainty that gnawed at his heart.

On the evening of the earl's birthday ball, Mathilda examined herself nervously in the cheval glass beside her dresser. She had spent more than half the afternoon preparing herself both mentally and physically for the night ahead. As the time of her departure for the Grange approached, Dolly, her abigail, had begun to look a little frazzled, but Mrs. Hettie Grey maintained her cheerful demeanour throughout with no sign of impatience. The frequent appearances of her housekeeper with offers of pots of tea and other refreshments warned Mathilda that her staff was caught up in the excitement she had not been able to conceal.

"That is a very lovely gown, my lady," Mrs. Walker said in awed tones from the doorway, where she had appeared with yet another tray. "No one will hold a candle to you for sure." She came into the chamber and set the tray down on the crowded dresser. "I thought you might like a cup of the mint tea my own mother used to make for such occasions, my lady. It soothes the nerves."

Mathilda wondered if she looked as nervous as she felt. It was so unlike her to expend excessive energy and time on her appearance. But tonight she had tried on and discarded at least a dozen gowns before settling on a new sea-green diaphanous, high-waisted ball gown in Italian taffeta, worn under a spider-gauze over-gown strewn with silver spangles.

"That is very kind of you, Mrs. Walker," she murmured distractedly. "Perhaps the silver gauze is not quite the thing with this gown, Hettie. What do you think? Should I wear the gold lace with seed pearls instead?"

"I would not advise it, my lady. The gold is too heavy for that pale green taffeta. The silver net gives the impression of airiness and fragility that is most becoming on you. Which jewels will you wear with it?"

"The emeralds?"

Mrs. Grey shook her head. "Too cumbersome. I would suggest the diamond and jade parure. The jade matches the taffeta, and the diamonds pick up the sparkle of the sequins. You will look like a fairy princess."

Mathilda wondered idly if she really wanted to appear as a fairy at all, but Hettie was right, the jade—ironically, a gift from James on their last Christmas together—did match the gown perfectly, and the dozens of small diamonds on the lacy setting created a shimmering effect on her bosom that was definitely magical. When she added the jade ear-bobs and bracelet, she felt as though she had left her old self behind and stepped into a wonderland where anything was possible.

She hoped fervently that appearances were not deceiving, because tonight she was hoping for a miracle of major proportions. Tonight she hoped that her shattered dreams of ten years before would be made whole again. Tonight, if all went as she hoped, Miles would claim not just her lips and her body as he had so far, but her heart as well—to have and to hold forever.

The drive to the Grange in her aunt's carriage passed all too quickly for Mathilda. Torn between her desire to see Miles again, to look into his eyes and see that tenderness she had glimpsed there yesterday, and her fear that she had misread his intentions, her nerves were stretched to breaking point when they arrived at the earl's front door. At the bottom of the grand curving staircase, where she stood with her mother, chatting vivaciously with a doting Lord Snowburn, her aunt, and a dozen other dinner guests waiting to be formally received by the countess and her son, Mathilda kept her eyes modestly lowered.

With half an ear, Mathilda listened to the chatter swirling around her. But she could not work up any enthusiasm for the trials of Mrs. Glover to find a decent downstairs maid to replace the hussy she had discovered disporting herself on the table in the pantry with the under-footman. Or for the vicar's losing battle with giant green caterpillars on his prize cabbages; or Lady Burk's despair of ever inducing little Freddy to memorize his Latin verbs. Or even for Mrs. Fraser's veiled hints that Miss Letitia Winters, the squire's rambunctious daughter, had landed herself in real trouble at last. Just as she had predicted last spring, the old gossip insisted quite as though she were personally responsible for the poor girl's predicament.

"My dear Aunt Agatha," an unctuous voice floated up the stairs from behind her, "I trust I find you restored to health." Sir Reginald pushed his way up to stand beside his mother and her party, earning several irate looks from guests who had arrived before him.

"There is nothing wrong with my health, Reggie," Lady Denton snapped crossly. "You would do well to look to your own, my boy. That inferior snuff you are always stuffing up your nose will be the death of you, believe me." She glanced with barely concealed horror at the pale yellow velvet coat he wore and the exaggeratedly high points to his cravat. "That is if your cravat does not strangle you first," she added with some relish. "And I must ask you to remove yourself from my train, boy. I did not wear this new gown so you might wipe your boots on it."

Mathilda hid a smile at her brother's flustered protest, but her amusement was short-lived. She felt a movement behind her and turned to find the handsome face of Lord George Bennett observing her. He bowed a greeting, and his thin lips stretched into a mocking smile.

"You are looking very lovely, as usual, my lady," he said close to her ear. "Pity your heart is as black as pitch, if indeed you have a heart at all." At her look of astonishment at this unexpected attack, he continued in the same intimate undertone. "Rumour has it that you are about to make that stuffed-shirt Southmoor the happiest of mortals." He raised an elegant brow, eyeing her speculatively. "Unless, of course, you have already done so, my sweet little tease," he added with a lecherous grin.

Mathilda's face froze. She stared at him icily, struggling to keep her expression from betraying how accurately the vicious remark had hit its mark. He could not possibly know about her illicit afternoon under the willows, could he? She took a deep breath to steady herself. It would never do to give a sewer rat the satisfaction of seeing her rattled. Her smile was cool. "I trust you are not planning to wager on it, my lord," she remarked in a bored voice, turning back to where her aunt was shredding Reggie's taste in clothes.

"What sane man would wear a waistcoat with pink frogs embroidered on it?" she demanded in such strident tones that several guests turned to stare.

"I warned your esteemed nephew that frogs were not quite the thing, my lady," Lord George added with a smirk, "and that to indulge oneself with pink ones was nothing short of a descent into dandyism of the most frivolous kind."

"Are you calling my nephew a dandy, sir?" Lady Denton turned her formidable gaze full on the duke's son, who suddenly seemed to find his cravat uncomfortably tight. Her aunt might not belong to the first ranks of the aristocracy, but that did not stop her caustic tongue from castigating pretentiousness when she found it. She was well known for speaking her mind to lord and peasant alike, and Mathilda waited with bated breath to see Lord George cut down to size for his impertinence.

She was to be deprived of this spectacle, for at that moment the guests began to move upstairs and Lord George prudently

fell back into place behind them. Before she was quite prepared for it, Mathilda found herself enveloped in the violet-
scented embrace of the countess, who was in high gig that
evening, her china-blue eyes sparkling with gaiety. She made
much of Mathilda's appearance, and to that lady's embarrassment turned to her son for confirmation.

"Is our Mathilda not a delightful sight, Miles?" the countess
cooed ecstatically, seemingly unaware of the tension that hovered between the couple.

"Indeed, she is," he responded, his voice low and caressing
as he raised her from the formal curtsy and lifted her gloved
fingers to his lips.

Mathilda dared not look up into his eyes. His tone of voice,
his touch, the smell of him battered her senses with reminders of
their intimacy. She felt completely undone by his proximity,
quite as though they were back in the warm sensual cocoon they
had shared beside the lake. She could sense that he was smiling;
the warmth of it brushed her skin. Her hand was still trapped in
his, and from his fingertips all manner of secret messages
seemed to flow. It was all quite improper, but the countess had
turned away to greet Lady Denton, leaving her alone with *him*.

How nonsensical, she thought. They were surrounded by
guests. The formal drawing room was filling up with people;
the staircase was crowded with them. She was not alone with
Miles. It only seemed that way. And she had lost her tongue
like a mere chit of a girl.

"I trust you have saved a waltz for me, Mathilda." His voice
washed over her like a soft summer breeze, and her knees trem-
bled. "And the supper dance. I insist upon that one. After all, this
is my birthday; I should be entitled to some privileges."

Her eyes swept up, stopping with a jolt at the level of his cravat, tied in some intricate creation she did not recognise. She saw
his mouth twitch into a smile and dredged up a response. "Of
course, my lord," she heard herself murmur primly before re-
trieving her hand and moving on to embrace his sisters, who had
been allowed to attend the dinner and ball in his honour.

EIGHTEEN

Mystery Lady

Starting with that first overwhelming sensation of joy at being in the same house, in the same room, with Miles, Mathilda's evening resembled a maelstrom of emotion.

Willy Hampton took her in to dinner. He appeared silently at her side in the crowded drawing room, his face wreathed in smiles. "I daresay poor old Miles is cursing his luck," he whispered over the noise of chatter and clinking of sherry glasses.

"Why ever is that?"

"His rank precludes his escorting you into the dining room. That is enough to make a dog weep. Look at the poor fellow, stuck with the Marchioness of Galsworthy, a more unworthy specimen of womanhood I have rarely seen."

"That is unkind of you, Willy," Mathilda whispered, glad that his irreverence had dispelled some of her nervousness. "The poor lady cannot help being a little hard of hearing." She could clearly hear the marchioness's voice trumpeting from across the room.

"Perhaps," he conceded, "that I might forgive. But I cannot forgive her constant carrying on about her dogs. She must have two dozen of them, and each one has a different story that her ladyship insists upon repeating at every gathering she attends. I wager I am not the only one tired of her incessant dog tales."

Luckily—or perhaps the countess had planned it that way—Mathilda found herself seated between Willy and Lord Snowburn. Her brother and Lord George sat at the end of the table, but Mathilda was close enough to Miles to know, without actually looking at him, that his eyes were often on her face. Others seemed to have noticed the earl's interest, for Lord Snowburn—who normally had eyes only for Lady Heath—twitted her about the grand conquest she had made. Was the announcement to be made at the ball? he wanted to know.

Mathilda wanted to know that, too. And since his lordship had not lowered his voice in asking his question, Mathilda was soon aware of other guests watching her surreptitiously, ears primed for gossip.

Although the Southmoor table was famous for the best fare to be had west of London, Mathilda could not have said what she ate. She put food into her mouth at regular intervals, but her attention was divided between Willy's humourous chatter on one hand, and the voice of the gentleman at the head of the table on the other. She could not hear much of Miles's actual words, but the sound of his voice, reaching her over the hubbub of hearty conversation and the clatter of cutlery and porcelain, washed over her like warm honey.

The earl led off the ball with his mother, but the second dance, which was a waltz, went to Mathilda. She was ecstatic. Surely by singling her out so publicly Miles was letting it be known that he . . . that he . . . Mathilda could not bring herself to finish the thought. She hoped desperately that she did not look like a moonstruck chit suffering her first *tendre* for a gentleman.

At this point her joy reached its zenith, and she allowed herself to smile up at him as they glided round the room together in perfect harmony. She felt giddy with happiness and ceased to care that the whole world could read the love in her eyes. She was on the brink of making a spectacle of herself, she realised, straining to rein in the smile that seemed to have taken up permanent residence on her face.

In Miles's arms, his eyes full of admiration, Mathilda felt herself become the fairy princess Mrs. Grey had predicted. This euphoria lasted right up to the supper dance, which she had promised to Miles. Basking in the memory of Miles's smile, she was even able to dance with her brother and Lord George without losing her composure. Sir Reginald did make a halfhearted attempt to champion his friend's cause, but when she laughed in his face at the notion of preferring that wastrel over the Earl of Southmoor, he retired in one of his nasty moods, warning her that she would be sorry.

Much later, Mathilda was to remember her brother's prophetic words.

Ironically, it was her new friend, Lady Sylvia Longueville, who brought her the first hint that all was not well shortly after supper.

"Nicholas received some extraordinary information from Jason Ransome," Lady Sylvia whispered breathlessly when she caught up with Mathilda between sets. "Jason came back from Town late this afternoon. He tells us that London is abuzz with a mysterious announcement."

"What announcement is that?" Mathilda asked lightly, too happy to pay attention to the gravity of her friend's expression.

Lady Sylvia looked at her askance. "Are you telling me you do not know, my dear? How can that be? Surely you are bamming me? A gentleman does not send off a notice to the *Gazette,* at least not a matrimonial notice without—" She stopped abruptly as if something odd had occurred to her. "Southmoor *has* made you an offer, I presume?"

Mathilda shook her head, bewildered, a little knot of uneasiness forming in her stomach at this peculiar turn of events.

"Not yet," she confessed without thinking. "I am expecting—" Mathilda bit off her words abruptly. She had promised herself not to expect anything from Miles, not to hope too fervently that she had touched his heart, not to count on receiving the offer that had, until yesterday, seemed the only honourable sequel to their intimacies at the lake. But of course she *had* expected, and hoped, and counted on his honour. She was still the dreamer waiting for miracles. But what if . . . She was almost afraid to ask.

"What did the announcement say?"

"Jason could not tell us. He did not actually see it himself. Nor did he bring the *Gazette* back with him. He merely said that the clubs were full of it, with wagers already on the books at White's that Southmoor would be left at the altar again." Lady Sylvia linked her arm in Mathilda's and drew her among the profusion of potted palms towards the terrace door, which stood open to the warm summer night.

"I am sorry that old spectre has risen up again to haunt you, dearest," Lady Sylvia said gently, leading Mathilda out onto the terrace, where strings of fairy lanterns flickered and danced in the moonlight. Several couples strolled about among the shrubbery, talking and laughing, and the scent of jasmine and heliotrope and roses tantalised the senses. It was a night for lovers.

Mathilda had imagined herself strolling in this same moonlight with Miles, sharing whispered words of love, hearing his promises of a lifetime of devotion, his offer of marriage. Receiving his kisses.

That image had suddenly blurred, the fairy lights wobbly and indistinct. Mathilda shuddered as an icy shard of alarm touched her heart. She pulled herself together with an effort. She must not succumb to the premonition of disaster that threatened to undo her.

"So the actual text of this announcement—if there is one— is still a mystery?" she mumbled through stiff lips.

"Oh, there is one all right," Lady Sylvia replied, demolishing Mathilda's effort to banish the fear expanding insidiously in her heart. "And it seems clear that Lord Southmoor's name is involved. The mystery is the lady. Nobody seems to know her. I found that very odd since, forgive me, my dear, your name would not be a mystery in this case. And there cannot be another woman. He has made his preference for you very clear for weeks now, and we all thought . . ."

Mathilda wanted to agree, but the words stuck in her throat.

At that moment they approached a group of young ladies

seated around a fountain, laughing at something amusing a
dainty blond beauty with pansy-blue eyes was saying. The tit-
tering ceased abruptly as Lady Sylvia and Mathilda passed by
on the other side of a low privet hedge. The silence was so absolute that Mathilda could draw no other conclusion than that
she had been the subject of the laughter. She smiled briefly at
one or two of the girls she knew, but their eyes slid away from
her gaze.

"I wonder what that was all about," Mathilda murmured,
trying to control her panic.

"I daresay the silly little gossipmongers have heard about
the mystery announcement," Lady Sylvia responded scath-
ingly.

"They may also have learned the name of the mystery lady,"
Mathilda added in a hollow voice. Some inner demon taunted
her that she was not that lady. The reflection brought her
whole world crumbling at her feet.

"I think we shall soon find out ourselves," her companion
remarked with an attempt at humour. "Here comes that old
biddy Mrs. Fraser. If anyone knows the secret, it will be she."

Mathilda cringed inwardly at the vindictive light she detected in Mrs. Fraser's stony little eyes as she walked briskly
towards them down the narrow path. There would be no
avoiding her, and in any case, Mathilda told herself fatalisti-
cally, she would have to know sooner or later.

"Ah, there you are, my dear Mathilda." She heard Mrs.
Fraser's high falsetto actually quaver in delight at the gossip
she was about to spew out. "Have you heard the wonderful
news?"

It took all Mathilda's sangfroid to feign interest in the
harpy's words. She would have much preferred to pick her up
by her skinny neck and drown her in the fountain. Instead, she
opted for insouciance and dredged up a supercilious smile.

"If you mean the mystery announcement in the *Gazette* that
has everyone in a twitter, that is old news already, my dear
lady." Mathilda refused to give the old Tabby the satisfaction

of seeing her distress, which had evidently been the harridan's intention.

The smug smile faded, but Mrs. Fraser had not yet exhausted all her ammunition. She rallied instantly.

"Then I am sure you can tell us who the mystery lady is, my dear. Who is this lucky Miss Amanda Champion the Earl of Southmoor has chosen for his bride?" Her false smile stretched her wrinkled face into the mask of a gargoyle.

Mathilda felt Sylvia's warning fingers dig into her arm. She was suddenly aware that her friend was practically holding her erect. She took a deep breath, gathering her strength to fight back the dizziness that blurred her vision. Staring directly into the old harridan's adder-like eyes, she forced her dry lips into a faint condescending smile.

"Yes, indeed I can," she lied without the slightest compunction. She felt Lady Sylvia tense beside her, and her smile broadened. In for a penny in for a pound, Mathilda thought, conscious of a wicked gratification when Mrs. Fraser's ferret face fell in astonishment. That would teach the old harridan to carry tales.

"Who is she?" Mrs. Fraser demanded harshly, unable to conceal her avid curiosity. Doubtless she was poised to spread the name far and wide as soon as it left Mathilda's lips.

Mathilda relaxed a little. So this was what it felt like to be cast aside for another? This searing pain ran through her veins as though some corrosive acid had invaded her body. It was excruciating. Everything she had wished for, everything she had truly expected to enjoy with Miles suddenly shrank into a hard core of pain where her heart used to be. He had given it all to another.

Another squeeze on her arm reminded Mathilda that she still had a role to play in this heart-wrenching melodrama.

"Who is she?" she repeated, shrugging as if the whole affair were tiresome beyond words. "I cannot say," she said, that part at least true. "You see, I promised not to reveal the secret."

"But surely . . ."

Lady Sylvia steered her firmly past Mrs. Fraser, who stood staring after them, gibbering and frothing with frustration.

"You deserve a role on Drury Lane with that performance, my dear," Lady Sylvia whispered as they meandered back towards the terrace. "You were superb. I envy you. Was any of it true?"

"Not a single word."

Miles stood making small talk with Lady Denton, whom he had just partnered through a lively quadrille, when he saw Willy Hampton beating a path across the dance floor towards him. Something about the set of his friend's face, devoid of its habitual smile, warned him that things were about to come to a head.

There had been growing tension among his guests during his supper dance with Mathilda. It was another waltz, and he had been looking forward to holding her in his arms again, but the heightened amount of attention they had aroused in the other couples on the floor told him that news of that ill-fated announcement had reached the Grange. Several of his house guests had driven out from London earlier that day to attend his birthday. Any one of them could have glanced at the *Gazette* or brought it to Bath. His plan was evolving exactly as he intended, but now that victory was so close at hand, Miles felt strangely devoid of satisfaction.

Mathilda had appeared to be unaware that they were the centre of attention, and that speculative stares followed them round the room. She was particularly ravishing tonight, her green spangled gown revealing just enough of her sweet bosom to remind him of the hidden delights he had enjoyed beside the lake. Her amber eyes were sparkling, and she smiled up at him with such trust and love that Miles felt more like a despicable cad every minute.

How would she react when she heard about the announcement, which she was bound to do at any moment? The thought had plagued him for several days, ever since he had sent the notice up to London with one of the grooms. He had more than once regretted writing the damning notice, but a stubborn, self-destructive streak in him had insisted that the game be played through to the bitter end. He had not waited so many years for personal vindication, he kept reminding himself, only to be cheated of satisfaction by a pair of amber eyes and a lovely smile.

This argument had sustained him since the day he had set eyes on Mathilda again in Hatchard's Book Shop. He had used it more frequently since she had returned to Rose Park, but in the past week it had begun to sound specious and uncomfortably gauche, more like the defence of a spoiled brat, a mere April-squire with more hair than wit, instead of the gentleman of rank and substance he had prided himself on being.

And now, as disaster crowded in upon him, Miles came face-to-face with an ugly realisation. By pushing this hideous game to its conclusion, he would wound Mathilda beyond bearing. And destroy any possibility of finding happiness for himself. For now, when it was too late, he saw that life would be unthinkable without Mathilda; she held his happiness in her small hands. Why had he not seen it sooner? Why had he not realised that his eye-for-an-eye philosophy—and his plan had been no less primitive than that sanctioned by Scripture—had no place in the game of love? Forgiveness was the secret of love. He saw it clearly now. Mathilda had known it all along, and told him so. Learn to forgive the past, she had said.

She had been right, of course, and he had been terribly wrong. Now that it was too late to stop the game, Miles recognised his reckless stupidity for what it was. A sop to his wounded pride. He had the sudden urge to take Mathilda by the hand and run off to the lake with her, to their secret place, where he had spent the most joyous moments of his life.

Out of the corner of his eye he had seen Lady Sylvia Longueville lead Mathilda behind the potted palms towards the terrace. He had little doubt what the subject of the countess's confidences would be. If only he could turn back the clock . . . He wanted to rush after her and try to explain, to beg her to accept his tarnished heart, unworthy as it was.

But it was too late for regrets. Mathilda would probably never want to speak to him again after the contents of that nefarious notice became known. Rumours were already spreading among his guests. The mildly curious stares that had followed them through the supper dance, and then into supper, had become frankly hostile now. At any moment his mother would descend upon him, demanding an explanation. Which he did not have.

Overcome with a sense of disaster, Miles closed his eyes for a moment, blotting out the events rushing to their climax. He opened them to find Willy standing next to him. Brown eyes glared into his for a moment, and Miles knew the moment of reckoning had arrived.

"I must speak with you *now,* Miles, if you please," Willy said without roundaboutation. He sketched a bow to the ladies and led the way back across the floor and down the stairs to the library.

The musicians struck up a cotillion, and Miles considered fobbing Willy off by claiming his duties as host. But then he did not truly want to escape this confrontation, one he had brought about with his own actions. And the set of his friend's shoulders warned him that it would serve no purpose. Willy would not be distracted. He had the bit in his mouth and would have his say. Miles had never seen Willy so angry.

Hampton led him into the library and closed the door. He stalked across to the carved oak desk that had been in the Stephens family for generations and picked up a folded newspaper. Miles did not have to ask which newspaper it was.

"Perhaps you will be good enough to explain this notice, Southmoor." Willy's voice was low but steely, and Miles knew there would be no point in pretending ignorance. Willy's use of his title had set aside all reliance on friendship to save him.

"I assume that is the *Gazette.*"

Willy snorted impatiently. "Of course it is the *Gazette.* Jeremy Foster brought me a copy down from London this afternoon. You can imagine my astonishment when I discovered a notice announcing your betrothal to a Miss Amanda Champion." He paused as though waiting for Miles to deny it.

"I have not seen this notice you speak of," Miles prevaricated.

"You do not deny having sent the thing to be published?"

"I was not aware I needed your permission to publish anything, Hampton," he retorted dryly.

"You can publish anything you bloody please," Willy burst out, his calm facade slipping. "But when you deliberately set out to hurt and humiliate a female I hold in very high regard, you will certainly answer to me for it, or I will know the reason why."

"I fail to see that it is any of your affair."

"I am making it my affair."

"Are you calling me out, Hampton?"

"If I have to. Unless, of course, you are willing to announce publicly that the *Gazette* made an embarrassing error, and that Miss Amanda Champion does not exist."

"Oh, but she does." Miles could not repress the flicker of an ironic smile.

"You actually *know* this female?" Willy sounded outraged.

"I appear to be betrothed to her, so I must do, old chap." Miles hated himself for this flippancy, but the tension in the room was stifling.

"Who in the blue blazes is she?" Willy's chin jutted ferociously.

Miles's lips thinned as he refused to answer. The silence that followed hung heavily in the room, bristling with tension and the imminent threat of violence.

NINETEEN

The Dust-Up

The library door slammed open, and a thunderous voice came from behind them. "Yes, who is this female inexplicably linked to you in this blasted notice, Southmoor?" Lord Longueville stood at the open door, hands on hips, glaring at Miles sternly.

Miles turned to stare at yet another friend who appeared to have taken up arms in Mathilda's defence. "Obliging of you, Longueville, to take an interest in my private affairs. But if you are thinking of calling me out over my choice of females, old chap, you will have to wait your turn. Hampton here has already issued his challenge."

Willy let out a crack of unpleasant laughter. "The devil fly away with such niceties as duels," he snapped. "I shall beat you to a pulp with my bare hands."

"Be my guest, old man," Miles hissed between clenched teeth.

As Hampton angrily discarded his coat, Longueville looking on with approval, Miles had visions of returning to the ballroom, his new blue silk coat in tatters and splattered with blood. Willy was not unskilled at boxing, but had no chance of touching him if it came to a bout of fisticuffs. Except that Miles would simply not defend himself against his friend. He would take the beating he richly deserved.

Willy rolled up his sleeves and addressed Miles again. "You are beneath contempt, sir. Drawing and quartering is too good for the likes of you. I am going to enjoy knocking your teeth down your throat!"

"And if the job isn't done to my satisfaction, I'll finish you off myself. My lady has expressly demanded you be made to pay," Longueville added.

Miles felt the force of Willy's outrage, measured the damage the powerfully built earl could inflict, and shuddered. He fervently hoped that his erstwhile friends would batter him senseless. Perhaps even disfigure him so badly that he would be a recluse for the rest of his life. If he lost Mathilda—which he no longer doubted he would—he would be a recluse anyway. His life would not be worth living. He almost wished the beating would start. It would block out some of the empty hopelessness that seemed to have settled into his soul.

"Who is this mysterious Miss Amanda Champion?" Willy demanded harshly, grabbing Miles roughly by the once elegant folds of his cravat.

"Her identity must stay hidden a while longer," Miles mumbled.

This seemed to enrage Hampton, who shook him violently by the cravat, effectively destroying an hour's careful effort to produce a masterpiece of elegance.

"Hold it a moment, Willy," Longueville protested. "If the lass does exist, then the dastard has deceived two innocent ladies with false promises of marriage."

"I never promised marriage to Mathilda. At least not recently," Miles clarified. He could not explain why he was being deliberately combative; perhaps because he needed his friends to remain enraged.

"But you *are* going to, are you not, my fine buck?" The words were softly spoken, but there was no mistaking the latent hostility in Hampton's voice.

For good measure, Willy jerked viciously on Miles's cravat. "And what about poor Miss Champion?" His innate sense of chivalry forced Willy to raise this unpleasant issue. "Do you intend to jilt the gel, Miles? Her reputation will be in shreds."

Knowing the true identity of Miss Amanda Champion, Miles was able to respond with an astonishing lack of feeling.

"I am happy to assure you gentlemen that Miss Champion has no reputation to speak of. And as for being jilted, she will doubtless survive. I did," he added bitterly. Particularly since the young lady would never learn that she had been betrothed to the Earl of Southmoor in the first place. Miles would take good care that she did not.

Hampton became visibly incensed at this brazen remark, and without warning took a swing at Miles, connecting a respectable left hook to his friend's chin while Longueville looked on in disgust.

Miles rocked backwards and would have sprawled on the Axminster carpet had Willy, still holding him by the cloth that had once passed as an elegant Mathematical, not yanked him upright.

"I see what you are about, y-you h-heartless jackstraw," Hampton stammered. "You have harboured a grudge against Mathilda for all these years, and think to pay her back in the same coin. Of all the scurvy tricks, this one takes the cake. A pox on you, I say." His right fist came up so quickly that Miles saw only a blur before knuckles connected solidly with his nose, knocking his head back with a painful crack.

Hampton pulled him upright again, then muttering a colourful oath under his breath, punched Miles in the solar plexus with enough force to send him spinning backwards to land in a heap on the floor.

All Miles could think of was that before these *friends* finished with him, his face would be reduced to mush and he would quite possibly be maimed for life. A just punishment for his ill-conceived revenge. Responding to Willy's solid hit, his nose was bleeding copiously. Miles felt the warm blood run down his chin and stared stupidly as the crimson drops fell on his pristine blue coat. The only coherent thought that went through his mind was that his mother would kill him if he got blood on her carpet. And Mathilda would never speak to him again.

He stared up at the two figures looming over him.

"Get up and take your punishment like a man," Hampton commanded, unexpectedly kicking him in the ribs.

"It seems infinitely safer down here," Miles muttered, wondering why he had never realised that the man he had known all his life as Sweet Willy for his unflinching good nature had a dark side that was quite dangerous.

Longueville leaned down and jerked Miles to his feet. "Well?" he snarled in a voice that would have done justice to his barbaric Norman ancestors. "Are you going to settle this affair honourably, or do we have to rearrange your phiz for you?"

Miles grimaced. What could be honourable in two ablebodied men beating another to a pulp? he wanted to ask, but thought better of it.

"Let us do it anyway," Hampton grunted, evidently primed for blood. He caught Miles by the ruined cravat again and raised his fist. Casually, he administered a quick jab to the left eye.

Miles felt a sharp pain as he rocked away from the blow. He could feel it begin to swell almost immediately. Willy grinned sadistically and drew back his fist for another jab.

Miles braced for the blow, but it never came.

A female voice cut across the tension in the room like a knife.

"Stop this senseless butchery immediately." Hysteria made the tone shrill and breathless. "What are you? Savages?"

Three pairs of eyes swiveled towards the door where Lady Parmenter stood, an expression of horrified outrage on her pale face. All motion ceased, and Hampton's arm hung harmlessly in midair.

Miles gaped at the vision in pale green framed in the doorway.

"Get away from him!"

Mathilda marched right up to the two men clustered around him and struck at them wildly with her fists. "Get away, I say. Barbarians," she spat, her face flushed, eyes flashing.

Miles thought she looked magnificent. And so very much out of reach.

The gentlemen fell back immediately. Mathilda stood like an avenging angel, pointing at the door with a trembling finger. "Out!" she stormed. "Get out of here, both of you. *Now,*" she cried, her voice rising dangerously. Under the barrage of her fury, the two gentlemen bowed to her greater claim to satisfaction from Miles.

"Mr. Hampton," she snapped. "I would be obliged of your escort home in a few minutes. After I have finished with this . . . this gentleman."

Hampton nodded. "Of course, my dear, anything you—"

"Thank you, sir," she cut in stiffly. "Now please go."

The two friends slipped out of the room, leaving Mathilda standing glaring at Miles. He straightened his shoulders, conscious of his partially closed left eye and the blood still flowing from his battered nose. He braced himself for the onslaught of fury of this wonderful female he had so harshly wronged.

Suddenly, a change came over Mathilda's face; her eyes widened and her mouth formed a silent exclamation of horror. She stood as though petrified for a long moment, then rushed to jerk the bell-rope. The butler must have been lurking in the hall outside, for the library door opened immediately and Harris hurried in, his normally placid face harried.

"Take off your coat," she ordered, without meeting Miles's eyes. "Harris, take his lordship's coat up to his valet and tell him to sponge off the blood immediately before it stains. Then bring it back here. And send down a fresh cravat. I will also require a bowl of warm water. Now, if you please."

Harris hurried away, his face impassive again, as though sopping up his master's blood and changing his clothes in the library was an everyday occurrence.

The silence became oppressive.

Miles could not take his eyes from Mathilda's face. He saw the signs of unhappiness there, the tense lines around her lovely mouth, the haunted expression in her amber eyes. He cursed himself for a heartless fool. Nothing, not even the satisfaction he had imagined he would derive from the success of his plan, was worth one instant of pain to this female who had captured his heart so completely. What could he possibly say that might explain, much less excuse, his despicable action?

When she finally spoke, he had to strain to hear the whispered words.

"Who is Miss Amanda Champion? At least have the courtesy to tell me who the mysterious lady is you are to wed."

TWENTY

Game's End

Only after the words had left her lips did Mathilda ask herself if she really wished to know who her rival was. What could it possibly matter now? Miles had made his choice, and she was not it. Why must she stir up more unhappiness for herself?

Furious at Miles for leading her to believe he loved her, and then making her the laughingstock of Bath society, Mathilda had stormed in from the terrace after her inauspicious encounter with Mrs. Fraser, bent on venting the full extent of her wrath.

"Where is he?" she had demanded sharply of the butler, who was standing at the top of the stairs, blinking as though he had seen a ghost.

"His lordship has gone down to the library, milady," Harris muttered with less than his accustomed aplomb.

Without giving a thought to the impropriety of her behaviour, Mathilda had lifted her skirts, raced down the stairs, and flung into the library. The gathering of gentlemen in their shirtsleeves had stopped her short. Only when she realised what they were about did she explode into a whirlwind of fury.

Now she was alone with Miles, and her angry question hung in the air between them.

With a slight grimace of resignation, Miles sighed, his shoulders sagging in a gesture that touched her heart.

"If I am ever to take a bride, my dear Mathilda—which appears increasingly unlikely—she will definitely not be Miss Amanda Champion."

Mathilda caught her breath in astonishment. "Why ever not?" she blurted. "Surely you cannot mean to—" She stopped abruptly, unable to finish her thought.

"I cannot wed Miss Champion because I love another, my dear. The lady I love," he continued in a husky voice, "the only one I have ever loved, would not wed me if I were the last man on earth. And I cannot blame her. I have treated her abominably. My case is hopeless."

His eyes had taken on a strange glitter and were focused upon her so intently, Mathilda felt her blood rush wildly through her veins. For a delirious moment she imagined that Miles was talking about her, but common sense told her she was being foolish. Whoever this mysterious Amanda Champion was, she stood between them like an evil spectre; this official bride-to-be could not be denied, whether Miles loved her or not.

Now there appeared to be, by his own confession, yet another female in his life, one he loved who would not have him. This development was simply beyond bizarre; it made her head spin.

With considerable effort, Mathilda pulled her eyes away from his mesmerizing stare. She must not build castles in Spain. How easy it was to fall into that trap. One seductive glance from those penetrating grey eyes and she was magically transformed into a blancmange. Where was her own fury of a moment ago, which she had fully intended to call down upon his handsome head? She must not forget that she was the injured party here, and the beating she had interrupted moments ago was well deserved. Miles had led her on and then callously announced his betrothal to another. He deserved none of her pity. She knew she must harden her heart.

Looking around desperately for something to break the tension, Mathilda's eyes fell on his blood-splattered cravat. As she watched, another drop of blood inched slowly down his chin to join the others. Seeing this as a welcome distraction until Harris returned with the warm water, Mathilda drew out her lace handkerchief and moved forward.

"Oh, dear me, you are a perfect mess," she fussed, reaching up to stanch the blood from his chin. It amused her to treat Miles as she had Brian after he fell out of the apple tree last week. "Although from what you have done to poor Miss Champion, I would say you deserve the thrashing your friends gave you. For myself, I would have you taken out and flogged," she added with certain gusto.

She felt his muscles move beneath her fingers as he said, "Amanda will never suffer a moment's discomfort over that damned announcement."

"How can she not if you refuse to honour it? Surely she must have some affection for you?"

"She has not seen me since the day of her birth, so I am sure she has no particular feelings for me at all."

"You have known her all her life? How could you break a young girl's heart like that, you odious creature?" Mathilda was appalled at this display of callousness, and her fingers pressed roughly on the earl's tender nose. She ignored his sharp intake of breath at the pain, dipping a cloth into the warm water Harris had brought in and applying it to the earl's bruised face.

"I shall require a cold poultice for that eye, Harris."

"Very well, my lady," the butler replied, leaving them alone again.

"Tell me, Mathilda," Miles said softly, his eyes fixed intently on her face. "Did I break your heart all those years ago?"

Mathilda's heart skipped a beat. Her first thought was to brush off the question, but suddenly she realised that the time had come for honesty between them. "Yes, you did, Miles. I was very young and perhaps foolish, with unrealistic expectations." She paused, then, dropping her voice, confessed the pain that had driven her into the arms of another man. "I thought you did not care."

"And James did, I take it?"

She smiled in tender remembrance of the man who had loved her enough to leave his country for her. A man who was not afraid to tell her so. "Yes," she said softly. "James was a wonderful husband. I cannot regret a moment of the time I spent with him. I am sorry if this hurts you, Miles, but I will not deny that I was very happy with James."

"You should not have to, my dear," he surprised her by saying after a pause. "I was a complete dolt not to see that James was the answer to any young girl's dreams, not me. I should not have been surprised when he won you away from me. But never think for one moment that I did not care, Mathilda. Perhaps I cared too much, for after I lost you, I could never bring myself to approach another woman."

Mathilda stared at him. This astonishing revelation left her more confused than ever. This was not the cool, remote gentleman she remembered. Besides, how could this be true if he had just told her himself that the only woman he loved would not have him? Who was this witless female anyway?

Harris returned with a poultice at that moment, and Mathilda busied herself in applying it to the earl's swollen eye. Miles had taken a seat in a ladder-backed chair, and closed his eyes. As she hovered above him, Mathilda sensed his unhappiness reaching out to envelop her, too. Her compassion was aroused, and it did little good to remind herself that this man she had trusted with her virtue and her heart had brutally betrayed her with a mysterious lady he appeared to care nothing about.

"I wish I had known all this at the time," she said when Harris again left them alone. "You never gave me a sign that you cared. Not even a chaste kiss in the chapel." She smiled at the memory of their not-so-chaste second visit to the ruined chapel.

"Would it have made any difference?" Miles had opened his right eye, which glittered with an emotion that Mathilda refused to put a name to. She took her time in responding, trying to understand the passions that had driven this man to deceive her as he had.

"Perhaps you would not have hated me so much," she said gently.

He sat up abruptly, the poultice falling from his eye. "I never hated you, Mathilda. Even in the darkest days after you and James left, I never hated you. You must believe me, my dear. I was furious with the whole world. I lost the love of my life; naturally I went into a black rage."

Strange talk indeed from the stiff-rumped Earl of Southmoor, but he looked so miserable that Mathilda's heart went out to him. She believed him; Miles had not hated her. From the way he talked, it appeared that she had broken his heart as well. She had found consolation; he had not. Perhaps she was incurably naïve, but she wanted to believe he might still love her.

"Then you merely wished to punish me for breaking my promise to you. Is that it?" She replaced the poultice over his swollen eye. "How ironic that all I could think of was that you had broken yours to me."

Mathilda reached out and loosened the twisted cravat, unwinding it carefully from his bruised neck. "If I had not arrived when I did, those *friends* of yours would have strangled you," she observed, examining the red marks critically.

"Better for everyone had they done so."

"Fustian! I will not listen to such rubbish."

It was not in Mathilda's nature to accept defeat so easily. She had been the mother of two rambunctious boys too long to give way to despair. The same protective tenderness she had called upon so many times with her boys rose up strongly in her now. She longed to take poor Miles's bruised head in her arms and assure him that hearts do not really break; they go on beating in spite of the most excruciating unhappiness. She should know. Had she not recently suffered the most galling blow a female could possibly endure? Her reputation and her heart had been publicly mocked by the man she had trusted.

And, despite everything he had done or not done, she still loved him. Perhaps she was a gullible simpleton, but of one thing Mathilda was perfectly certain. She had given herself and her heart to this man beside the lake, and she could not change that even had she wished it. She was irrevocably his, whether he loved her or not. No matter how many mysterious ladies he had in his past.

Mathilda smiled gently and stroked his forehead. He sighed—perhaps with pleasure?—but did not open his eyes. Her gaze slid down his bruised nose to his lips, now wiped clean of blood. Lips that could make her delirious with their slightest kiss. Of their own volition her fingers trailed down his angular cheek to the corner of his mouth. Dare she touch it? She felt his lips curl up in a smile as if he read her mind, then his hand shot up and grasped her wrist, flattening her palm against the warmth of his mouth.

"I have wanted to do that since you came in, my love," he whispered, his warm breath playing havoc with her senses. "But I was afraid you would slap my face for me."

The unexpected endearment sent shivers of excitement skittering through her. His one good eye opened and stared up at her lovingly. "And why would I do that, my lord?" she demanded, ruthlessly suppressing the urge to fling her arms round his neck and cover those provoking lips with kisses. There was still some plain talking to be done by this gentleman before she could lower the defences of her heart again.

The smile faded from his gaze, but he did not release her. "I have been an ignorant, selfish lout for so long, my dear, that I cannot find the words to beg your forgiveness. I do not deserve it, of course, so I dare not ask it of you."

"Perhaps you might start by asking Miss Amanda Champion to forgive your cavalier appropriation of her name for your ignoble ends," Mathilda suggested.

"Amanda—you might as well know it—is the ten-year-old daughter of a distant, *very* distant, third cousin of my mother's.

They live in Yorkshire and never come anywhere near London. I shall make everything right with her, I promise."

"And perhaps send her a generous gift for her next birthday?"

"Absolutely. Consider it done, my love." He nibbled tenderly on her fingers one by one.

Disregarding the endearment and this quite inappropriate behaviour with difficulty, Mathilda maintained a severe expression. If the rogue imagined he was getting off so easily, she had other plans for him.

"Having disposed of Miss Champion," she said crisply, "and before you ask me to forgive your devious and dastardly behaviour, I suggest you ask the other mysterious lady in your life if *she* can forgive you. Perhaps if she can bring herself to gloss over your gross misconduct, I may find it possible to put the incident behind me and go back to being a loving mother to my boys and forget all about . . ." She had almost said it, but for some odd reason Mathilda could not say that she was prepared to give up on love.

His one good eye took on a tender expression, and he kissed her palm again. "Forget all about what, my love?" When she did not reply, he placed his other hand on her waist and drew her close against his side. "I trust you will not give up on love, my sweet Mathilda. Or on me. I could not bear to lose you again."

"Oh, I am not going anywhere," she murmured innocently. "And I do not believe you should be holding me like this. It is most unseemly. What if Willy were to return?"

He glanced at her sharply. "What the blazes has Hampton to do with anything?"

Mathilda smiled sweetly. "You do not want me to give up on love. You said so yourself. Well, I have a confession to make. It is entirely possible that dear Mr. Hampton might be encouraged to . . . that is, he has shown a definite—"

Miles stood up abruptly, the poultice falling unheeded to the carpet. "The devil fly away with Hampton and his impertinence," he roared, gripping her firmly round the waist and pulling her against him. "The devious little rat. He assured me that—" He stopped suddenly and glared down at her. "You are teasing me." His voice fell into a sensuous murmur. "You are a silly goose, my love, if you think I will let another man take you to the altar. Again. The next time you walk down the aisle, my girl, it will be with me and no other. Do you understand me?"

"Perfectly, my lord." He grinned triumphantly and bent his head towards her; but before their lips met, Mathilda raised a hand. "Except for one thing." By this time it was obvious to Mathilda that she herself was the other mysterious lady in the earl's life, and that he had—in a roundabout way—confessed his love for her. But some perverse part of her demanded more.

His one eye took on a dangerous glint. "What thing, my love?"

"You have not yet asked me, Miles." She flashed her most scintillating smile, amused at the sudden uncertainty in his gaze. "I do believe it is customary to make an offer before one dashes off announcements to the *Gazette.*"

He gazed at her lovingly. "I gather that if you can jest about it, you have forgiven me, my love." He brushed her lips with his, tempting her to stand on tiptoe to nibble his chin.

"Perhaps," she agreed between nibbles.

"Then you will marry me?"

"If you ask me nicely, I will certainly consider it."

Miles groaned, then pulled her more closely against him, bending her curves to fit into his own body. His kiss was searing and left Mathilda without the strength to resist. "That will teach you to trifle with a gentleman's heart, you saucy wench." Then he stepped back and, holding one of her hands in his, went down on one knee and addressed her formally.

"Mathilda Charlotte Heath, will you make me the happiest man alive?"

She paused, savouring the moment. Instinct told her the

promise she was about to make was one she would never break. She smiled down at him, her eyes misting over. Coatless, sans cravat, with his hair in disarray, black eye and swollen nose, the Earl of Southmoor might not be looking his best, but to Mathilda, he was the handsomest man in the world. And he was hers. At last.

"Yes, oh yes," she whispered before she was engulfed in a rib-cracking hug that confirmed her belief that forgiving Miles had been the wisest decision of her life.